MORE PRAISE FOR
ELAINE BARBIERI!

"Exceptional . . . exciting adventure, dark obsessions, deep passions and redeeming love . . . readers will find themselves captivated!"

—*Romantic Times* on *Dance of the Flame*

"Captivating! Elaine Barbieri does a terrific job creating a fresh, exciting plot!"

—*Literary Times* on *Dangerous Virtues: Honesty*

"Ms. Barbieri writes a multidimensional story with several subplots and enough adventure, action and romance to satisfy any western romance fan."

—*Romantic Times* on *Dangerous Virtues: Purity*

"*Chastity* adds excitement, adventure, danger and riveting action to a magical series!"

—*Romantic Times* on *Dangerous Virtues: Chastity*

"A powerful story that evokes every human emotion possible . . . pure reading pleasure . . . a must read."

—*Rendezvous* on *Tattered Silk*

PRISONER OF LOVE

Crouching down beside her in the dim light of the nearby lamp, Night Raven stared down into Edwina's sleeping face. Golden hair, smooth skin, small features tranquilly composed. . . .

Night Raven covered her mouth with his hand. Edwina stirred. Her eyes flew open wide. He felt the jolt that shook her.

"Struggle is useless, Edwina."

Her startled response muffled by the hand clamped tight over her mouth, Edwina stared at Night Raven with disbelief. She was dreaming. She had to be.

Crouched over her, black hair spilling over the broad width of his bare shoulders, Night Raven whispered in the white man's tongue. "Our time together has come full circle, Edwina. I was your prisoner, and now you are mine."

NIGHT RAVEN

Elaine Barbieri

LEISURE BOOKS NEW YORK CITY

*To my parents, Evelyn and Andrew Favati, who inspired my
belief in true, enduring love, and whose
memory is with me always.*

A LEISURE BOOK®

June 2000

Published by

Dorchester Publishing Co., Inc.
276 Fifth Avenue
New York, NY 10001

ISBN 0-8439-4723-3

NIGHT RAVEN

Prologue

The sound of fluttering wings was eerily familiar.

The fluttering grew louder, and Night Raven stirred in his sleep. A blurred scene gradually materialized in his mind, then came into sudden focus. He saw a rainswept battlefield where many of his enemy lay dying. Above it, a raven circled with harsh, mocking calls. He waited, his anticipation growing as the bird circled lower to feast on his enemy's flesh. His heart pounded in expectation of final vengeance when the raven alighted on a motionless blue-coated form, then turned to look at him.

He saw the eye of the raven. *It was his own.*

The moment of ultimate retribution was at hand, and Night Raven held his breath—only to be shocked into incredulity when the raven lowered itself gently against the body of the fallen soldier and stretched out its wings to shield the man from the falling rain.

Night Raven awakened with a start. The same dream had returned to turn the sweetness of victory to ashes, but he knew its assault was not yet complete. The unwanted images lingered in his mind as he turned toward the woman who lay on his blanket beside him. The relentless grip of the dream intensified, briefly altering Dawn Woman's black hair to a shimmering gold, changing dark eyes that flickered open to a brilliant blue, transforming angular features into the delicate face of a woman he had never met—but whom he knew he would not forget.

Dawn Woman's musky scent touched his nostrils. She stirred, then stilled, and Night Raven's jaw tightened. The dream had revealed all too clearly that Dawn Woman was no different from the many women before her. She would provide no more than momentary satiation, which could not dispel the tormenting images of the raven, and of the golden-haired woman who haunted him.

Night Raven threw back the blanket and stood up abruptly. Shards of silver moonlight pierced the branches overhead to glint against the contours of his powerful frame. With eyes of fierce gold, he stared down at the sleeping woman.

A flush of anger suffused him. He was not the weak, confused winged creature in his dream! He knew who he was! He was Night Raven—a Sioux warrior who stood proud, alone and strong, dedicated to vengeance!

He needed *no one*.

Chapter One

Brilliant morning sunlight shone on a fort yard
that was tensely silent. Standing in the shadows near her quarters, Edwina Keene surveyed
the ominous tableau. Armed soldiers were concealed on the fort walls, their eyes trained on
the wilderness terrain beyond the fort gates.
Others were posted in strategic locations near
the civilian lodging, while the remainder of the
fort's contingent, rifles ready, was poised in
defensive positions within the log walls.
Frowning, Major Locke moved among the
men, checking the armaments and issuing
gruff commands.

Attack was imminent.

The unnatural quiet prevailed and Edwina's

14

delicate features tightened. She had left the
safety of the civilian quarters where she'd been
herded with the women and children a short
time earlier. Her reaction was the same as it
had been a few months previous, when she had
ignored the worsening situation with the Sioux
and traveled to Fort John Carter in response to
Margaret's appeal for help. She had known
then that her place was with her ailing friend—
just as she knew now where her place was.

Across the fort yard, Major Locke turned
unexpectedly in her direction, and Edwina's
expression hardened. She saw the revealing
twist of his lips when he snapped a short command to a recruit crouched nearby. Jumping to
his feet, the slender youth made haste to her
side and addressed her bluntly.

"Ma'am, Major Locke says he wants you to go
back to stay with the women, where you
belong."

The bastard!

"You can tell the major that I *am* where I
belong."

"Ma'am, the major said—"

"I don't care what he said. I've lived in this
part of the country all my life. I know it just as
well as he does. I can take care of myself."

"Ma'am—"

"I'm stayin' right where I am! And make sure
you tell the major *exactly* what I said."

"Yes, ma'am."

Edwina glanced again at the major as the soldier sprinted back across the yard. He was glowering at her. Edwina watched as the trooper relayed her response. The major shot her a glare of pure antipathy before he turned to address Captain Rice, who stood nearby. The exchange between the two men was brief.

Edwina watched as Captain Craig Rice approached, brown brows furrowed, the fiery color of his hair in bright contrast with the military blue of his uniform. She could tell from the set of his slender frame that he was angry. His fair skin colored revealingly as he said, "This isn't the time to oppose the major, Edwina. The Sioux are going to attack any minute."

"*Any* time's a good time to oppose him!"

"He wanted me to place you under arrest, but I told him I'd talk some sense into you."

"Talk some sense into *me?* The Sioux wouldn't be attackin' right now if it wasn't for him! You know that as well as I do! He knew Lieutenant Ford was itchin' to take Sioux scalps when he sent him out to locate that Sioux encampment. He knew Ford wouldn't leave anybody alive if he found it."

"Lieutenant Ford was at Fort Madden. He saw what the Sioux left behind when they attacked."

"Ford attacked a *peaceful* camp—defenseless

women and children! Are you sayin' he was right to slaughter them all?"

"No, but—"

"Major Locke praised Ford for his actions!"

"The major's been fighting Indians a long time, Edwina."

"He's been fightin' them *too* long, if you ask me! There'll never be peace in this territory while he's commandin' Fort John Carter because he won't be satisfied until he kills every last Sioux! He's responsible for what's happenin' now."

"Whether he is or not, you're not accomplishing anything by exposing yourself to danger."

"I can take care of myself!"

"That's beside the point! You're providing a distraction that we can't afford."

"I said, I can take care of myself!"

"Edwina, I'm asking you, as a favor to me."

The softening of Craig's tone halted Edwina's protests. He was Margaret's husband and a dear friend. The three of them were closer than family. The only problem was that somewhere along the line, Craig had begun feeling responsible for her, a situation she had tried desperately to discourage. She knew who would be distracted by concerns for her safety if she stayed where she was. Craig would.

Damn.

"I'm not asking you to abandon your princi-

17

ples, Edwina. I'm only asking you to take reasonable cover."

Silence.

"Edwina . . ."

"You're not tellin' me to go back to stay with the women, *where I belong?*"

"No. I know you too well for that."

Yes, he did.

"Just move back out of the major's sight. He has a plan. If it works, you won't be—"

"They're coming!"

A barrage of gunfire erupted at the sentry's shouted warning. Thrusting her suddenly backwards into her quarters, Craig ordered, "Stay under cover!"

"But—"

"Do what I say, dammit!"

Not waiting for her response, Craig dashed back across the fort yard to join his men.

The gunfire grew more intense and Edwina's throat tightened. Yes, she knew her place. Despite her greatest wish to the contrary, Dr. Edwina Keene would soon be needed here.

The attack escalated.

Concealed behind a rise some distance from the fort, Night Raven held his mount under rigid control. His muscular frame quivered in anxious anticipation as the conflict continued. At his rear, a great force of mounted warriors waited as impatiently as he.

Night Raven glanced at Jumping Bull; the war chief sat his horse motionlessly. The older man's visage betrayed no sign of the furor that Night Raven knew pounded within his noble chest as well. Jumping Bull's plan was going well. An hour earlier, an army patrol had raced back to the fort to warn that a Sioux war party was approaching. The soldiers did not know, however, that they had seen only a small part of the party—the part that Jumping Bull had *allowed* them to see. Jumping Bull had then ordered only that small portion of the war party to attack the fort, so the warriors could pretend to be driven back by the firepower from behind the walls.

Night Raven sneered. Jumping Bull knew well what would happen then. So great was the fort commander's hunger for Sioux blood, he would order his men out in pursuit of the fleeing braves. He would leave only a nominal force behind to protect the fort in presumption of an easy victory. He would not be expecting the great Sioux force that lay in wait. The soldiers would ride headlong into their midst, and when it was over, the fort would be in ashes.

Night Raven's face heated under the black war paint he had so skillfully applied. The lives of the bluecoats for the lives of an innocent camp! It would be fitting vengeance, but his long-standing thirst for retribution would not be so easily quenched.

Forcing aside all other thoughts, Night Raven watched the progress of the attack more intently. The war party had begun to retreat as planned. He could almost hear the laughter behind the log walls and the soldiers' derisive calls as his Sioux brothers pretended to flee.

The retreating warriors rode toward the hidden force at a frantic pace, but Night Raven's gaze remained fixed on the fort gates. He waited, jubilation jolting through him when the gates opened and mounted soldiers burst out in pursuit.

Fools who believed the Sioux suffered fear!

Dupes who assumed Sioux vengeance would be so easily abandoned!

Jumping Bull withheld the signal as the retreating warriors raced nearer, their dust luring the soldiers on.

A little longer. A little closer.

Jumping Bull brought his hand down sharply as the fleeing warriors pounded past them, and Night Raven spurred his mount forward. His war cry resounded with those of his brothers as they leaped out into the enemy's view and rode toward them in full force!

But something was wrong.

The soldiers did not panic at their unexpected appearance. They did not hesitate at the overwhelming size of the war party suddenly racing toward them. Instead, as if prearranged, the mounted contingent separated in two and fell to the sides of the open terrain, creating a wide path down the center that left the Sioux warriors in clear view of the fort.

As if prearranged.

The boom of cannon shook the earth! Night Raven struggled to control his terrified mount as the shot struck the ground nearby. Pelted by debris as bloodied warriors fell around him, he heard a second boom . . . a third!

Agonized cries of pain surrounded him. The shrill whinnies of fallen ponies reverberated in his ears.

Another boom. Another.

Their ruse had been turned against them!

Pandemonium reigned as the warriors scrambled to escape the power of the great gun. Gunfire cracked through the grainy mist, increasing the carnage. Floundering within the acrid black clouds of death, Night Raven realized that the mounted contingent was firing on them from established points of safety even as the cannon continued its deadly assault.

A blood rage rose inside him as his brothers continued to fall, and Night Raven forced his mount forward. He would not run. He would take life for life. He would make his enemy see that the Sioux heart did not falter. He would—

The world exploded in a sudden roar of sound. The blast pierced Night Raven's body with pain, hurling him high into the air as his horse disappeared from beneath him.

21

Night Raven's body struck the earth with shuddering impact, but he was suddenly numb. He could no longer smell the gunpowder cloud that blotted out the sun. He could not feel the dirt between his teeth, or taste the blood that filled his mouth.

Sound faded.

Light dimmed.

A thought flashed across Night Raven's mind before the light failed. He was not yet prepared to die.

"No."

"What do you mean, no?"

"I mean I won't let you go into that cell to treat that murdering heathen, Edwina! Leave him as he is to live or die! He doesn't deserve anything more!"

Edwina struggled for control. The Sioux attack had ended hours earlier. It had been brief and costly. The patrol that had been dispatched to draw out the concealed Sioux war party had not emerged unscathed, but the greatest loss of lives had been among the Sioux warriors, who still lay where they had fallen, in clear view of the fort.

Edwina's hand closed spasmodically on the small black bag she carried. The leather case had been her father's. It was all she had left of the slender, stoop-shouldered man who had dedicated his life to the easing of physical misery.

Edwina mentally corrected that thought. No, her father had left her much more than a worn medical bag.

"He's a savage, Edwina! You didn't see him out there, but everybody on the walls did! He was leading the charge against the men we sent out. He would've been the first one to put a torch to the fort if the battle had gone their way!"

"I've already taken care of the wounded soldiers, Craig." She motioned toward the small, barred structure in the center of the fort yard. "But there's another wounded man in that cell."

"That wounded man is *Night Raven*, Edwina." Satisfied at her start of surprise, Craig continued, "I knew you'd recognize the name. There aren't many people in this area of the country who wouldn't."

"How do you know it's Night Raven?"

"It couldn't be anybody else. The men recognized him the minute they saw him. He stands head and shoulders above most of his tribe, but even if it wasn't for his size, his war paint—that totally blackened face with the white lightning bolt painted on each cheek—couldn't be missed. He's too dangerous for you to handle."

"He's dangerous—but he's still a human being."

"There's nothing *human* about him! He's an animal bent on killing, and that's the truth of it! I'm not going to let you go in there."

"Major Locke asked me to look at his wounds."

Craig flushed to the roots of his hair. "I suppose I should've expected that."

Edwina hadn't expected it. She had been surprised when Major Locke singled out one wounded Indian to be taken prisoner, but she had been stunned when the major requested that she treat his wounds.

Craig's expression sobered. "Did it ever occur to you that you might be doing that Indian a favor if you let him die?"

"A favor?"

"Why do you suppose Major Locke singled Night Raven out to be taken prisoner when he left all the other Indians where they fell? Every trooper in this fort was itching to take Night Raven's scalp, but he wouldn't let them. It isn't because he's forbidden his men to take scalps, if that's what you're thinking, or because he didn't want to give the Sioux the satisfaction of being able to say Night Raven died nobly on the battlefield."

When Edwina did not respond, Craig pressed on. "Think about it. You know how Locke feels about you. Do you think he'd ask for your help if he didn't have something up his sleeve? You know what he's like. As far as he's concerned, the only good Indian is a dead Indian. The only reason he'd ask you to treat Night Raven's wounds would be because he's got plans for him."

"Plans?"

"It's no secret that Washington isn't pleased with the way Locke's been handling things out here. But if Locke could notify Washington that he'd captured the most dangerous Sioux in this area, he might turn that thinking around. Locke *needs* Night Raven, and he needs him healthy, so he can march him through the territory to show off his prize. He wants to see to it that Night Raven is put on trial—and you can bet he'll be standing right there, claiming the credit when they hang him."

Craig's brown eyes pinned her. "Don't do it, Edwina. Let that Indian die. It's better that way. It's a truer justice."

Silent, Edwina held Craig's gaze. She knew he was right about everything he said. She had seen through Major Locke the first time she met him. Locke's swaggering step, the ragged cut of his graying hair and beard, and the buckskin jacket he chose to wear instead of his military blue—even the feather he wore tucked in the band of his hat—were deviations from standard military garb devised to draw attention to himself and broaden his already colorful reputation as an Indian fighter. She had been at odds with him from the moment she rode through the fort gates. The bastard almost laughed when she said she was a doctor! She had gotten that same reaction before, but the bias usually disappeared after she proved herself. It didn't with Locke. He made his thoughts very clear. She didn't know her place. She was trying to prove she was smarter than a man. Worst of all, she was a good doctor, which infuriated him. If the fort hadn't been so badly in need of her services when the fever took hold a few months earlier, she was sure he would have tossed her out the first time she stood up to him.

As for Night Raven, if half the stories she had heard about him were true—

"Edwina . . ."

Aware of the irony of the situation, Edwina replied, "The last thing I want to do is to help Major Locke, Craig, but that Indian in there's bleedin' blood just like any other man. Try to understand . . . I can't stand by and let him die."

Craig's flush deepened. "Your father didn't do you any favors when he passed that bag on to you, you know."

"I've had that same thought often enough."

Edwina saw the almost imperceptible shake of Craig's head before he said, "All right, but you're not going into that cell alone."

"Whatever you say."

"A guard will stay with you the whole time."

"All right."

A lingering resentment rang in his tone as Craig turned toward the guard at the cell door and ordered, "Open it up, corporal."

A lock turning. A creaking door.

Night Raven stirred. Pain ravaged his chest with every breath, but he kept the encroaching darkness at bay. He did not remember how he came to be there, but he knew where he was. He was in the fort jail, where the stench of former inmates was so strong and foul that his stomach had almost rebelled upon his first awakening a short time earlier.

Night Raven searched the fragmented thoughts whirling in his mind. He remembered the anticipation of battle. He recalled riding out gloriously to face the enemy . . . and he remembered the roar of the fort's great guns.

Jumping Bull had not known that cannon awaited them.

Pain stabbed sharply again, and Night Raven reached weakly for the wound in his chest. The bleeding had begun anew, as it did each time he attempted to move. He had been removed from the field of battle where he might die as a warrior—another way in which his enemy sought to dishonor him.

Voices intruded again into Night Raven's thoughts. He heard the sound of approaching footsteps.

Night Raven closed his eyes and waited.

* * *

The stench of the prison cell was overwhelming. Edwina faltered momentarily, as unprepared for it as she was for the dank squalor of the small, airless structure. The dirt floor was rank with the smell of human waste and decaying debris, and she fought to suppress a spontaneous gagging as she approached the cot against the wall, where the Indian lay.

"Are you all right, Edwina?"

Edwina did not reply to Craig's concerned question. Instead, she leaned over the cot, noting that it was fetid and stained as she assessed the motionless Indian in the single ray of light that shone through the small, barred window. His eyes were closed and his breathing was shallow. Blood had pooled underneath him from a chest wound that had almost stopped bleeding. She could neither judge his color nor distinguish his features underneath his black war paint. She pressed her hand to his forehead. His skin was as cold as ice.

Edwina addressed him softly. "Night Raven, can you hear me?"

When there was no reply, she turned toward Craig. "Does he understand English, Craig?"

"I don't know."

Edwina tried again. "Night Raven, can you hear me?"

Still no response.

28

Edwina removed the stethoscope from her bag and pressed it against the Indian's bare chest. She listened intently, relieved when she heard a heartbeat that was weak but surprisingly steady. She examined him briefly, finding that although his body was covered with cuts and abrasions, he appeared to have only one bullet wound.

Assessing her patient's massive proportions for a silent moment, Edwina turned toward Craig again.

"I need your help to lift him so I can look at his back."

His resentment obvious, Craig rolled the Indian roughly to his side, allowing Edwina the glimpse she needed. Nodding, she instructed, "Lay him back—*gently*, please."

Hardly aware of Craig's snort, Edwina took a bandage from her bag and pressed it tightly against the wound. She felt the jolt that shook the Indian and looked up at his face. His eyes were still closed, yet he had felt pain.

Suspicious, Edwina scrutinized the Indian a moment longer. Well, conscious or not, he needed help quickly.

Edwina looked back at Craig. "The bullet's still in his chest. I have to take it out, but I can't do it here."

"You're going to have to."

"I don't have time to argue with you, Craig! This place is filthy and the light is bad. I can't work on this man here if you expect him to live."

"You know how I feel about that."

Edwina hesitated. "I'll go to Major Locke if I have to."

No reply.

Edwina stood up and started toward the door. Halting her with a hand on her arm, Craig whispered, "Let him die, Edwina. His life's going to be a living hell if he survives."

"Are you goin' to help me move him or not?"

Regretting her harshness when Craig's jaw hardened, Edwina added more softly, "If you think Major Locke will refuse consent, that's another matter."

"Locke's consent has nothing to do with it."

"Craig, he starts bleedin' every time he's moved. The truth is, he might not even survive bein' carried across the yard, but we need to get him to my quarters as soon as possible."

"To your quarters?" Craig shook his head. "No, that's out of the question."

"Where else can we take him? It would cause a riot if we put him in with the rest of the wounded. Craig . . . please . . . I have no choice, and neither do you. Let's both just do what we have to do and put everythin' else aside for now."

Craig remained silent.

"Craig . . ."

Craig turned toward the guard. "Get some

men in here to transport this Indian, then report to Major Locke and tell him we're moving the prisoner so Dr. Keene can operate on him."

The guard's retreating footsteps echoed behind her as Edwina looked back at the prisoner. She studied his blackened face more closely. The Indian's eyelids moved, but they remained closed. She resumed her pressure on his wound and his muscles twitched spasmodically.

Heavy footsteps turned Edwina toward the soldiers who entered the cell as Craig ordered, "Take the prisoner to Dr. Keene's quarters."

The four frowning soldiers carried the Indian across the fort yard. Edwina saw her patient's eyelids flutter again as the entourage entered her room.

"Put him on my bed."

"No!" Craig's response was immediate. "Put him on the floor. I'll have a cot sent in."

"I can't wait for you to hunt up a cot!" Her patience short, Edwina repeated, "Put him on my bed."

Craig turned stiffly toward his men. "You heard Dr. Keene. Put him on her bed." Turning back to her, he added more softly, "I hope you don't regret this, Edwina."

Leaning over the still Indian moments later, Edwina was hardly aware that Craig had left the room.

* * *

He was weakening. Each breath he took was more excruciating than the last.

Night Raven suppressed a grunt of pain, aware that the last of his strength was rapidly failing as the woman probed his wound. Fragments of the exchanges he had overheard minutes earlier spun dizzyingly in his mind.

He's a savage, Edwina! There's nothing human about him!

Locke wants you to make Night Raven healthy again, so he can hang him!

His life's going to be a living hell if he survives.

Rage touched his mind.

The woman—*Edwina*—was leaning closer now. He smelled her scent. He felt her breath against his cheek.

Pain stabbed deeper, momentarily stealing his consciousness.

"Night Raven . . ."

The woman's anxious tone called him back and his rage stirred anew. She would make him well again so he could face a more demeaning death!

Hatred infused Night Raven's reeling thoughts. He would suffer this woman's touch and healing care, but the final triumph would be his! He would rise again, stronger and more knowledgeable of his enemy, and he would then wreak the vengeance that temporarily eluded him.

Night Raven struggled to retain consciousness a moment longer. He had heard the feigned concern in the woman's voice. He had felt the mockery of her gentle touch—but he had yet to look upon the face that masked her deception. He needed to see her! He needed to memorize each and every line of her face for the day when he would claim his retribution!

Night Raven's breathing was strained. His eyelids were heavy. With the last of his draining strength, he forced his eyes open at the same moment that the woman turned away from him to call out, "I need some help here, corporal!"

With the woman's face averted, Night Raven was able to see only her hair of shimmering gold. . . .

The woman turned back abruptly to look down at him and he saw eyes that were a brilliant blue. . . .

Staring transfixed through slitted eyelids, Night Raven saw the delicate, familiar features of a woman he had beheld only in the shadows of his mind.

Recognition rocked through Night Raven.

Yes . . . it was *she!*

Chapter Two

Bright magenta streaks colored the cloudless sky over Fort John Carter. The fort gates were tight and secure and the walls were heavily guarded. The din of battle had long since faded and the frantic aftermath had gradually slowed. A day begun in tense anticipation and rising fear was ending—but Edwina's work was far from over.

Returning from another round of tending the wounded, Edwina was weary beyond words as she pushed open the door of her room and walked inside. Night Raven lay silent and unmoving on her bed. She met the gaze of the youthful guard standing nearby, who responded with obvious resentment to her unspoken question.

"He ain't moved a muscle. Not even once. For a minute there, I thought he'd stopped breathin', but—"

Corporal Thompson concluded his statement abruptly. Remaining unvoiced was his poorly concealed disappointment that his assessment had been wrong.

Suddenly exhausted, Edwina replied, "I'll take over from here, Thompson. You can go back to your quarters now."

"Ma'am . . ." Thompson's beardless face creased in a frown. "I got orders to stay with the prisoner. Major Locke wants a man on guard here at all times."

"You can guard the prisoner from outside the door. I don't want somebody standin' over me."

"That Injun might wake up, ma'am, and if he does—"

"*If* he does . . ." Edwina paused, "he'll be lucky if he has the strength to open his eyes."

"Ma'am, I can't—"

"Outside . . . please." At the fellow's obvious perplexity, she added, "Don't worry. I'll call if I need you."

Waiting until the door closed behind the reluctant soldier, Edwina turned back toward her patient.

Hours had passed since the wounded Indian

was brought to her room. She had met the greatest challenge ever to her skill in removing a bullet that had lodged critically close to his lung.

Edwina studied Night Raven more closely. The man's proportions were menacing. His size, combined with the black war paint that still covered his face, and dark hair long enough to reach past his broad shoulders, made him fearsome, even with the bandage that contrasted so sharply with the sun-darkened color of his skin.

Edwina pressed her palm to Night Raven's forehead. She frowned at the realization that it was growing warmer, then checked the bandage again. The bleeding had stopped, but she was hindered in assessing his color by the war paint staining his skin.

She had treated Night Raven's critical wound, but she had yet to treat other, countless abrasions that needed to be washed free of the residue of battle. She had postponed that task when called back to the bedside of one of the wounded soldiers. She was keenly aware that if Night Raven had been any other man, the women of the fort would have volunteered to help her with his care, but Night Raven wasn't any other man, and no help was forthcoming.

Edwina stared at her silent patient a moment

longer. Another irony—this man, this hated enemy—was the only man in the fort whom the women refused to tend, yet he was the only man in the fort whose life was at immediate risk.

Let him die, Edwina. His life will be a living hell if he survives.

She only wished she could.

"Thompson . . ." The door opened with a snap and Edwina addressed the trooper directly. "I need a bucket of fresh water, some clean cloths, and bandages."

"For *him*, ma'am?"

Edwina's light eyes narrowed at his frown. "Does it matter who it's for?"

"Yes, ma'am, it does." The soldier's head bobbed resolutely. "I heard the ladies of the fort tell Major Locke that they won't be providin' no supplies for no savages."

"What did the major say to that?"

"He didn't say nothin', ma'am."

"Is that so?" Edwina was suddenly bristling. "In that case, you can deliver this message directly to the major—that I don't appreciate his lack of support when my tendin' to the prisoner was *his* idea in the first place! You can also tell him that I know what he's up to, and I expect fresh bandages, food, and anythin' else I need for the prisoner, or he might not get the opportunity he's hopin' for."

"Ma'am . . . ?"

"Just tell Major Locke what I said. He'll know what I mean."

"Ma'am, I'm guardin' this Injun. I can't leave."

"I told you before, this man's too weak to lift a finger. Just do what I said. Knowin' Major Locke, if somethin' happens to the prisoner because of your inaction, you'll be the one to suffer."

Leaving her last statement to hang on the air, Edwina waited. She watched as his smooth face flushed and then he nodded. She turned back toward the bed when the door closed behind him.

It had been a hard day, and it wasn't near its end, despite the darkness rapidly closing in. None of the soldiers' wounds were critical, but the bone in Sergeant Miller's leg had been shattered when he was knocked from his horse. He was in great pain. Corporal McNulty's shoulder wound had numbed his entire arm. She needed to watch him closely. Private Wallace's hand was going to be a problem; she couldn't be sure about the damage to Corporal Hale's knee; and Private Neil was still disoriented after falling from the wall.

And she was tired . . . so tired.

Closing her eyes, Edwina willed herself to relax. Extending her arms slowly upward, she cupped her hands at the back of her head and arched her back, stretching aching muscles cramped from the intense day's work. Suddenly aware that several strands had come loose from the careless knot confining her hair, she removed the few remaining pins and let the heavy mass drop onto her shoulders. She then slid her fingers into the strands at her temples to massage away her tension, unconsciously groaning in relief.

A sensual awareness prickled the back of her neck, and Edwina snapped her eyes open and looked at the bed where Night Raven lay. She had the fleeting sensation that he was looking back at her.

Edwina walked closer to her motionless patient. His eyes were closed, but she could almost swear—

Damn that war paint!

Her jaw tight, Edwina turned back toward the door.

"Corporal! Where's that water?"

Major John Randolph Locke's lean face twitched. Struggling to suppress the fury that shook his wiry frame, he demanded, "Repeat that again, corporal!"

The young soldier responded promptly. "The doc . . . I mean Miss Keene said she don't appreciate your lack of support, since her takin' care of Night Raven was your idea in the first place. She said she needs fresh bandages and food for that Injun. She said she knows what you're up to, and she expects to get anythin' she needs for the prisoner or you might not get the opportunity you're waitin' for."

"She sent you to me with that message?"

"Yes, sir."

Outrage flooded Locke's bearded cheeks with hot color. He'd had all he could take of Miss Edwina Keene! She had been a thorn in his side since her arrival at the fort months earlier, when she boldly announced that she was a doctor. The concept was idiotic then, and it was idiotic now! The only service she performed was the same service women had always performed—nursing the sick—yet, with a keen sense of timing and minimal skills, she had gained an exalted position with the inhabitants of the fort. She had opposed his authority every step of the way, and had informed him just as boldly that she did not intend to leave until Margaret Rice's child was safely delivered into the world. He would have thrown her out on the spot if not for the fort sentiment in her favor.

Major Locke's jaw hardened. Edwina Keene didn't know her place, and he had witnessed firsthand the problems that could cause. His own father had turned to drink and then suicide, rather than face life with an overbearing second wife who traded on his weaknesses. Were it not for his uncle, the retired army offi-

40

cer who'd rescued him from that woman's clutches and arranged for his education, he would not be the man he was now, a celebrated military Indian fighter who knew no equal on the frontier.

His emotions raging, Major Locke took a stabilizing breath. He had refused to recognize the word *surrender* in his dealings with the Sioux, and he had long since decided that annihilation was the only remedy for the Indian problem. He had only recently discovered, however, that dealing with Miss Edwina Keene was far more complex.

Major Locke straightened his spine, his anger tempered by a growing sense of satisfaction. He had thwarted the Sioux attack and earned himself the admiration of the fort, but it was his action in capturing Night Raven that had been truly inspired. Edwina Keene believed she understood his full agenda in taking Night Raven prisoner. She had threatened him, but her threat had little bite, because she didn't guess his superior strategy. As the situation now stood, he couldn't possibly lose. If Night Raven were restored to health, Washington would be informed that Major Locke was the man responsible for capturing one of the most dangerous Indians on the frontier. He would arrange to be present at the savage's trial and hanging, and the accolade would be his.

Major Locke entertained that thought for a

moment of true enjoyment. Of course, the savage might die under Edwina Keene's care, but his secondary purpose would still have been achieved. Sentiment at the fort was already turning against her. Fool that she was, the woman had openly demanded that the savage be removed to *her* room and be placed in *her* bed. The women of the fort were outraged. Even he had been shocked. Miss Keene had made her second mistake by sending her present message to him by the obviously disapproving young corporal, who was sure to pass it along. He'd see to it that the corporal passed along another thought as well, and as soon as the fort turned firmly against Edwina Keene, he would throw her out on her ear.

The young corporal shifted uncomfortably and Locke responded, "So, Miss Keene is hoping to make everyone believe it was my idea to give that Indian personal care. I suppose I should have expected some such nonsense." Major Locke raised his chin. "Make sure Miss Keene gets everything she needs for the prisoner."

"Sir, the women said—"

"Night Raven is Miss Keene's patient. I don't like Indians, corporal, and I don't like seeing Miss Keene treating that murdering savage better than she treats our own brave soldiers, but she's in charge of the prisoner until he's well enough to hang, and I have to go along with her. See that she gets what she wants. That's an order."

"Yes, sir."

The door clicked shut behind Corporal Thompson, and Major Locke resisted a smile. Yes, as things now stood, he couldn't possibly lose.

Yes, it was *she!*

Night Raven's eyes remained closed as the woman approached the bed and stood over him. He felt the heat of her perusal as images of the scene he had just witnessed flashed through his mind.

He saw Edwina standing at the foot of his bed, her eyes closed as she stretched her arms upward, then arched her back to boldly flaunt before him the womanly beauty he had glimpsed only in the shadows of his dream. The heavy golden strands that haunted his thoughts had tumbled onto her shoulders, and she had slid her fingers through the glittering mass and taunted him with soft sounds of yearning.

Night Raven's heart pounded, increasing his dizziness, and a familiar anger soared. His body was impotent against the woman's designs, but his mind was not deceived. The shaman's vision of a raven that had foreshadowed his birth declared that his destiny would not be ordinary. The echoes of his mother's and brother's dying cries had established the path he now trod. Only he had survived the massacre that had brought his youth to an end. Since then his pursuit of retribution had been relentless. He had earned the respect of his fellow braves, the admiration of the women of his tribe, and the hatred of his enemy—yet the disturbing dream had returned time and again to haunt him, and the specter of the golden-haired woman had allowed him no peace.

But the woman had emerged from the shadows at last. She now had a name, and all was suddenly clear. Edwina was the final challenge to his destiny—the test of his worthiness to lead his people to ultimate victory. He would accept that challenge . . . and he would prevail.

His strength abruptly failing, Night Raven felt consciousness ebb. The heat consuming him soared hotter with a suddenness that stole his breath, shattering his thoughts into shards that became whispers as sharp as a blade.

Hair of glittering gold deceives you.
Eyes of brilliant blue speak lies.
Delicate features seek to beguile you.
Womanly beauty aspires to destroy you.
She is your enemy!

"Did Major Locke send me a reply, Thompson?"

The young soldier had reappeared at Edwina's door a few minutes earlier, water bucket and supplies in hand. He entered the room without comment and placed the bucket beside the bed and the bandages on the table. Edwina was immediately suspicious. This was too easy.

Edwina prompted, "Did he?"

Turning back toward her, the corporal replied with obvious resentment, "No, ma'am, Major Locke didn't send no answer to your message."

"He must've had some reaction."

"He reacted, all right. The major don't like Injuns no better than most of us do, and he don't like that Injun bein' treated better than a white man. I'm thinkin' if the major had his way, that Injun would've stayed in that jail cell where he belonged—but he says you're in charge of the prisoner for now, and I'm to see that you get what you want for him."

Edwina seethed. Locke was directing the hostility of the fort toward her, and she had played right into his hands.

A bitter smile twisted her lips. "Thanks, corporal."

The young man burst out, "If it was up to me, I would've left that murderin' Injun for the buzzards!" He added with obvious resentment, "Is that all you need, ma'am?"

Edwina's expression sobered. "That's all for now. I'll call you if I need you."

The young soldier left the room, obviously glad to be dismissed. Edwina thought it ironic that she, who had treated so many savage wounds inflicted by the Sioux, was now being called an Indian lover. Thompson's attitude was probably reflected a dozen times over within the fort. Major Locke hated her, and he was as shrewd as he was relentless. He was determined to get her out of his fort, one way or another.

Frowning, Edwina snatched up the soap from the washstand and approached the bed. She had no choice about what she had to do.

Edwina filled the basin beside the bed and soaped a cloth. The Indian's eyes remained closed as she scrubbed his forehead clear of the black dye. The skin beneath was smooth and touched by the sun to an appealing russet hue. The realization that the cloth warmed quickly—too quickly—tightened her frown. His temperature was rising.

Edwina rubbed the lather against the Indian's closed eyelids and cheekbones, and across full lips that moved under her touch. Her hand stilled when his face was finally washed clean of the intimidating war paint. She suddenly realized that she had clearly exposed Night Raven's face to his enemy for the first time.

Edwina was uncomfortably aware that the face of this Sioux demon was unexpectedly handsome. His features were strong, but fine, his brows and lashes slight slashes of color

46

against the warm tone of his skin. The sharp
sculpting of his cheekbones and firm jaw might
have appeared menacing if not for full lips that
were slightly parted, revealing even, white
teeth. Strangely, an aura of power remained
about the man despite his debilitated state,
and she—

Edwina gasped as Night Raven's eyes
opened unexpectedly. Jumping back spontaneously at the sight of his piercing, gold-eyed
stare, she was struck with the thought that he
was aptly named: His hair was black as a
raven's wing and his gaze as penetrating as
that feathered creature's stare. And if the stories about him were true, he possessed the
intelligence and cunning of his namesake as
well.

A handsome and cunning savage.

Night Raven's eyes closed just as abruptly as
they had opened, and Edwina breathed a
relieved breath. Ignoring the rapid pounding of
her heart, she went back to the task at hand,
forcing herself to keep in mind that she was a
doctor, and it made no difference that this man
was the enemy. He was wounded and needed
her care.

The countless cuts and abrasions on Night
Raven's massive shoulders and chest had been
washed free of debris when Edwina sat back at
last, frowning at the bloody stains on his
leather leggings. Aware that she had no choice,

she sliced him free of their restriction so she could assess the wounds beneath.

Flushed hotly when Night Raven's naked body was revealed in its entirety, Edwina muttered a soft curse. What was wrong with her? The sight of a naked man wasn't new to her, and all male bodies were alike.

Edwina's gaze lingered.

No . . . they were not.

Her task finally completed, Edwina stood up and drew the coverlet up to Night Raven's waist. Aware that his temperature was still rising, she moistened a cloth in the bucket of fresh water and applied the cold compress to his forehead and cheeks. She pressed the moist cloth to his lips.

Night Raven mumbled a hoarse, indecipherable sound, and Edwina leaned closer. She cried out in alarm when his eyes flew open again and his hand clamped around her wrist. He went limp as the door burst open behind her and Corporal Thompson ran into the room, gun drawn.

"What happened, ma'am?"

Edwina was somehow unable to respond.

"Ma'am?"

"N . . . nothin'." Breathless, Edwina struggled for control. "I almost spilled the water. Everythin's fine."

"You look pale, ma'am."

"I'm tired, that's all."

Edwina turned back to Night Raven as Thompson left the room. His eyes were closed and his breathing was steady. He had fallen into an unsettled sleep.

If he was really sleeping . . .

Her knees suddenly weak, Edwina sat abruptly on the chair beside the bed. She needed to get her emotions in hand. Whatever this man was or had been, he was now as weak as a kitten.

The raven's wings had been clipped.

Edwina shook her head. She needed rest, all right. She needed to close her eyes, if only for a few minutes.

Just a few minutes.

He was hot . . . so hot.

Unable to move, Night Raven struggled against the fire that seared him. His eyelids were heavy and his limbs were unresponsive. Finally forcing his eyes open, he saw that instead of the hide shelter of his tipi, heavy log walls surrounded him. Reality penetrated Night Raven's fevered mind. He lay in a white man's bed, burning heat consuming him as his life drained away.

Night Raven's unsteady gaze halted abruptly on the pool of gold that lay beside his hand. He stretched out his fingers to touch it. The pool shimmered briefly, then shifted to reveal the delicate features of the woman's face.

Night Raven went still. Edwina lay sleeping with her head resting on the bed beside him. Her golden hair was cool against his palm. Her skin was light and flawless. Her lips were parted. She was the woman of the shadows who had lain beside him in his dreams, but he was not dreaming now.

A knock sounded on the door.

Edwina stirred, but she did not awaken.

Another knock.

Edwina did not respond.

The door burst open.

Night Raven closed his eyes as a bluecoat rushed toward them.

"Edwina! Are you all right?"

Edwina started as Craig rushed to her side. She stood up abruptly, disoriented, and Craig reached out to support her as she swayed.

"Are you awake, Edwina?"

"Of course I'm awake!"

"You were asleep!"

"No, I wasn't!"

"Edwina . . ."

"I was restin'."

"Look at me, Edwina!"

"I *am* lookin' at you. Are you tryin' to make me mad, Craig?"

Craig paused to bring his emotions under control. For a moment, when he'd first seen Edwina lying there, he had thought—

50

"You were asleep, Edwina . . . with your head lying on that savage's bed. Do you realize how dangerous that was? Look at the size of that man! He could break your neck with a twist of his hand!"

"I wasn't in danger."

"You weren't?" Craig paused again, his anger rising. "Don't tell me you expect that savage to appreciate anything you're doing for him."

"Appreciation has nothin' to do with it."

"The fact that you're a woman won't make any difference to him, either."

"I know that better than you do, Craig."

"Then what makes you think—"

"The man in that bed has hardly moved since I removed the bullet from his chest. He'll be lucky if he lives."

"No, he won't."

Edwina remained silent, and Craig's gaze locked with hers. She was still standing in the circle of his supportive embrace and Craig felt the heat of that contact to the tips of his toes. He turned abruptly toward the corporal standing in the doorway behind him.

"Wait outside, Thompson. Everything's under control here."

The door clicked closed and Craig rasped, "You scared the life out of me, Edwina! I knocked twice, and you didn't answer. When I opened the door and saw you lying so limp beside that savage—"

Suddenly contrite, Edwina responded, "I'm sorry, Craig. I didn't mean to scare you. I guess I really was asleep."

"You know how Margaret and I worry about you."

"You shouldn't. I can take care of myself."

"So you say."

"I can!"

Feelings long held in check burst forth as Craig grated, "You take too many chances, Edwina. You shouldn't travel alone in this country, with no one to watch out for you, and you shouldn't be subjecting yourself to danger to take care of a murdering savage!"

"We've had this conversation before, Craig."

"I know . . ." Craig recited stiffly, " 'I'm a doctor. I go where I'm needed.' "

"It's not a joke!"

"I didn't mean it to be."

"My father spent his life on this frontier. My mother lost her life working by his side."

"I'm not asking you to give up that cause, Edwina. I know doctors are needed out here. I just want you to take reasonable precautions."

"What would reasonable precautions include, Craig? An armed guard wherever I go?"

"Edwina . . ."

"I don't need anybody to take care of me!"

"You do, dammit!"

Craig paused again, suddenly aware that he was shaking. That was the crux of it, he knew.

52

Edwina needed someone to take care of her—
and for longer than he cared to recall, he had
wanted desperately to be that someone.
Edwina had remained blind to his feelings, but
Margaret had not. He had turned to Margaret
for consolation, and when the futility of his
love for Edwina became more than he could
bear, Margaret was there. He loved Margaret
and the child she was about to bear him, but
Edwina was—

Halting his straying thoughts, Craig continued, "You're asking for trouble, Edwina."

"I'm doin' my job!"

"If that Indian had awakened, there's no
telling what might've happened!"

Edwina stiffened. "I'm tired of this conversation."

"You're so damned stubborn!"

"Am I?" Edwina held his gaze for long
moments before she continued more softly, "I
suppose I am a trial to you and Margaret, and
I'm sorry about that, Craig. You've always been
so supportive of me. You've respected me for
the person I am, rather than for the woman
you think I should be."

"Edwina . . ."

"But I want you to understand, I'll never be
the woman you wish I could be."

Craig's heart was pounding. He wanted to
tell Edwina that he had never wanted to
change her. He had just *wanted* her—and now

that that time was past, he just wanted to keep her safe . . . and close . . . so he could love her from a distance as he always would, without worrying that one day he might not be there when she needed him most.

Edwina's eyes held his . . . clear eyes . . . trusting eyes. That trust held him silent.

A choking sound from the bed behind them turned Edwina from him abruptly. Beside the bed in a moment, she touched Night Raven's forehead, then looked back at Craig, her expression strained.

"I need a bucket of cold water, Craig—as cold as I can get it. This man's burning up. If I don't get his fever down, he won't make it through the night."

Craig did not dare respond.

"Craig, please."

The clear blue of Edwina's gaze destroyed his resistance. Resigned, Craig turned toward the door and called out the order.

He had taken only a few steps away from Edwina's quarters when an approaching trooper halted and addressed him directly.

"Major Locke wants to see you, Captain."

Night Raven's heavy eyelids stirred as Edwina pressed a cup to his lips.

"Drink."

He recalled an image of Edwina in the blue-coat's arms—his face close to hers . . .

"Drink, Night Raven."

She spoke his name sharply.

"Night Raven . . ."

But her agitation did not match his.

"Can you understand me?"

Yes, he understood her . . . better than she knew.

Edwina tilted the cup to pour the liquid between his lips. She cursed when it spilled onto the bed. Frustration entered her tone as she grated, "If you knew what the people in this fort would say if they saw me giving you Army medicine, you'd drink it fast enough—just for spite!"

Night Raven separated his lips.

"That's right." Edwina's voice grew hopeful. "Drink."

Night Raven felt the bitter liquid touch his tongue. He heard her sigh of relief as he swallowed. He saw momentary doubt flash in her eyes.

"If I didn't know better, I'd think—"

The cooling baths continued.

"You're makin' a mistake—a big one, Edwina! You're turnin' the fort against you!" Margaret's round face was flushed. Her breathing had not yet returned to normal. Seven months pregnant, she had waddled across the fort yard at a pace that had left her almost dizzy; she was hoping that she could get back to her quarters before Craig realized she was gone. She had arrived in Edwina's room minutes earlier, but Edwina had hardly looked up from her motionless Indian patient or paid any attention to what she said.

Annoyed, Margaret pushed a straying strand of brown hair back from her heavily freckled face and demanded, "Edwina, are you listenin' to me?"

Edwina turned fully toward her at last, and Margaret was struck, as she always was, by her friend's unaffected beauty. Amazed, she realized that in a plain, wrinkled, bloodstained dress, with her hair disheveled and her face lined with fatigue, Edwina had somehow reached another level of beauty. She remembered how jealous she had been of Edwina's fine features and bright hair when they first met as children—until she realized that Edwina didn't really care how pretty she was. Fast friends ever since, they had shared each other's joys and sorrows, had weathered the deaths of their mothers, and had sworn youthful promises of fidelity that they had somehow managed to keep despite conflicts both expressed and unspoken.

Until now.

"I heard everythin' you said, Margaret." Edwina's tone was clipped. "I didn't answer because I'm busy, and because you didn't say anythin' I don't already know."

"I know what you're tryin' to do. You're tryin' to make me think I'm makin' a mountain out of a molehill, but it's not goin' to work." Margaret advanced a few steps closer to the bed. "Look at that fella! He's not just another patient! He's a savage! He probably can't even count the number of men he's already killed, and now you're savin' him so's he can kill some more."

Edwina's lips tightened with disapproval. "That's Bertha Charles talkin', not you."

Margaret felt the flush that flooded her face. Bertha Charles—big, buxom, bold, and bellicose—a moose of a woman. Edwina and she had laughed about that shortly after she arrived at the fort, but times had changed. "I know you never liked Bertha. You know I don't really like her, either, but she's right this time, and the women of the fort are behind her." Margaret paused. "The whole fort's callin' you an Injun lover, Edwina."

Edwina's chin moved up a revealing notch. "Are *you* callin' me an Injun lover, too?"

The heat of tears warmed Margaret's eyelids. Edwina, who was closer than a sister . . . She had not hesitated to send her a plea for help when she was sick, despite the distance between them. Edwina had traveled the danger-filled miles to her side without hesitation. Edwina had nursed her through the fever and saved the life that moved so vigorously inside her.

Margaret swallowed against the lump in her

throat. "You know I'd never do that. I'm just tryin' to warn you that you're makin' enemies and you're—"

The door was pushed open unexpectedly and Margaret took a spontaneous backward step at the sight of Craig standing in the opening. He entered and advanced to her side. He spoke softly, but his fair skin was flushed with anger.

"What are you doing here, Margaret? I asked you not to leave our quarters tonight. The yard's patrolled, but those savages could still be hanging around, hoping to get over the walls."

"You couldn't talk sense into Edwina, so I knew it was up to me."

"Craig . . ." Craig turned stiffly toward Edwina as her tired smile flashed. "Maybe you should take Margaret back to your quarters. Nothin' either of you has to say will change anythin' here, and there's no point in gettin' Margaret involved in all the trouble that's bein' stirred up. Things will settle down once emotions start to cool."

Silent for a moment, Craig responded softly, "You weren't listening to a word I said earlier, Edwina, and you don't really understand what people are sayin'. You demanded that that Indian be removed from his cell and taken to your room."

"The cell was filthy. He didn't stand a chance there. Where else could I have him brought?"

"He belongs in a cell—not in your *bed*."

Edwina's gaze grew icy. "Are you sayin' that the women of this fort are insinuatin' that I intend doin' somethin' else here besides tryin' to save this Injun's life?"

"This man is the *enemy*. He belongs in a cell."

"Major Locke's the one who wanted this Injun taken prisoner. Major Locke asked me to look at his wounds. He put Night Raven's life in my hands. If I did any less for him than I'd do for any other patient—just because he's an Injun—I'd be no better than a murderer."

"A murderer . . . like him."

"I'm not a judge, Craig! I'm a doctor!"

"He should go back to that cell, where he belongs."

"I'll make the decision as to where he belongs!"

"Listen to Craig, Edwina!" Margaret's voice was a desperate plea. "He won't be able to protect you much longer."

Edwina stilled. "What are you sayin', Margaret?"

Silence.

"Margaret?"

Margaret glanced at Craig's flushed face. She began reluctantly, "Things aren't goin' to settle down for a while. Major Locke's goin' to see to that."

"What happened?"

"Craig's disobeyin' orders by bein' here right now."

"Disobeyin' orders by comin' to see *me?*"

"Major Locke ordered Craig to stay away from you . . . and to keep me away from you, too."

Edwina turned toward Craig, her color rising. "Is that true, Craig?"

"Send that Indian back to his cell, Edwina." Craig spoke softly. "It's the only thing to do." Not waiting for Edwina's reply, Craig urged, "Let's go, Margaret."

"No."

The silent plea in Craig's eyes tore at Margaret's heart as he pressed, "I don't want you walking back across the yard alone."

Margaret withheld a sob. She loved Craig. She had always loved him . . . even when he was immune to the love in her eyes each time she looked at him. She loved the bright color of his hair and the freckles that darkened each time he was exposed to the sun. She loved the way he walked, the way he talked, the way he smiled; the day he asked her to be his wife was the happiest one of her life. She had always known he'd never love her in the same way she loved him, but that knowledge had no effect on what she felt each time he as much as whispered her name. But although she loved him . . .

"You're my husband, Craig, but I won't let you or anybody else make me abandon Edwina!"

"Go with him, Margaret." The weariness in Edwina's voice was suddenly acute. It turned Margaret back toward her as Edwina continued, "Craig's right. Emotions are runnin' high now, and it isn't good for you to get upset."

"But—"

"I can handle things here. I'll feel better if you leave."

"I won't go!"

"Do you remember when we were children, Margaret . . ." Edwina continued softly, a small smile returning to her lips, ". . . when you wanted to come to see me when I was so sick with the fever? Your pa made you stay away— because he knew there was nothin' to gain if you caught the fever, too." Edwina paused. "It's the same thing now. There's nothing to gain by lettin' this trouble rub off on you and Craig."

The sadness inside Margaret deepened. "You're my friend. I want to stay."

"Enough damage has been done for now. I want you to go."

"But—"

"Go, please."

Margaret hesitated, her throat tight. Edwina was right. Edwina was always right, but—

Margaret was still protesting when the door closed behind her.

Satisfaction stirred Night Raven's clouded brain as the door closed behind the bluecoat and his woman. The plain woman's shrill voice had awakened him from his heated world of pain, and he had listened and learned. The bluecoat then appeared, and he had learned more.

He was alone with Edwina again.

Night Raven watched as Edwina moved around the room, unconscious of his scrutiny. The fort commander sought to strike fear in Edwina's heart, but he could not. The people of the fort thought to threaten her, but they failed. The bluecoat named Craig and his woman hoped to change Edwina from the woman she was, but they were unsuccessful as well. All of them thought they knew Edwina, and all were wrong. Only he knew the truth.

Gratification stirred within Night Raven.

The truth was, Edwina was *his*.

Chapter Three

The keening and wailing continued. The bitter sounds of mourning resounded with heartrending woe as dawn lifted the shadows of night from the Sioux camp.

Jumping Bull raised the flap of his tipi, grief a deadening weight in his breast. The great guns at the fort had been unexpected. His braves had been no match for their power. Many had lost their lives. His proud warriors had shown no fear and had ridden bravely into the face of death, but the suffering of his people was not lessened by their valorous displays.

Jumping Bull's strong shoulders slumped and his graying head bowed. His gaze lingered on Willow Woman as she stepped out of her

63

dead husband's tipi. Her body trembling, her hair coarsely cropped, her arms and legs slashed and bleeding from the self-inflicted wounds of her grief, she threw herself upon the ground in unbridled torment.

Jumping Bull turned at a shriek behind him. Emerging from the tipi she had shared with Eagle Heart, Morning Bird writhed in pain, her arms flailing, her hand dripping blood where she had severed a finger in overwhelming torment.

Jumping Bull glimpsed Laughing Water, White Antelope, Spear Woman, all widows of the failed attack, their cries a chorus of sorrow he could not evade.

Brave warriors stood in sober observance. Children gathered in tearful groups. Behind and around him the sounds of anguish multiplied, deepening with the rising of the sun and growing greater with each beat of his people's hearts.

Jumping Bull breathed deeply of the purifying smoke that rose from Lone Dog's tipi. He tried to absorb comfort from the shaman's lamenting chants, but consolation eluded him.

The dark sorrow of death prevailed.

Jumping Bull walked to the tipi at the edge of the camp that he had visited many times before. Apprehension tingled down his spine as he neared. Where he had expected echoes of personal anguish to match his own . . . he heard only silence.

Jumping Bull pushed aside the flap of Seeing Woman's tipi. He stopped short when Seeing Woman turned toward him. Stunned, he saw her lined face was dry of tears; she stood motionless, awaiting his entrance.

A rush of fury replaced Jumping Bull's former trepidation. Advancing toward her, he snarled, "Your coldness shames you, Seeing Woman! Night Raven was the son of your heart! The bravest of warriors, he fell in battle without fear! He was more a son to me than those of my own loins. You alone are left of his blood to mourn him—yet your eyes are dry!"

Jumping Bull's blood thundered at Seeing Woman's silence.

"Speak, woman! Tell me why you dishonor Night Raven in this way!"

Seeing Woman remained motionless under his verbal assault. His rage abruptly draining away, Jumping Bull viewed in the subtle lift of her chin the remnants of a slenderness and grace that was once unmatched. He saw not neat braids streaked with gray but a flow of black hair that gleamed in the sun. He saw not a womanly face touched by the passage of years but a youthful countenance of inordinate beauty. He saw not lips composed in a sober line but a radiant smile that touched his heart—and he saw eyes that glowed with life—unlike the sightless eyes that now returned his stare.

Sadness overwhelmed Jumping Bull. He was a chief of his people. He was respected by all within the camp, and his status was second to no other. He had wives who served his needs, and his generosity to them and others was as well known as his exploits in battle, but his heart was filled with despair. Night Raven, the son of his spirit, had slipped from life on a bloody battlefield, and the only woman who had ever filled his heart was forever beyond him.

Jumping Bull urged more softly, "Speak to me, Seeing Woman. Tell me, so I may understand why you do not mourn."

Seeing Woman approached, halting so close that her familiar scent filled his nostrils as she raised her hand to touch his cheek. Smoothing the skin there with her palm, she whispered, "Your cheeks are also dry. I am glad. I would not have Jumping Bull shed unnecessary tears."

"Unnecessary tears?"

"Many died in the thunder of the white man's cannon. I mourn them, but I do not weep for the one close to both our hearts."

Jumping Bull's heart seemed to stop.

"Night Raven lives."

His heart leaped.

"The shadows before my eyes cleared as the

night deepened. I saw him then—Night Raven, his face washed clean of war paint, his eyes closed."

"Dead . . . you saw him dead!"

"No!" Placing the flat of her hand against Jumping Bull's chest, where his heart pounded with furious intensity, Seeing Woman halted his protest. "I saw him breathing deep. I saw the mark of the white man's bullet, a wound carefully tended and bathed . . . and I saw the room where he lay in a white man's bed."

"In a white man's bed?"

"And I heard his thoughts! I felt the anger and driving need for vengeance that spurs the beating of his heart."

"He is dead. I saw him fall."

"Jumping Bull . . ." Pain flashed in Seeing Woman's sightless eyes. "Cries of mourning echo within the camp. Many have died, but Night Raven lives!"

Sensing that his doubts were fading, Seeing Woman continued more softly, "Night Raven is the tie that binds us. That tie remains unbroken. It lives, growing stronger with every breath Night Raven breathes. Night Raven would have you put aside your grief and rejoice."

Seeing Woman paused. Her expression abruptly sobered.

"And he would have you prepare . . . for he will return."

* * *

"I don't like being challenged, Captain!"

Drawing his wiry frame up to its full height, Major Locke faced Captain Rice with rising annoyance. The sun had barely risen. He had come to his office earlier than usual, expecting to spend the morning drafting his report to Washington. He had been up most of the night, outlining it in his mind. He intended to describe in detail the plan he had used to defeat the enemy. He would avoid any mention of himself and would extol the virtues of the men under his command without reference to any particular individual, thereby turning the praise back on himself. He would be subtle in making sure his superiors understood that he, alone, was responsible for the capture of one of the most bloodthirsty savages on the western frontier. He would then add a request to assume *personal responsibility* for Night Raven until the savage was brought to final justice under the law—thereby ensuring that his name would be forever linked with his victory over the infamous enemy warrior.

Major Locke's annoyance heightened as he stared at the officer standing stiffly in front of him. He didn't like having Captain Rice interfere with his morning plans. In truth, he didn't like Captain Rice, either. Rice's blazing red hair was personally distasteful to him, the fellow's exaggerated spit and polish was the exact opposite of the manner of dress he had adopted, and Rice's strict adherence to military procedure was a silent challenge to the method of command he had developed over years of Indian wars. He had no patience for the man.

Nor did he have patience for Rice's formal protest against the order he had issued the previous day regarding Edwina Keene. The man's tenuous control was obvious in the stiffness of his shoulders and the set of his jaw. Rice was furious, but he failed to realize that his manner only aggravated the irritation he stirred at the mere mention of the abrasive Miss Keene.

Locke continued sharply, "Let me set one thing straight with you before we go on, Captain. You refer to Miss Keene as *Doctor* Keene. I've made my feelings clear on the subject of Miss Keene's claim to being a certified medical doctor. I won't allow any man in my command to address her by that title until I'm sure it's valid. As for my direct order that you refrain from any personal contact with Miss Keene, it's my opinion that your close association with her could possibly influence the performance of your duty under present conditions, and that the result could be detrimental to the fort's welfare. That order stands until the prisoner is returned to his cell."

"I would like to restate my formal protest of that order, sir." Captain Rice's voice was strained. "Having achieved the rank of captain in the U.S. Army, I feel I've proved that I'm capable of performing my duty under any circumstances."

"Unfortunately, Captain, what *you* feel you've proved doesn't matter much to me. Your protest is denied! And let me make another point. You disobeyed a direct order last night when you went to Miss Keene's quarters."

"Sir, Miss Keene and I—"

"Yes, I know all about *'Miss Keene and I . . .'*"

"Sir—" Captain Rice's fair complexion heated. "My association with Miss Keene is totally respectable."

"I don't care whether it is or not! The situation in this fort is volatile. Resentment against Miss Keene is high. I won't have one of my officers openly agitating the residents of this fort, who stand in righteous protest against Miss Keene's demand that the prisoner be taken to her quarters to be given *special* care."

"Openly agitating, sir? My association with Miss Keene is purely personal."

"You're proving my point!"

"My private friendships aren't the army's concern."

"You have no private life in this fort, Captain! In case I need to be more explicit, let me repeat—you are to refrain from any personal contact with Miss Keene until further notice. That order includes Mrs. Rice, and will remain in effect until I formally rescind it. Is that clear?"

"Sir—"

"Is that clear?"

"Yes, sir!"

"That's all, Captain."

Struggling to control his anger, Major Locke remained stiff-faced as Captain Rice exited the room. Staring at the closed door, he cursed under his breath. He had half a mind to throw the impudent bastard into the same cell Night Raven had vacated—but he wouldn't be that foolish. He had no desire to do anything that might distract the fort's attention from its growing disapproval of Edwina Keene—who was doing his dirty work for him. He had no doubt that she would do her best to restore the Indian savage to health just to prove she was better than any male doctor.

Locke turned toward the office window where the sun shed its golden glow on a fort yard just coming to life with the new day. He breathed deeply of the brisk morning air. He had grown truly fond of the wilderness frontier with its vast, wide-open spaces and endless opportunities. It was made for a man like he, who was destined for greatness and who wasn't afraid to grasp the opportunities presented. Yes, once he had rid the frontier of the Sioux lice infesting it, it would be as close to perfect as any place could be.

Locke's bearded face twitched in a brief smile. It would be a new day for him, indeed, when Night Raven stood healthy, strong, and in chains, as the court pronounced his fate. With a bit of luck, he might even be rewarded for his accomplishment by being given a free hand in dealing with the Sioux—so the extermination could begin.

Locke's short laughter was harsh. How it would gall Miss Edwina Keene if she knew she was providing a large forward thrust in that direction.

Miss Edwina Keene, who despised him as much as he despised her.

Night Raven will return.

The words she had uttered to Jumping Bull with such confidence moments earlier remained vivid in Seeing Woman's mind.

Jumping Bull's distinctive step faded from Seeing Woman's hearing, drowned out by the tearful laments still resounding in the camp. She remembered rushing to join the expectant crowd when the returning war party was sighted. The abrupt silence that fell as it neared needed no explanation. She had waited, listening as the warriors dismounted, hoping for Night Raven's touch on her arm, for the sound of his voice speaking the reassurance that he was alive and well. The black well of despair into which she fell when she learned he had not returned was familiar and deep.

Seeing Woman stared into the darkness that would forever enclose her. She unconsciously stroked the jagged scars on her arms, aware that her legs were similarly marked. The past rose before her sightless eyes with a sudden clarity that left her breathless. She saw Spotted Wolf, and love squeezed her heart. He stood tall and strong, smiling at her in a way that he did for no other. She saw his lips move with whispered words of love as he held his arms out to her, inviting her in.

A sob of joy escaped Seeing Woman's lips. She had known Spotted Wolf all her life: she had tolerated him as the older brother of her friend; she had liked him as the boy whose smile was always warm for her; she had loved him as the bold, handsome brave who won her heart; but her love had increased a hundred fold for the husband who esteemed her above all else. She had considered herself the most fortunate of all young maidens when Spotted Wolf paid her court; and when they married, she believed her happiness was complete.

But time passed, and no children came to them. In her despair, her heart bleeding with every word, she had urged Spotted Wolf to take another wife—but he would not. She had turned to Jumping Bull, Spotted Wolf's dear friend, imploring him to speak to Spotted Wolf so her husband would not be denied the son he so deserved, but Jumping Bull's efforts were to no avail. Her husband's love for her seeming to grow stronger, his body ever more eager for her flesh. Spotted Wolf wanted no other woman, and her selfish heart silently throbbed with joy at knowing she would share him with no other.

Seeing Woman took a shaky breath. She had been ill and unable to travel with the camp on the fateful day of the massacre. Left behind, she could only shudder in horror at the knowledge that the women and children who had gone ahead with the main party had been slaughtered by the bluecoats. Her widowed sister, Morning Sun, and her two sons were among them.

Then she learned that Night Raven, the elder of her sister's sons, had survived.

Night Raven was a badly wounded boy of ten summers when she took him into the tipi she shared with Spotted Wolf. The greatness foreshadowed by the shaman's vision of a raven at the time of Night Raven's birth was evident even then—in the boy's powerful stature, which surpassed all other youths, and in the keen mind the boy exhibited. It was then that the reason the Great Spirit had withheld children from her became suddenly clear. Night Raven had been marked for greatness, and

Spotted Wolf and she had been chosen to help him on his way.

With Night Raven's coming to their tipi, the circle of love within was completed. She had not realized, however, that the circle was meant to be broken.

A soft wail rose in Seeing Woman's throat. She saw again the image of Jumping Bull, his head bowed as he brought Spotted Wolf's body home. Jumping Bull sought to console her, but her grief was inconsolable. Her hair shorn and her arms and legs bloodied by her own blade, she lay in the brush for days, convulsed by a torment that almost stole her life. Were it not for Night Raven, who sought her out and brought her home, she would not have survived her sorrow.

Jumping Bull, ever Spotted Wolf's friend, provided for Night Raven and her in her widowhood, but Night Raven would not be satisfied with Jumping Bull's generosity. Taking up Spotted Wolf's shield, he demanded to ride with Jumping Bull in Spotted Wolf's place. His youthful heart was hardened to vengeance, and his bravery was unmatched. The bond that formed between Jumping Bull and Night Raven grew firm and fast, bringing them solace, but her own grief at Spotted Wolf's death remained. She knew at last that it could be relieved in only one way.

The ceremony was brief. The bloom of youth was still on her cheeks when she invited the honorable widows of the village to her tipi and gave them feast. She listened as they spoke of their faithfulness to their husbands, and then spoke of her own. When all had been said, she "bit the knife," vowing to be ever faithful to the great warrior she had loved and lost. So strong was her love that she did not fear the curse that would befall her if that vow was broken.

Her emotions again under control, Seeing Woman raised her head high. She did not lament her misfortune when her eyes grew dark and her vision faded, for she was rewarded with sight that others did not possess. She saw many things with that sight, and it was secretly whispered by some that a part of her was *Wicasa*, wise above all, a term allowed only for the wise men of their village. But of everything she had seen with her sightless eyes, most precious of all was the vision of Night Raven that had appeared the previous night.

Seeing Woman's throat choked tight. Even now the steady pounding of Night Raven's heart echoed in her ears. The waiting would be hard, but she knew Night Raven would return.

Seeing Woman closed her eyes as tears rose.

Night Raven, the son who was not really her own.

Jumping Bull, who loved and was loved without spoken acknowledgement.

All were blessings that filled her life with—

At the sound of a stealthy step outside her tipi, Seeing Woman stilled. She called out aloud.

"Who comes?"

No response.

"Speak."

Silence.

Suddenly trembling, Seeing Woman spoke more boldly.

"What're you doin', Corporal?"

Edwina stood rigidly in the doorway of her room, her attention focused on the burly soldier who stood menacingly over Night Raven's bed, his gun drawn. When he made no response, she addressed him again.

"I asked you what you're doin', Corporal!"

Corporal William Smart turned sharply toward her, and Edwina felt a familiar aversion. She had never like the looks of his beefy face, yellow teeth, and shifty eyes. She had left her quarters at dawn to visit the ward where the wounded soldiers were recuperating, only to discover that Corporal Smart had replaced Corporal Thompson on guard outside her door during the night. Her discomfort became concern when Smart entered her quarters to stand guard beside Night Raven's bed, but concern became alarm when she'd returned a few minutes earlier to find Smart standing over Night Raven's bed, his finger tight on the trigger of his gun.

Smart's snarling reply sent a chill down her spine.

"This Injun ain't as sick as he's makin' out to be. He's playin' a game with you."

"Oh, is that so, Doctor?"

Advancing into the room, Edwina slipped between Smart and the bed, forcing the corporal a few steps backward. "I didn't need to be a doctor to feel that Injun watchin' me out of the corner of his eye while you was gone!" he spat. "And I didn't need to be a doctor to see him close them eyes when I came closer! The bastard's just makin' out he's sick! He's waitin' for a chance to—"

"Get out of here, Corporal. I'm the doctor here. I say whether this man's sick or well, and I don't answer to you."

"He's makin' a fool out of you! He's makin' a fool out of us all!"

"Don't make me report you to Major Locke."

"The major wouldn't say nothin'. He ain't an Injun lover like you!"

Edwina stiffened.

"The major wouldn't like nothin' better than for me to put a bullet through this Injun's head right here and now."

"Get out."

"And that's the way it would've been if it wasn't for people like you who—"

"Get out of this room—now!"

"Injun lover!"

Following Smart's lagging steps to the door, Edwina slammed it shut behind him, then stood trembling with fury as his taunt lingered.

Drawing her emotions under control, Edwina turned back to the bed to assess her patient. She had bathed the fever from Night Raven's body for the greater portion of the night and had then slipped into an exhausted sleep, only to awaken with a start of guilt when she saw dawn creeping through the window. Her guilt was relieved when she saw that Night Raven's temperature appeared to have stabilized. She had then taken the lamp behind a conveniently placed screen and quickly washed the grime of the previous day from her face and shoulders before slipping into fresh clothing and leaving to check on her other patients.

Edwina leaned closer to the bed and pressed her palm to Night Raven's forehead as he slept. Yes, he was cooler.

Edwina scrutinized him more closely—the clear, russet skin; the chiseled features motionless in sleep. Her heart skipped a beat. She had no doubt that Night Raven was several inches over the mark of six feet. His shoulders were as impressive as his height; his chest was powerful and deep, and the long length of his arms and legs was all muscle and sinew; yet there was an aura about him, a sense of power from within, that was more potent than his physical proportions. That aura lured her inexplicably, raising a keen awareness within her. The touch of his gaze was almost physical. His silence seemed to speak to her in ways that sent tremors down her spine. It was almost as if those gold eyes that had met hers so briefly had looked down deep inside her, to a part of her that she herself did not know—as if his silent voice called out to that part of her, compelling her to answer.

Edwina took a backward step. Night Raven was intimidating in so many ways, even in his present condition, but she had no doubt that standing tall, at full strength, he could stop a man's heart.

Or a woman's.

He could crush your neck with one hand.

The truth of Craig's warning was very clear.

Forcing that last thought from her mind, Edwina quickly checked Night Raven's wounds. Through it all, he did not stir.

Sleeping . . . or pretending? She couldn't be sure, but she consoled herself that he was so weak it didn't matter. She had already decided that she'd see to it Corporal Smart never darkened her doorway again, but in another day or so . . . yes, she'd bring the guard in to stand beside Night Raven's bed. It would be safer that way.

Disturbed by that concession, Edwina noticed that a plate of food and a cup of broth had been delivered in her absence. Turning back toward the bed, she prompted, "Night Raven, are you awake?"

Night Raven's eyes opened unexpectedly and Edwina's heart again leaped. Damn those gold eyes!

But his eyes were closing again.

"No, don't go back to sleep. Try to stay awake. I have some broth for you. It'll give you strength."

No response.

Edwina reached for the cup beside her and held it within Night Raven's line of vision. "This . . . for you. It'll make you—"

His eyes closed.

Cursing, Edwina placed the cup back on the table. Frustrated, she mumbled, "I'm wastin' my breath. He doesn't understand a word I say."

Edwina stared at Night Raven's still face.

". . . not a single word."

"Who comes? Speak."

Gratified at the halting breaths that betrayed Seeing Woman's anxiety, Running Deer stood peering into the older woman's tipi. She allowed the silence to stretch longer, with deliberate malice. The old woman's uneasiness was evident in her stance, in the tilt of her head as she strained to identify the sounds around her. That pleased Running Deer.

Entering the tipi at last, Running Deer closed the flap behind her. She raised her chin, her thin lips twisting with contempt. She had seen Jumping Bull leave this tipi. She had watched his comings and goings many times.

The angry knot of jealousy within Running Deer twisted tight. She was the youngest of Jumping Bull's wives. Jumping Bull was her father's friend and he had taken her into his tipi a year earlier when Black Dog was killed. Her comely features and slender form had made her much desired within the camp before Black Dog's death, but she had desired a man who did not glance her way, and she had spurned her many suitors. Jumping Bull had offered for her when she was left without a man to provide for her, and she had gladly accepted the union, despite the difference in age between them. She had foreseen great advantage to her in their union. Jumping Bull's other wives were old. She had been sure she would give Jumping Bull sons—sons who would supplant the harsh and unfeeling Night Raven in his eyes—and she had eagerly anticipated the day when she would become the most favored and powerful of his wives.

But her ambitions had been thwarted.

Jumping Bull's attentions to her had been meager, and it had not taken her long to understand why.

At first she had thought little of Jumping Bull's attentions to this woman whose hair was gray, whose skin was marked by age, and whose eyes could not even see the great warrior who paid her homage. She had believed they were inspired by pity. She had known she erred when she witnessed for the first time the warmth in their exchanges. Her angry protests were met with words of warning from Trailing Mist, the first of Jumping Bull's wives. Winter Flower, his second wife, had not been so kind.

"Speak, you who enter."

Running Deer tossed back the black, heavy hair that was so admired within the camp. She straightened her slender shoulders as Seeing Woman advanced falteringly toward her. Of the same age as Jumping Bull, Seeing Woman had grown weak with the years as Jumping Bull had grown stronger. Yet, old and sightless, she had somehow managed to bewitch Jumping Bull's mind—but the woman would not hold Jumping Bull captive much longer.

"Speak."

"It is Running Deer, Seeing Woman." Running Deer spoke abruptly. She smiled as the old woman jumped. She continued with feigned solicitude, "I waited to speak, uncertain whether I should intrude on your sorrow."

"My sorrow is for those who mourn the loved ones they have lost. I am not among them."

"But Night Raven—"

"Night Raven lives."

"Jumping Bull said he saw him fall."

"I have seen Night Raven. He is alive."

"You have seen him?"

"Last night, here, in my tipi."

A smile grew on Running Deer's lips. Night Raven's death had touched Seeing Woman's mind. The spell she had cast over Jumping Bull could not survive, and Jumping Bull would then see her as the aged witch she truly was. It was only a matter of time.

"Do not rejoice, Running Deer."

Running Deer's smile froze. "I rejoice that Night Raven lives."

Seeing Woman's sightless eyes devoured her.

"I share your happiness, and Jumping Bull's."

"You would . . . if you were wise."

"What do you mean?"

"You are young, Running Deer. There is much you must yet learn."

Running Deer's temper flared. "I am not so young that I do not know that you and Jumping Bull are—"

"Caution, Running Deer!" Seeing Woman's soft voice hardened. "Words harshly spoken linger long."

Running Deer forced the return of her smile.

"We speak at odds, Seeing Woman, but that was not my purpose in coming." She raised the bowl she carried toward Seeing Woman. "I come from Trailing Mist, who sends you food from her campfire. I will tell her that you have seen Night Raven, and that he lives. She will be glad that Jumping Bull's sorrow is lessened."

"Jumping Bull is a good husband to you."

Running Deer raised her chin a notch. "Yes, he is."

"He is kind and generous."

"Yes."

"He is gentle and fair in all things."

"Yes."

"—but he is unforgiving of deceit."

Running Deer stiffened.

Seeing Woman extended her hands to accept the bowl. "You may tell Trailing Mist that I thank her. You may tell her that Night Raven will repay her for her generosity when he returns."

Running Deer dropped the flap of Seeing Woman's tipi behind her, her good humor restored by the woman's parting words. The old woman was crazy. Night Raven was dead, and she was glad. His body was now as cold as his heart.

Running Deer smoothed a strand of hair back from her clear cheek. Her beauty was unmatched in the village. Her skin was fine, her body firm, and her features small. With his mind freed of Seeing Woman's spell, Jumping Bull would view her clearly, and he would want her. The other old women who were his wives were no match for her. She would soon rule Jumping Bull's heart.

Running Deer followed a direct path back to her tipi—head lowered to hide her smile from those who were mourning.

No, he was not sleeping . . . and he understood Edwina, far better than she knew.

Night Raven watched through slitted eyes as Edwina busied herself tidying up the room. He had awakened earlier that morning, before the light of day fully dawned, with a certainty that despite his pain, he was going to live. He had then watched Edwina's shadow reflected against the screen hiding her from direct view. Her womanly outline had taunted him mercilessly as she bathed—graceful neck, proud shoulders, rounded breasts—feminine curves that had moved sinuously, enticing him, mocking his weakness.

Night Raven studied Edwina surreptitiously as she approached him again. Her hair was neatly combed, and her freshly washed skin glowed. He pretended sleep as she leaned over him. The sweet scent of her skin filled his nostrils as a golden lock brushed his cheek with warmth.

Hair of glittering gold deceives you.

Pain surged unexpectedly, and Night Raven opened his eyes, gasping. Edwina leaned closer, the glorious blue of her eyes filled with concern.

Eyes of brilliant blue speak lies.

"What's wrong, Night Raven?"

Frustration touched Edwina's expression when he did not respond. She stared at him in silence, unaware that his pain faded while she was near. She picked up the cup from the table beside her.

"You need to eat somethin'."

Edwina raised the spoon to his lips, but he refused it.

"You need to eat somethin' if you want to get well." She pressed the spoon to his lips again. "Eat."

Night Raven turned away. Something tugged deep inside him and he looked back to find that the lines of concern on Edwina's face had deepened.

Delicate features seek to beguile you.

Ignoring the mocking voice, Night Raven separated his lips to accept the nourishment Edwina offered.

Edwina sat beside him as she fed him the broth. Her lips were smooth and lightly tinged with color. She wiped a drop from his cheek and her gaze locked with his. Her breasts heaved with a startled breath and she turned away abruptly, her hand trembling as she placed the empty cup back on the table.

Frowning, she stood up abruptly. The morning sun shone through the window, illuminating her with a radiant beam of gold as she paused.

Womanly beauty aspires to destroy you.

He would accept that challenge willingly.

She is your enemy.

He would meet the challenge and emerge victorious.

He swore that it would be so.

Shaken, Edwina looked down at Night Raven. He was sleeping again, but his eyes had spoken to her just moments ago when they met hers. Their message had left her trembling.

A sudden rush of panic turned Edwina toward the door. Her steps halted as reason returned. Why was she running? Where was she running to? She had been forbidden Craig's company, the residents of the fort had turned against her, and she couldn't go to Margaret and chance causing her dangerous stress. She had been denied any support she could possibly seek within the fort.

Damn the devious Major Locke! His plan was working well. With no one speaking up for her, and so many speaking out against her, the situation could only worsen. But she'd be double damned if she'd let him back her down.

Edwina glanced back at Night Raven.

An Injun lover, was she?

Edwina turned toward the door. Major Locke had a lot to learn if he thought he had won—and he was about to get his first lesson.

Jumping Bull walked toward the rise where his pony was tethered, where the sounds of the camp's sorrow were muted. The midday sun beat warmly on his head as he gazed out at undulating grasses that stretched as far as the eye could see. The golden glow of the vista did not lighten his heavily burdened heart. Seeing Woman's words had brought him bittersweet joy. Night Raven was alive . . . but he was a prisoner of bluecoats who would like nothing more than to see him hanged by the neck and left to rot in the sun, as had been the fate of other Sioux warriors before him.

Jumping Bull's frown lightened. He remembered Seeing Woman's joy when she'd said Night Raven would return. It brought to mind the image of Seeing Woman when she was young, and a familiar guilt stirred. He recalled his hunger for her, and his despair when she chose Spotted Wolf, his close friend, in his stead. He remembered that the death of his friend was a blow to his heart that was tempered only by the hope that Seeing Woman might turn to him in her grief. But Seeing Woman's love for Spotted Wolf had survived his death, and it was not to be.

Guilt stabbed deeper. Seeing Woman's eyes

were now sightless because of *him*. He had brought the curse upon her by insinuating himself into her life and joining Seeing Woman's spirit with his, even though her body remained pure, by sharing Night Raven with her as the son he could never have, and by holding Seeing Woman close to him through the years—*closer* to him than any other.

The ache within Jumping Bull expanded. He was a chief of his people, but he did not possess the power to open Seeing Woman's eyes so she could again view the world around her, so she could see that as the years passed, each new line on her cheek etched her beauty more deeply, and each gray hair added greater luster to the radiance that glowed from within her.

"Jumping Bull . . ."

Jumping Bull turned at the sound at a voice behind him. Running Deer approached, her slender body moving with the fluid ease of youth, her clear eyes bright. Halting beside him, she pressed her hand against his heart and whispered, "I saw you in the distance. Your great shoulders were bowed with sorrow, and my heart sorrowed as well. I long to offer you consolation, my husband."

Running Deer's intrusion into his moment of introspection brought back Jumping Bull's frown. Running Deer was young. She believed youth allowed her privileges that it did not, and he was displeased by her presumption. She was the wife he had taken to repay a brave warrior for his friendship, but he had quickly learned that she was too young to feel more than the beat of her own heart.

Running Deer took his hand and attempted to draw him toward a shaded bower nearby. She turned back toward him when he did not follow. Her gaze bold, she whispered, "I wish to give myself to you, Jumping Bull."

A girl, when he dreamed of a woman.

Jumping Bull's response was grave. "Return to your tipi, Running Deer. I seek a different consolation on this day of mourning for my people."

The disbelief that flashed across Running Deer's face at his response did not escape Jumping Bull. The anger she could not conceal was in the harsh line of her lips and the stiff set of her shoulders as she walked away—but he did not care. On this day of mourning, he did not lament the hurt feelings of a spoiled child. Instead, he grieved for the many brave warriors who were lost . . . for a love that was forever denied him . . . and for the son he treasured who was not his own—a son who had yet to return.

"Corporal Smart is guardin' my quarters. I want him replaced."

"Is that an order, Miss Keene?"

Major Locke's smile was a frozen grimace. Under other circumstances, Edwina was certain she might have shuddered from its freezing bite, but she was long past allowing this man's anger to affect her. Three of the wounded soldiers in her care had taken a turn for the worse that morning, demanding her constant attention during the previous hours. She had labored unassisted under the critical eyes and sharp comments of the women of the fort, and had finally turned on them with a harangue that was probably still echoing through the infirmary. She had then returned to her quarters to find Corporal Smart again flaunting his gun in Night Raven's face. No, Major Locke's frozen grimace didn't scare her, and she wouldn't tolerate Corporal Smart's presence in her quarters a minute longer.

Edwina replied coolly, "A command or a request . . . I don't care what you consider it, but I want Corporal Smart replaced *now*."

Edwina's response hung heavily on the silence between them before Locke answered. "It may come as a surprise to you, Miss Keene, but *I'm* the commander of this fort."

"I know that."

"That means I'm in charge, not you!"

"That's where you're wrong."

"Wrong, am I?"

"Yes, Major, you're wrong, because *I'm* in charge where my patients are concerned—that is, unless you want to assume responsibility for their welfare."

"As commandant of this fort, I'm responsible for the welfare of everyone in it."

"You're not a doctor."

"Neither are you."

Her jaw locking tight, Edwina replied through gritted teeth, "You have my official resignation, Major. The wounded men in this fort are now *your* patients."

Turning away from Major Locke without waiting for a response, Edwina reached for the doorknob. She paused only briefly at the choking sound behind her before pulling the door open.

"Come back here, Miss Keene."

Edwina glanced back at Major Locke, her expression cold. "I'm done talkin'."

"I'm not!"

Edwina took a step.

"I'm warning you . . ."

Edwina look back at him again. Major Locke's color was apoplectic as he repeated slowly, with rigid control, "Come back in here and close the door."

Edwina turned to face him and pushed the door closed behind her. Were Locke any other man, his high color, clipped breathing, and furious trembling might have caused her concern, but Locke wasn't any other man.

Instead, Edwina waited until he burst out "All right, you win! I'll have Corporal Smart removed from your door. I'll instruct my men that any requests from you with regard to Night Raven are to be handled promptly and without exception. I'll even allow you to choose the men you want on guard at your quarters—but I want to make one thing very clear."

Advancing to stand threateningly close, so close that Edwina was subjected to the pungent odor of his perspiration, Locke rasped, "By giving you total control over your Indian patient, I'm assigning you total responsibility for his health as well. In other words, Miss Keene, if Night Raven doesn't survive, I'll make an official report to my superiors that he died because your skills were inadequate and your care negligent."

"Is that supposed to scare me, Major?" Edwina stared back at him. "The army wants Night Raven dead anyway."

"But the army doesn't want him dead *now*, Miss Keene. The army wants him alive, so he can be tried for the entire western frontier to see, and hanged for his crimes, from the highest tree we can find."

Edwina held Locke's gaze without flinching.

"I thought the army was sent here to *civilize* the frontier, Major."

"I wouldn't expect an Indian lover to recognize the subtle distinctions involved."

"Call me an Injun lover if you want, but there's one thing I know for sure. You can't civilize a dead man."

Refusing to take a backward step at the sight of Major Locke's clenched fists, Edwina added, "But if that's the way you want it, it's fine with me. From here on in, Night Raven is *my* responsibility."

"Until he's well enough to stand for the hangman."

The sudden rise of bile to her throat twisted Edwina's lips into a grimace.

"What's the matter, Miss Keene? Bitten off more than you can chew?"

Her momentary squeamishness gone, Edwina responded, "It occurs to me, Major, that I might be askin' *you* the same question before too long."

Major Locke's muttered curse did not escape her ears as Edwina stalked out of the room.

There she was. She was leaving Major Locke's office, and it was clear that things hadn't gone well.

Drawing back into the twilight shadows of the fort yard, Craig waited as Edwina neared.

"Edwina."

Edwina jerked to a halt. "Craig! What are you doin' here?"

Regretting his furtive behavior, Craig snatched Edwina back between the fort buildings. He raised a cautionary finger to his lips.

Edwina glanced out into the fort yard, then whispered, "Are you crazy? This is just what Locke's waitin' for!"

"Why did he call you to his office, Edwina?"

"He didn't call me."

"You went to see him of your own accord?"

"I went to give him a taste of his own medicine. He didn't like the taste." Edwina's fleeting smile faded. "We shouldn't be talkin', Craig. There's nothin' Locke would like better than to get at me through you, but you'd be the one to pay for it."

"I'm sorry, Edwina. I failed you."

"What are you sayin'?"

Craig paused in reply. He should have realized Edwina wouldn't understand. She had always been blind to the fact that he loved her. She couldn't possibly know that when he'd finally accepted the reality that she would never return his feelings, when he'd allowed himself to love Margaret and to marry her, he had promised himself that whatever happened, he would protect Edwina and keep her safe. It was a selfish promise, he knew, but it was a promise to which he was committed.

"Craig . . ."

"You came to the fort because of Margaret, because of your feelings for her and our baby. It was my duty to see that you didn't suffer for it."

Edwina gave a short laugh. She touched his cheek lightly. "I guess I should apologize, too, because I've done nothin' but make trouble for you with the major since I got here."

Her sympathetic touch was almost more than he could bear. Craig grasped Edwina's hand and held it fast. Her hand was warm and lightly callused—toughened by circumstance, but with heat at the heart—just like her. He'd always love her.

"Don't look at me like that, Craig. Just stop worryin'."

"Locke's out to get you, Edwina . . . and he's ruthless."

"I know, but he's met his match."

"I'm sorry you got involved in this because of Margaret and me."

"Tell me somethin', Craig." Edwina's delicate features sobered. "If the situation was reversed, would you and Margaret have hesitated to come to my aid?"

"No, but—"

"No buts. I love you both, Craig."

Craig's heart thundered.

"You're family."

Family . . .

"You'd better go, Craig." Edwina scanned the

fort yard. "Someone's goin' to see us here, and you'll be in trouble."

"I don't care."

"I do." Edwina's smile sliced at his heart as she whispered, "Tell Margaret not to worry about anythin', either."

"Listen to me, Edwina." Struggling against his emotions, Craig whispered, "I want to say something. I know Major Locke's trying to force you out of this fort."

"He can't make me leave this fort a minute before I'm ready. I won't let him."

"But if any of it gets to be too much for you to handle, if Night Raven causes you a problem, if you need me for anything at all, I want you to let me know. Lee, Thompson, Murray, Pitts—any one of them would get your message to me."

"It would ruin your career to go against Locke's orders."

"Just send for me."

Edwina frowned. "I'd better go."

Edwina's eyes were so blue that they burned him. If he was another kind of man—

But he wasn't another kind of man. Instead, never more sincere, Craig whispered, "Remember what I said, Edwina. If you need me, I'll be there."

Edwina was suddenly frowning. "There is one thing. Major Locke said I could choose the guards to be stationed at my door. Which men would you choose, Craig?"

"Corporals Lee, Thompson—"

"No, not Thompson."

Craig frowned. "Why not Thompson?"

Edwina shook her head. "Who else, Craig?"

"Murray, Pitts, or Anderson."

He was still frowning when Edwina whispered, "I'll be all right."

She was gone before he had a chance to reply.

Night was falling.

Jumping Bull surveyed the Sioux camp as the day of mourning came to an end. The sorrowful wails had gone hoarse. The tears had dried and had then begun falling again. Purifying smoke filled the air, but hearts were heavy and spirits low.

Jumping Bull turned back to his tipi. The day had been long and his body was weary. The faces of fallen warriors remained in his mind, overshadowed by worry about Night Raven.

Sounds of movement within his tipi halted Jumping Bull's steps as he approached. His wives' tipis were silent nearby. He would have no patience for Running Deer if she awaited him. The comfort she offered him was not of the heart.

Jumping Bull lifted the flap of his tipi, paus-

99

ing as Trailing Mist turned toward him. The years they had shared were many. There was a comfort between them that had no need for words.

Jumping Bull lay down on his blanket, and Trailing Mist lay beside him. Her presence there was familiar and her arms were warm. The womanly softness the years had added to her body was comforting. She was a good wife who valued him as he valued her. She asked no questions when he spoke the name of another in the night. Instead, she held him closer, and his heart warmed to the love she gave him.

Jumping Bull turned to Trailing Mist. Her body soothed the ache within him—Trailing Mist, in whose eyes he saw the reflection of another.

Night was falling.

Weary, Edwina looked at the cot that had been delivered to her quarters in her absence. It was flat and hard, but it beckoned her with relentless appeal.

At a sound, Edwina turned toward the bed behind her. She looked at her sleeping patient. He still had not spoken a word. She approached him and touched her palm to his forehead. It was cool, as it had been all day. She had barely gotten him to drink another cup of broth before his eyes closed, but he was healing.

Edwina glanced at the door as a shadow

passed by. Corporal Smart had been replaced on guard by Corporal Lee, who was on the top of the list she had submitted to Major Locke. Major Locke would make her pay for that minor victory before all was said and done, she was sure.

Edwina looked back at Night Raven. In the short time since this silent Sioux had entered her life, friends had become enemies, and enemies had become friends.

Edwina amended that last thought. Night Raven was not her friend. She had become *his* ally, but he had not become hers. She was certain that of the many emotions she had sensed in Night Raven's gaze, friendship was not among them.

Edwina whispered to her sleeping patient, "You're my responsibility now, did you know that, Night Raven? Major Locke put your care into my hands—bastard that he is. And you'd better get well, because he's goin' to hang me if you don't." She paused, adding with a bitter twist of her lips, "Of course, if you do get well, he's goin' to hang *you* . . . from the highest tree he can find."

Sobering, Edwina stared at the sleeping Sioux. A peculiar knot deep inside clenched tight. She had no doubt that the men of the Sioux camp were lamenting the great warrior they had lost, but she suspected the women were lamenting a loss of another kind entirely.

Suddenly weary, Edwina mumbled, "Everybody's worrin' about you gettin' up and murderin' me in my sleep. But you know somethin'? Even if you did, I'd be too tired to care."

Walking the few steps to her cot, Edwina lay down and closed her eyes. Her mind wandered as sleep grew near.

Life was strange. Margaret and Craig were sick with worry about her. They loved her, and love was such a responsibility.

Night Raven's life was her responsibility. Did that mean his death would be her responsibility, too?

No.

Yes.

Maybe.

Damn.

Night had fallen. Night Raven stared at the cot close by where Edwina lay. Her breathing was slow and deep. She was sleeping.

Edwina had spoken to him, believing him unable to comprehend the white man's tongue. He had listened, and he had learned.

The bluecoats had given him nothing that they did not intend to take away. He had not expected more.

The major had put his life into Edwina's hands. That was as it should be—for it would not be long before her life would be in his.

Chapter Four

Edwina lay hot and moist beneath him. She closed her arms around him, drawing him more tightly against her. The sheen of her skin glowed in the semidarkness. It was smooth, without blemish. He tasted the rise of her cheek, the curve of her jaw. He brushed her lips with his and heard her soft cry of yearning.

Night Raven covered her mouth with his, and the sweet taste of her surged through him. He drank from her lips, long and deep, his hunger for her soaring. She was the vision beyond his reach, his torment and his joy, but she was not now eluding him.

Edwina's lips separated under his. Her body welcomed him in. He sank deep inside her and the wonder within him rose. She spoke to him, tender words of love that were sweet to his ears. Her light eyes held his—their color as true as the endless expanse above them.

Night Raven plunged deeper into the intimate warmth that held him. Edwina cried out softly as the moment of fulfillment rapidly neared.

Then she halted him abruptly. She trembled, loving words flowing from her heart. She waited for his response—but he could not speak to her. Not yet. It was not time.

She urged him to reply, her own love gradually dimming as his silence continued. He wanted to tell her . . . he wanted to speak, but—

She began struggling beneath him. Eyes formerly filled with love grew dark with anger. He attempted to hold her fast, but she wrenched herself free. She ran from him, but he could not follow. His arms were heavy, his legs were weak. He reached out toward her, imploring . . .

Night Raven awakened with a jolt. The darkness of the fort room surrounded him. Momentarily disoriented, he raised his head and saw the cot a few feet away where Edwina lay. She was sleeping, her expression serene, the glittering gold of her hair vibrant even in the darkness. She moved in her sleep, turning more fully toward him. The previous moments remained so vivid in his mind that the taste of her was still in his mouth, her scent in his nostrils. Her words of yearning echoed in his ears.

Edwina's lips separated. She whispered unintelligible words in her sleep and his heart began to race.

Suddenly aware that he was shuddering, Night Raven sneered with disdain at his vulnerability. Edwina tempted him to betray himself, even in his dreams, but he would not succumb to her entreaties.

Three nights had passed since the fort cannon had brought injury to him and disaster to his people. He had maintained his silence during that time and his silence had served him well. He was healing, but he was still weak. A few more days and his arms would be strong again, his legs quick, and then his time would come.

Night Raven glanced at the window where another dawn was rapidly yielding to the light of day.

A heavy knock sounded on the door.

Edwina bolted upright in bed. She glanced toward him, but he did not move. The knock came again and Edwina jumped to her feet.

Jumping Bull drew back on the reins, pausing to survey the land surrounding him as daylight stretched hungry fingers across the sky. The tipis of his people were coming into view on the horizon—the camp where sounds of

105

mourning had gradually dimmed, although hearts were still heavy.

Jumping Bull glanced at White Bear's mount, where it snorted at the end of a lead rope. He had brought home many of his warriors' mounts in the years past. Each time it grew more difficult than the last, but today sorrow had been replaced by a burning need for vengeance.

The sun's first rays grew rapidly brighter as Jumping Bull nudged his mount into motion again. He was anxious to return to the one who awaited him.

Emotions stirred Jumping Bull's heart as he neared the camp. His strong shoulders were erect, his expression stoic as he searched out a particular face among those who milled at the edge of the clearing. He felt the contact of eyes that could not see. Seeing Woman sensed his approach.

Dismounting beside her, Jumping Bull spoke the three words Seeing Woman waited to hear.

"It is done."

"I won't stand for it!"

Still disoriented from being awakened so abruptly minutes earlier, Edwina moved between Corporal Smart and Night Raven as Smart attempted to secure Night Raven's wrists to the bed. Smart glared, pushing her roughly aside with his beefy bulk as he turned toward the guard who had followed him into the room.

"Get her out of my way, Pitts, or there's goin' to be trouble."

"Step back, please ma'am," Pitts requested.

Aware that she had no recourse, Edwina responded to Pitts's soft-spoken entreaty with a stiff nod. Seething, she watched as Smart grasped Night Raven's wrist and looped a coil of rope around it. Night Raven made no protest, but his gaze cut deep.

"What're you lookin' at, heathen?"

Edwina was trembling with fury. "He doesn't speak our language, Smart."

"No? Well, I'm thinkin' there's no way he won't understand what I'm doin' now."

Jerking the rope tight, Smart secured Night Raven's wrist to the bed. Night Raven made no sound, but the almost indiscernible twitch of his eyes betrayed him.

"That rope is too tight. You'll cut off his circulation."

"I'd cut off more than that if I had my way."

"And you call him a savage!"

"That's right, *ma'am.*" Smart looped another coil of rope around Night Raven's ankle and jerked it down against the bed. "But nobody calls me an Injun lover."

"Get out of here, Smart!"

"You can't chase me out of here like you did before, not before I do the job Major Locke sent me here to do. He gave you leeway for a while, but he ain't takin' no chance of this Injun gettin' away."

"Use your eyes, Smart! Does the prisoner look like he's strong enough or stupid enough to try to escape from a well-armed fort where every man's waitin' for the chance to kill him?"

"I'm usin' my eyes, all right"—Smart's expression was hot with hatred—"and what I'm seein' is a savage who'd slit my throat just for the fun of it if he got the chance."

"Like you'd do to him."

"That's right, and I ain't ashamed to admit it. I seen this bastard's work . . ."

"Just like he's seen yours."

"Injun lover! You make me sick."

Edwina was shuddering. "Do what you came here to do and get out! It'll be *undone* soon enough."

"I hope you do try to let this Injun loose after I leave"—Smart glanced at the guard standing silently behind him—" 'cause Pitts here has orders. Ask him. Go ahead. He'll tell you. If you untie the prisoner, he has orders to report it to the major so's the prisoner can be sent back to the cell where he belongs."

"Is that right, Pitts?"

"Yes, ma'am. It is."

Edwina looked back at Night Raven. His expression remained impassive despite the ropes cutting into his flesh.

Agitated, Edwina waited until the last rope was tied. She then ordered, "Now get out of here, Smart."

Smart's jowled face creased in a twisted smile. "You want me out of here?" He took a threatening step toward her. "Fine. My fun's over. As a matter of fact, I ain't had so much fun since I was up on that fort wall, pickin' off them Injuns like fish in a barrel."

"Get out."

Still trembling when the door closed behind Smart, Edwina turned back to the bed. Her hands were on the ropes when Pitts spoke up.

"Don't do that, ma'am."

"I can't leave my patient like this, Pitts."

"I got orders."

"It's only been four days since this man was shot in the chest and lost half the blood in his body."

"The major's thinkin' that Injun might be recuperatin' faster than you think. That's how them Injuns are."

"*I'm* this man's doctor."

"The major says—"

"I'd appreciate it if you'd go back outside, Corporal."

"Ma'am, if you let him loose, I'll have to report it to the major."

"I won't. You have my word. Please leave."

Edwina turned back toward Night Raven as the door clicked shut behind her. Her stomach squeezed tight. Her patient's arms were secured spread-eagled to the side of the bed. His feet protruded from the coverlet, tied the same way. It was cruel and unnecessary . . . inhumane.

Night Raven's gaze caught and held hers and Edwina gasped. No, he wasn't impassive. He was angry and ready to kill . . . and somehow, he blamed her!

Bobbie Ray walked slowly through the vast, sun-drenched wilderness surrounding him. His path was uncertain, and his legs were weak. In all his nine years, he had never been so thirsty. He squinted up at the sun. His head ached and he knew from the heat in his freckled cheeks that his skin was burning. He felt as if he had been walking endlessly. He was beginning to think the fort would never come into view.

Bobbie wiped the sweat from his forehead with a stubby hand. His clothes were dirty and soaked with perspiration, and his stomach was empty. He flattened his palm to shield his eyes and stared into the distance. The heat rose from the ground in wavering columns that blurred the landscape, but he could almost see—

Bobbie's heart jumped a beat as the scene cleared. He saw the outline of a fort! It had to be John Carter. He was almost there!

* * *

Rage infused Night Raven as Edwina stood beside the bed, looking down at him. It was afternoon, and he had spent the hours since dawn bound like an animal. If his strength had fully returned, he would snap the feeble bonds that secured him. He would find the bluecoat who had spat his hatred of the Sioux as he tied the ropes, and he would drive his knife deep.

Edwina turned away from him abruptly and walked to the window. She pretended to be saddened by his discomfort.

Delicate features seek to deceive you.

Night Raven raised his chin. No, he would not allow her to deceive him. He jerked covertly at the ropes, his anger fierce. He could feel his strength returning.

Edwina's profile was etched against the light streaming from the yard beyond. His rage was boundless, but it did not dim the effect of Edwina's beauty on his senses. Her beauty drew him. It rushed through his veins each time she looked his way. His mind raced ahead to the time when he would be free to make his dreams become reality, when he would stroke her sweet flesh and bring to life a passion that would make him victorious.

A sudden commotion in the fort yard drew Edwina's attention. She tensed, her body like that of a graceful wild creature whose senses were suddenly alerted. She turned and walked swiftly to the door. As she pulled it open, the shouts grew louder.

"Get Major Locke! Hurry up, Rogers! Somebody's out there, comin' toward the fort. He's on foot."

The scramble in the fort yard was instantaneous. The Sioux attack four days earlier was still fresh in the minds of all. Rogers bolted toward the major's office. The spyglass was still pressed to the lookout's eye when Major Locke appeared in the yard.

Advancing toward the wall with long, heavy strides, Major Locke called out, "Report, Corporal Porter. Who's approaching? Is it an Indian?"

His eye to the glass, Porter mumbled under his breath to the soldier beside him, "I don't know no Injun who'd walk up to this fort in broad daylight."

"Porter!"

"Yes, sir, I'm lookin'."

Porter adjusted the glass. He called out, "It ain't a man, sir! It's a boy!"

"A boy?"

"He ain't too big, neither, maybe ten or so—no more. He's staggerin'. It don't look like he's goin' to make it, sir."

"You're sure it's not an Indian?"

"I ain't never seen an Injun with hair that yellow, sir."

Standing beside Major Locke, Rogers offered, "I'll go out and get the boy, sir."

"When I give the order, and not before."

"He fell down, sir!" Porter turned briefly toward the men gathered below him before raising the glass back to his eye. "Looks like he's havin' trouble gettin' up."

"Major . . ."

"Another word out of you, Rogers, and you'll be on report."

Refusing to turn at the sound of a familiar step, Locke heard the brief exchange behind him before Captain Rice addressed him directly.

"Porter says there's a boy out there who needs help, sir."

Locke turned sharply toward the tight-lipped officer behind him. "I'm not deaf, Captain. I heard him."

Rice waited impatiently for him to continue, and Locke almost smiled. Rice had been heading for an out-and-out confrontation with him since he had put the obnoxious Miss Keene off-limits. Rice's control was slipping a little more with each passing hour.

Rice's jaw twitched revealingly. "Sir . . . the boy—"

"That boy may be a trap the Sioux have set for us. They may be out there, hiding, waiting for a patrol to be sent out so they can ambush it."

"I don't think so, sir."

"I'm not interested in what you think, Captain."

Stiff-jawed, Rice questioned, "What's your plan, sir?"

"I'm going to wait."

"How long, sir?"

"Don't press me, Captain."

Rice's jaw hardened to stone. "I'll get the boy, Major."

"No."

"I'm making an official request."

"No."

Rice moved a step closer. His voice dropped to a confidential tone when he addressed Major Locke again.

"The reputation of the fort will suffer badly if something happens to the boy out there while we're waiting in here."

"Are you telling me you're concerned about the fort's image, Captain?"

"I'm thinking about the reputation of the fort, sir, but the boy is my main concern."

Locke's thin face twisted into a sneer. "All right, Captain, if you're so worried about a boy we know nothing about, go out there and get him—but remember, you volunteered!"

The fort gates swung open as Captain Rice mounted.

Standing in the fort yard where the commotion had drawn her, Edwina withheld a gasp of dismay as Craig lowered the boy's inert form down into waiting hands. The boy was unconscious. His fair skin was scorched by the sun and his breathing was short and fast.

Edwina ordered, "Take him to my quarters. Hurry up!"

Dismounting, Craig shook his head. "I don't think that's a good idea with that Sioux in there."

His complexion florid, Major Locke spat, "*I'll* make the decision where the boy is taken, Captain."

Edwina interjected angrily, "We don't have time to argue. The sooner this boy gets attention, the better."

"Take him to your room, then, Miss Keene—if you insist on exposing him to danger."

Aware that Locke hoped to goad her, Edwina did not bother to reply. Instead, she turned toward the soldier holding the unconscious boy. "You heard Major Locke. Take the boy to my quarters. He can be moved later if anybody feels he isn't safe there." When the uncertain fellow didn't move, she urged, "Hurry up! We have no time to waste."

"Edwina . . ."

Pained at the realization that to speak to Craig with the major nearby would only make matters worse, Edwina followed resolutely behind as the unconscious boy was carried away.

"My name's Bobbie Ray."

The day was waning. The boy had regained

consciousness earlier and had then fallen into a more normal sleep. He had slept most of the day before waking again a few minutes earlier.

Edwina's relief was sweet. She had seen the effects of dehydration and overexposure to the sun before. The boy's body temperature had been mounting. Working frantically to reduce the heat, she had pulled the linens from the cot and soaked them in a bucket of water. She had then shocked the soldiers silently observing by wrapping the boy, clothes and all, in the saturated sheets. She had endured clucking sounds of disapproval behind her when the boy started trembling violently, but when the hour was over, the boy's body temperature was normal and his eyes were open. Now he was talking.

A trace of disorientation remained as the boy continued, "I'm not sure how long I was walkin', ma'am. My pa and me got separated from the wagon train when we lost a wheel. Then my pa rode off to hunt up somethin' for us to eat . . . but he didn't come back. I waited with the wagon for two days before I went out lookin' for him—but my horse threw me and ran off. I've been walkin' ever since, tryin' to get here." The boy paused for a breath. "This is Fort John Carter, ain't it?"

"Yes, this is Fort John Carter." Major Locke stepped up beside the bed, responding in Edwina's stead. "Were you headed here?"

"My pa said we'd be passin' the fort on our way. I figure he'll look for me here when he sees I'm gone."

"It was foolish of you to leave your wagon. You've caused a lot of unnecessary trouble by not waiting for your father to return. I'll be sure to tell him so when he comes to claim you."

Edwina glared at Major Locke. The man didn't have a stitch of compassion in him! He hadn't even bothered to inquire about the boy's condition until he was notified that the child had recovered enough to speak. He had entered the room minutes earlier and had actually smiled when he saw Night Raven bound to the bed.

Major Locke turned toward Edwina, his voice emotionless. "The boy looks well enough. I want him out of your quarters."

"It's late, Major." Edwina struggled to keep her tone civil. "It's better if he stays where I can watch him until mornin'."

Major Locke glanced around him with obvious contempt. His gaze lingered on Night Raven before he replied, "I don't think the boy will be in much danger with the Indian safely secured, but he'll be better off staying with one of the officer's wives—among his own kind."

"He'll be better off here tonight."

Major Locke's small eyes pinned her. "I'll be sure to pass along your lack of confidence in the ladies of the fort, Miss Keene. I'm sure they'll appreciate it."

"I'm not worried about any imagined slight the ladies of the fort might think I intended."

"I'll be sure to pass that along, too."

"You can do anythin' that suits you, Major, just as long as you leave the boy here so I can watch him durin' the night."

"As usual, Miss Keene, I'll defer to your request—just as long as you remember that his safety is in your hands."

Noting the boy's silence after Major Locke left the room, Edwina questioned softly, "What Major Locke said didn't scare you, did it, Bobbie—about that Injun bein' a savage and you bein' in danger?"

"I don't listen to people who talk like that, ma'am." Bobbie shrugged. "My pa always says there's good and bad in all people, and a man's got to find out for himself which way it is."

"Your pa sounds like a good man, Bobbie."

"He is, and he's smart, too." Bobbie's eyes filled unexpectedly. "That's why I couldn't figure how he came to get lost like he did."

"Don't worry about that now." Swallowing past the sudden lump in her own throat, Edwina pulled the coverlet up to Bobbie's waist. "Your pa will find you. He won't stop lookin' until he does. I know I wouldn't."

Bobbie's smile wobbled.

"I'll be sleepin' in this chair beside your cot.

If you're not feelin' good during the night, you wake me up, you hear?"

"Yes, ma'am."

Her young patient settled, Edwina glanced up at Night Raven. He had closed his eyes, but she knew he wasn't sleeping. How could he be? He had been tied like an animal all day. Every muscle in his body had to be aching. Even if everything said about him was true, she couldn't let him stay like that all night.

Edwina walked to the door and pulled it open.

"Ma'am?" His dark brows furrowed, Corporal Anderson turned toward her. "Is somethin' wrong?"

"I'm goin' to untie Night Raven's ankles for the night, and I'm goin' to fix it so there's a little more slack in the ropes on his wrists."

"Ma'am, Major Locke wants that Injun tied just the way he is."

"He won't be able to get out of bed, if that's what the major's worryin' about. He'll just be able to move enough to sleep a little more comfortably."

"Ma'am, please, I'll have to report you to Major Locke, and Captain Rice wouldn't like that."

Edwina raised a weary hand to her head. "I don't want the prisoner to escape any more than you do, Corporal. If I thought there was a chance of that happenin', I'd leave him tied the way he is."

"Ma'am . . ."

"I'm only tellin' you because I didn't want to break the promise I made to Pitts this mornin'."

"Ma'am . . ."

"You can check the ropes yourself if you like."

Anderson glanced briefly around him, then lowered his voice. "Well, if the prisoner's ankles worked loose under the blanket durin' the night but his wrists were still tied, I guess it wouldn't matter too much—especially if I didn't know nothin' about it and his ankles was tied again in the mornin'."

"Thanks, Corporal."

Edwina smiled, then closed the door. She felt the heat of Night Raven's perusal as she approached him, and a familiar knot clenched inside her. She had tended this man's wounds for four days. She had tried to communicate with him and had not gotten a single word of response in return. She had fought for his welfare and comfort every step of the way—yet, with one sweep of those peculiar gold eyes, he reminded her that she was his enemy.

What was it about this man that made her conscious of him in ways she couldn't quite comprehend? Why did she struggle to penetrate his silence? How had she suddenly become his defender . . . especially since she had as much reason as everyone else in the fort to hate him?

The answers eluded her. What she did know was that somewhere along the line, the choice had been made for her, and she was committed to it.

Yet, with just one sweep of those peculiar gold eyes . . .

Edwina raised her chin defensively as she reached the bed. It would be a while before Night Raven was restored to his former strength, but there was nothing infirm about the way he looked at her . . . as if biding his time.

Her fingers suddenly clumsy, Edwina struggled to untie Night Raven's ankles. The heat of his stare burned her as she adjusted the ropes on his wrists—yet when she was done and she looked up, Night Raven deliberately closed his eyes.

Her tone caustic, Edwina grated, "You're welcome."

Irritated, she walked to the window and looked out at the darkened sky as the future loomed with growing uncertainty before her. She glanced at the cot where Bobbie lay. The boy was sleeping again. It occurred to her that the boy was probably wiser than she: He was taking the rest he needed before facing his own uncertain future.

Sighing, Edwina sat in the upholstered chair beside the boy and closed her eyes. In a few minutes, she would be sleeping, too.

Bobbie stirred, then opened his eyes to the darkness of the lady doctor's quarters. Everything was quiet. He looked at the chair beside the bed. The lady doctor was sleeping.

Bobbie threw back the coverlet and stood up slowly. He waited for the dizziness to go away. He knew it would. He had taken sick from the sun once before and it had passed, just like this time.

Pushing his light hair back from his forehead, Bobbie walked toward the bed where the Indian lay. He knew how to walk without making a sound. That lesson had been taught to him with great patience.

Beside the bed at last, Bobbie looked down at the great Sioux warrior lying there. His eyes were closed.

Bobbie leaned toward him. He whispered, *"How, kola!"*

Night Raven's eyes immediately opened. *"How,* White Bear."

His eyes bright even in the darkness, Bobbie whispered, "Jumping Bull sent me, Night Raven. I've come to rescue you, just like you rescued me!"

Night Raven smiled.

Chapter Five

"Eat your breakfast, Bobbie."

Bobbie looked up at Mrs. Sinclair. It was morning again, the second one he had spent in Sergeant and Mrs. Sinclair's quarters. Major Locke had sent a soldier to take him to stay with Mrs. Sinclair after that first night in Miss Keene's room. The major said he needed to live with them until his pa came to get him. He had wanted to stay with Miss Keene so he could be close to Night Raven, but Night Raven had made it clear when they secretly talked that he should do everything he was told until the time was right.

Bobbie attempted a smile. Mrs. Sinclair was

a pretty lady, but she wasn't as pretty as Miss Keene. And she wasn't as nice, because she treated him like a baby. She told him to eat even if he wasn't hungry, and sleep when he wasn't tired.

"You're not eating, Bobbie."

"I'm not hungry."

"Eat your breakfast or you'll sit at that table until you do."

Bobbie remained silent. His ma had never said things like that to him—or he hoped she never had. He couldn't remember too much about her. She had died too long ago. His pa had raised him, and his pa never talked to him like that.

Bobbie blinked back tears. His pa never did come back when he went out to hunt up some food that day, and Bobbie had gone out looking for him, just the way he'd told the story. The only difference between his story and reality was that Night Raven was the one who'd found him after he had wandered in the tall grass for so long—not knowing which way to go, hungrier and thirstier than he had ever thought he could be, with his head burning hot and his body feeling like it was on fire. He remembered lying in that grass and opening his eyes to see Night Raven sitting on his horse, looking down at him.

Night Raven was bigger than his pa. He had never seen anybody like the great Sioux warrior before, and he was afraid, but Night Raven swooped him up and carried him to a shady place to cool off. He gave him water and made a bed for him in the cool grasses, and when he was sick afterwards, Night Raven talked to him and promised not to leave him. Night Raven took care of him, and when his head wasn't hot anymore and his stomach was settled, Night Raven took him back to the Sioux camp.

Night Raven didn't have a woman and couldn't keep him until his pa was found, but Singing Bird was quiet and kind, and she welcomed him into her tipi. He liked her and Many Faces, who was a brave warrior—but no warrior was braver than Night Raven.

Bobbie lowered his head in sorrowful remembrance. Night Raven was sad, too, when he brought back his pa's saddlebags, which was all that was left of him. Night Raven said his pa was killed when his horse fell and threw him. Night Raven then offered to take him back to his people if that was what he wanted—but Bobbie told him that wasn't what he wanted. He wanted to stay with Night Raven.

Night Raven was so brave. He was so strong, and he was the fiercest warrior of all the tribe. Night Raven had had a vision, and that vision guided him. Everyone knew that Night Raven would live long and bravely, and that he would lead the Sioux to victory over the people who wanted to kill them.

Bobbie's lips pressed tight. Some boys in the tribe had said that the white man was their enemy, and because his skin was white and his hair yellow, he was their enemy, too. But they didn't say that when Night Raven was nearby . . . and after a while, they stopped saying it at all.

It was Night Raven who gave him his name. Night Raven said he could read his heart, and that in his heart was the courage of a bear. Night Raven called him White Bear, and Bobbie was proud. He was proud when Singing Bird made him the clothing of a Sioux boy, too, and he had not worn his old clothing again until the great chief, Jumping Bull, came to speak to him a few days ago.

"Don't daydream, Bobbie! Finish your breakfast!"

He was so proud when Jumping Bull asked him to help rescue Night Raven. He had fasted the day before Jumping Bull and he set out, just as Jumping Bull told him, so his plight would look real. He had not protested when Jumping Bull showed him the direction, then left him miles from the fort in the darkness before dawn so his weariness would not be suspect when he arrived there. He knew how important it was for him to be accepted and allowed the freedom of the fort, and he had closed his mind to all discomfort, just as Night Raven had taught him. He hadn't expected to locate Night Raven so easily and he was glad; but although he was sure Night Raven would soon be well enough to escape, the waiting was hard.

"Bobbie . . ."

Bobbie's pale brows drew into a frown. He didn't like what everybody at the fort said about Night Raven . . . that he was a savage and a killer. He had even heard Mrs. Sinclair say that she was waiting for the day they'd hang him higher than a kite. Night Raven was a warrior. He was the bravest of all. He fought to protect his people.

"Bobbie!"

Bobbie looked again at Mrs. Sinclair, then picked up his spoon. He needed to go to Miss Keene's quarters. He needed to talk to Night Raven again, to see if it was time.

"When you finish eating, you can go out-side." Mrs. Sinclair's narrow face grew pinched. "Captain Rice ordered the men to clean out the cell where they're going to put Night Raven. He's doing it for Edwina Keene, of course, because he knows she'll insist on going in there to check that Indian's wounds, and he says it isn't fit for a lady in there. The men resent it, and I don't blame them."

Bobbie's small face wrinkled quizzically. "That place in the fort yard? They're goin' to put Night Raven in there?"

"That's right! Sergeant Sinclair says Major

Locke's going to move that Indian into the cell as soon as all the water they're splashing in there dries out. That means tomorrow, I guess—and he's going to do it whether Edwina likes it or not. It's about time, too! That woman's been treating that savage like a king."

"It smells bad in that cell."

"It's no worse than that savage deserves!"

"I wouldn't like it in there."

"Well, you don't have to worry about that, do you? Nobody would put *you* there"—Mrs. Sinclair stared at him pointedly—"unless you refused to finish your breakfast."

Bobbie raised his spoon to his mouth.

Seeing Woman listened to the sounds of the new day as she went about her morning duties. She heard the sound of light footsteps passing. The women of the camp went to get living water—water fresh from the stream—for the new day and all that would happen in it.

Seeing Woman listened more intently. She heard heavier footsteps. The men walked to the rise where the horses grazed. She heard their muted conversation in passing.

Seeing Woman moved to the entrance of her tipi and lifted the flap. The morning breeze touched her face, and she breathed deeply. She heard a dog barking. She heard a weeping cry. She heard a child call his mother's name. The sounds of the camp continued around her, but above it all throbbed the sound that had been with her through the night. Night Raven's heartbeat echoed in her ears, growing ever stronger.

Seeing Woman heard a familiar step.

"Blue Shell . . ." The squaw halted as Seeing Woman addressed her. "Has Jumping Bull yet returned to his tipi?" she asked.

"No. Trailing Mist awaits him."

Running Deer's angry voice interrupted sharply. "Jumping Bull's tipi has been empty for two days and nights, Seeing Woman. It was my thought to ask *you* when Jumping Bull would return, since Jumping Bull speaks to you as he speaks to no other—not even his wives, who await him."

Irritated by her tone, Seeing Woman replied, "Jumping Bull speaks when he wishes to speak . . . and to those he wishes to speak to."

Seeing Woman heard Blue Shell depart, heard Running Deer's footsteps draw nearer. She knew they stood alone as Running Deer hissed boldly, "Your power over Jumping Bull nears its end, old woman! Your imaginings will leave him empty-handed, and he will despise you for your folly!"

"Take care with the words you speak, Running Deer. They may yet rebound on you."

"I'm not afraid of you!"

"You would do well to respect—"

"To respect a blind old woman whose mind wanders?"

"To respect one who sees with more than her eyes."

"You wait for Jumping Bull's return . . . but it is *I* who will welcome him! It is I who will offer Jumping Bull my young body when his heart is emptied of the dreams you have fostered there—when he realizes that Night Raven is dead!"

"Night Raven lives."

Running Deer's laughter was shrill. "Jumping Bull will forget his sorrow in *my* arms when he returns, and your power over him will cease."

"Jumping Bull will return with a lightened heart because—"

"I will listen no more!"

Running Deer struck her heavily, and Seeing Woman staggered backward. She fell to the ground, crying out Night Raven's name as she struck her head a numbing blow.

A jolt shuddered through Night Raven, awakening him to the early morning silence of Edwina's quarters. He felt a stabbing pain that was not his own. He sensed a hot spill of blood.

Night Raven glanced around the empty room, suddenly panic-stricken. He jerked at the bonds on his wrists. He glanced at the doorway. Something had happened. He could wait to be free no longer.

Night Raven's agitated thoughts halted abruptly at the sound of movement outside the door. He heard the guard's gruff inquiry.

"Where are you goin', kid?"

White Bear's youthful voice responded, "I lost a button off my shirt and Mrs. Sinclair told me to look for it in Miss Keene's quarters. She'll be mad if I don't find it."

"A button! Hell, them clothes are almost fallin' off your back!"

"She'll be mad if I don't find it."

"Yeah, I know that woman, all right." A pause. "Go ahead . . . but don't go anywheres near that Injun."

"I'm just goin' to look for my button."

Night Raven waited as the door opened.

"Don't listen to them women, ma'am."

Corporal McNulty glanced at the three women standing imperiously beside the door of the infirmary, glaring disapproval at Edwina as she removed the bandage from his shoulder and examined his wound. He looked back at her, his brown eyes sympathetic.

"I don't know what's the matter with them, ma'am. Captain Rice was in here. He explained everythin' to us, about how Major Locke ordered you to tend to that Injun's wounds so he'd be fit for trial."

"Craig did that?"

"He sure did, ma'am."

"Well . . ." Edwina smiled. It was just like Craig to find a way to support her, even if it was indirectly. Wanting to be perfectly truthful, she continued, "Major Locke didn't really *order* me to tend to Night Raven."

"He might just as well. We all know that. And like Captain Rice said, that Injun wouldn't be livin' now if he had stayed in that cell the way it was. And since you couldn't bring him in here, you didn't have no choice but to do what you did."

"You mean . . . puttin' him in my own bed."

Corporal McNulty flushed. "There was no use tendin' to him if you wasn't goin' to do your best for him. That Bertha Charles is just jealous. She never did like the way everybody was singin' your praises after the fever hit the fort and all."

"Well, nobody's singin' my praises now."

"I am, ma'am."

Her throat suddenly tight, Edwina looked up at the earnest young soldier. She had always liked Jim McNulty. He had always struck her as being more serious than the rest, and she'd heard Craig remark that he was one of the best soldiers he'd seen in a long time. He had been in a lot of pain, and she had done her best for him. She didn't usually look for applause, but McNulty's appreciative words and support were a welcome sound in the roar of disapproval surrounding her.

Edwina replied softly, "Thanks. I appreciate that, but I think the women are just scared about everythin' that's happened, and they aren't thinkin' straight."

"They ain't got no right to blame you for somethin' that ain't your doin'. Anyways, they won't be havin' nothin' to complain about after tomorrow."

Edwina's hand stilled. "Tomorrow?"

"Captain Rice has some of the fellas cleanin' out the cell in the yard right now, so's that Injun can be moved in there as soon as it's ready."

Edwina stiffened, a slow anger rising. "Nobody told me about that."

"The talk is that Major Locke figures that Sioux's had it easy long enough."

Edwina's jaw tightened. So much for Locke's word.

"I didn't mean to upset you, ma'am."

Edwina forced a smile. "Your shoulder's doin' fine." Affixing the bandage in place, she continued, "You can start movin' at your own speed now, but don't rush things, or you'll break that wound open again."

"Ma'am . . ."

"You didn't upset me, Jim." Edwina stood up. "You made me feel much better than I did when I came in here."

"Is that right?" McNulty's smile was suddenly bright.

"I'll see you tomorrow."

McNulty's smile was still beaming when Edwina turned away and headed for the door.

"Stop where you are, kid!"

Bobbie looked up at the guards at the fort gates. There were two of them with rifles in their hands. The gates were open, as they had been most of the morning while patrols came and went. He knew what he had to do.

Bobbie responded, "I just want to go outside to look for my pa."

The shorter soldier snapped, "You ain't goin' nowhere. It ain't safe for you out there."

"My pa should be gettin' here soon. I just want to walk out a little ways. I won't get lost again. My pa would never find me if I did."

"You ain't goin' out!"

"My pa might be lookin' at the fort through his spyglass right now. He'd be happy if he saw me."

"Look, kid—"

"Let him go, Parker," the taller guard interrupted. "The kid ain't stupid. He got himself here, didn't he? So, he ain't goin' to get himself lost again by just walkin' out a few feet from the gate."

"What if Locke sees him?"

"What if he does?"

The shorter fellow considered that thought, then grated, "All right, go ahead, but we'll be watchin' you."

His heart pounding loudly, Bobbie walked out through the gates and stood boldly, in clear view, staring into the distance. Raising his hands to his mouth, he called out, "Where are you? Are you out there? Can you hear me? Everythin's all right. You can come and get me now!"

When silence was his only reply, he raised his hands to his mouth and called out again, then again.

Long, silent minutes later, Bobbie walked back into the fort. The guards were frowning.

"Sorry, kid."

Bobbie's smile was genuinely bright. "He's out there, all right. He heard me, too, and he's goin' to come and get me, you'll see."

"Is it true?"

Edwina was fuming. She had waited the greater part of the day for the opportunity to see Major Locke, who was "too busy to talk to her at present." She had visited the cell that the resentful soldiers were preparing for Night Raven, and it had taken all the control she possessed not to speak to Craig, who was directing their efforts.

That bastard, Locke! He had reneged on his promise not to interfere with her treatment of

Night Raven, but he had not rescinded the order for Craig to disassociate himself from her. The truth was, she didn't need to talk to Craig. One look at the frustrated expression on his fair face was enough to confirm that everything Corporal McNulty had told her was true.

The setting sun was visible through his office window when Edwina was allowed into Locke's office at last, and her temper was short. Locke looked up at her, his expression so smug that she could barely control her anger as she demanded, "Do you intend to put Night Raven back into that cell tomorrow?"

"I'd alter my tone if I were you, Miss Keene."

"But you aren't me. If you were, you would've kept our bargain!"

"What bargain was that?"

"The bargain we made when I agreed to continue tending the wounded—that you'd leave Night Raven's care to me."

"That hasn't changed. You can still tend to Night Raven's wounds. You'll just have to go to his cell to do it."

"And if I refuse to go into that filthy hole?"

"Then Night Raven will be the one to suffer, won't he?"

"And you'll lose the opportunity to emerge a hero out of this."

"I *am* a hero, Miss Keene."

Edwina remained silent. She saw Locke's color rise as he continued, "In any case, it's obvious that the murdering Sioux is out of danger. From what I understand, he's recuperating well."

"Who told you that? Doctor Smart?"

"Your sarcasm isn't doing your case any good, Miss Keene."

"I'm Night Raven's doctor, and I say he isn't well enough to survive in that filthy cesspool you call a cell."

"I've taken your insistent criticisms seriously, Miss Keene. I've ordered the cell to be cleaned."

"*You* ordered it to be cleaned . . ."

"Let's put it this way: I *allowed* it to be cleaned."

"So you can claim you did your best if Night Raven's condition changes for the worse while he's in there."

"My reasons are my business."

Edwina drew back an angry step. "I want to make an official protest against Night Raven's removal to that cell. I won't be responsible for his condition if he's put in there."

"Too late. Everyone in the fort already considers you responsible."

"Bastard!"

His expression furious, Major Locke shouted toward the door, "Guard, Miss Keene is leaving! Escort her to her quarters!"

"I don't need an escort."

"You have one anyway, Miss Keene, because

what I say goes in this fort—and I advise you not to forget it."

Edwina turned toward the door with hardly a glance at the grim-faced guard at her side. No, she wouldn't forget it.

The night had darkened. Healing smoke rose in white puffs from the smoke hole in Lone Dog's tipi as Running Deer stood concealed in the shadows beyond the hide walls. She listened to the concerned voices within.

"Seeing Woman's wound heals, but her mind remains in the shadows." Lone Dog's rasping voice was easily identifiable as he addressed Trailing Mist. "The healing smoke does not bring her back to us because her heart is heavy at Night Raven's death."

Trailing Mist's voice rang with true concern as she responded, "Seeing Woman grieves for those lost in battle, but she saw Night Raven alive and well in the darkness before her eyes. She believes he will return. My husband told me so."

Running Deer could almost see the aging shaman's frown as he replied, "Yet the heaviness in Seeing Woman's heart remains. Her mind wanders in a place where my healing songs cannot touch her. She is beyond my reach."

Trailing Mist's moan of sorrow brought a sneer to Running Deer's face. The woman was a fool! She had hastened to Seeing Woman's aid on hearing of her "accident" and had remained at the old woman's side—proving that she actually revered the woman who kept their husband from them.

Running Deer raised her chin in silent defiance. But not she! She had called for help after Seeing Woman did not rise from her fall. Aware that no one had witnessed their exchange, she had forced herself to appear concerned when she explained that Seeing Woman had stumbled. She had known that even if Seeing Woman should open her eyes again and tell what had really happened, no one would believe the ramblings of a blind old woman who had already caused so many to doubt her.

The voices from within Lone Dog's tipi trailed to a halt. New smoke rose to the night sky in acrid puffs as Lone Dog's chants began anew, and true satisfaction expanded within Running Deer. She need hear no more.

Running Deer turned back toward her tipi with a smile. Night Raven was gone. Seeing Woman would soon follow. Jumping Bull would then be hers.

"I don't feel good, Miss Keene."

Edwina looked down at Bobbie Ray's flushed face. She had finally calmed down after her irritating confrontation with Major Locke, and an equally frustrating session with Night Raven while she fed him his nightly meal and was subjected to stubborn silence. Bobbie had shown up at her door only a few minutes earlier. The sun had long since set and she was preparing to put an end to the disheartening day.

Edwina touched Bobbie's forehead and frowned. The boy's sunburned skin was hot, but not seriously so, yet his expression was pitiful. She scrutinized the nine-year-old more closely. He looked anxious—but he didn't look sick. Bending down so she faced him at his own level, she questioned, "Does something hurt you, Bobbie?"

"My head hurts and my stomach don't feel good . . . and I feel hot."

Briefly silent, Edwina then asked, "Don't you like stayin' with Mrs. Sinclair?"

Avoiding her eye, Bobbie shrugged. "She's all right, but she keeps tellin' me what to do. My pa never bossed me like she does."

"She's tryin' to do well by you, Bobbie."

"Yeah . . . but I'd rather be here."

"Mrs. Sinclair wouldn't like it if you stayed here when she's supposed to be takin' care of you."

"She wouldn't mind if you told her I was sick."

"But you aren't sick, are you?"

Bobbie's eyes met hers. "Well, I am, kinda. I

get a headache from all her talkin', and my stomach hurts when she makes me eat what I don't want to eat."

"But you're not sick."

"I am sick . . . of stayin' there, Miss Keene. Let me stay here. Just for tonight, that's all. I won't ask to stay longer. I promise."

"But—"

"Please, Miss Keene. It's important."

Edwina considered the boy's anxious expression. She'd had a taste of Emily Sinclair's rigid personality, and she truly sympathized.

"Please."

"Well, if it's 'important.'" Noting the relief in Bobbie's flashing grin, Edwina called out to the guard at the door, "Anderson, Bobbie's not feelin' well. I'd appreciate it if you could send somebody to tell Mrs. Sinclair that he's goin' to stay here tonight."

Glancing back at Bobbie unexpectedly, Edwina saw him looking at Night Raven, and she warned, "Stay away from him, Bobbie. Night Raven's very angry tonight. He knows somethin's goin' on. He can't hurt you because he can't move out of that bed, but I don't want him doin' anythin' that might scare you."

"Does Night Raven scare you, Miss Keene?" Bobbie asked.

Startled by the question, Edwina glanced at the Sioux warrior. She wondered how he would look if those full lips were composed in a smile . . . or if there was joy in his eyes, instead of hatred.

Night Raven turned unexpectedly toward her, his gold eyes locking heatedly with hers, and she barely restrained a gasp.

"Miss Keene?"

Glancing back at Bobbie, Edwina forced herself to respond, "No, he doesn't scare me."

"That's good."

Pausing at the boy's unexpected reply, Edwina asked, "Why is that good?"

" 'Cause my pa always said that you can't see the good in people if you tell yourself there ain't any."

"Yes . . . well, just as long as you stay away from him." Edwina unconsciously sighed. "I'm tired. I'm goin' to sleep. You can take the cot. I'll be comfortable in the chair."

"No, I'll take the chair, Miss Keene. I'm smaller. I fit it better."

"No, Bobbie, you can—"

But Bobbie was already curling up in the chair, and Edwina didn't have the strength to argue. She glanced at Night Raven. He had deliberately looked away the moment Bobbie entered the room, making it obvious he wanted no contact with the boy. She wondered what was going through his mind right now . . . why she had the feeling that despite his present indignity, this enigmatic savage had not for a moment considered surrendering to his circumstances ... that he was awaiting the opportunity to turn on her.

Suddenly disgusted with herself, Edwina brought her thoughts to an abrupt halt. No, she would not succumb to this Sioux warrior's silent intimidation. She was as strong as he was—even stronger. She'd show him that he couldn't back her down.

Night Raven held her gaze boldly as she walked to his bedside. Refusing to reveal the inner quaking his silent antagonism evoked, Edwina released his ankle bonds. He moved his legs under the coverlet. The movement showed no sign of frailty and Edwina's heart jumped. Maybe Major Locke was right, after all. Maybe Night Raven *was* recuperating faster than she believed. Maybe he was just waiting for her to make a mistake so he could escape and wreak his vengeance. Maybe everyone would be safer when he was lying in that cell, where he didn't stand a chance of escape.

Night Raven's gaze did not falter.

And maybe she was doing exactly what she had sworn she would not—allowing him to intimidate her.

Granting herself the satisfaction of a vocal response, Edwina declared softly, "You don't scare me, Night Raven. You don't scare me at all."

Turning away from the bed, Edwina took a

deep breath, aware that her heart was pounding. She was tired . . . too tired to deal with this
savage who somehow shook her to the core.

Glancing a last time at Bobbie, Edwina lay
down on the cot. Bobbie was already breathing
slowly and evenly. Well, like it or not, after one
more night her patient would be confined in a
cell where everyone seemed to want him to be,
and the stress of the past few days would be
relieved.

One more night.

The night stretched long. Night Raven studied
the sounds of even breathing that filled the
darkness. He waited, then made a soft,
whistling call. The darkness stirred, forming a
small figure that moved quietly to his side.

"I waited for you to call me, just like you
said, Night Raven."

"Untie my wrists quickly, White Bear."

Night Raven's anxiety deepened as the boy
fumbled. Edwina had been tense. Her sleep
was restless. He had been forced to wait longer
than he would have chosen before he was certain she slept deeply enough for safety.

White Bear produced a knife. The blade
glinted in the meager light as he cut the rope.
With one hand free, Night Raven loosened the
rope on his other wrist, then drew himself to a
seated position in the bed. Pain shot through

his arms and back. His legs were heavy, slow to respond to his will.

"We have to hurry, Night Raven."

Night Raven drew himself to his feet. He stood uncertainly, his chest aching and his muscles screaming a protest as he snatched up the breech cloth lying nearby and stepped into his moccasins.

"Night Raven . . ."

Night Raven accepted the knife White Bear held out to him. Casting the pain from his mind, he took one step, then another. Heat surged through his veins, and he felt his strength returning. Two more steps and he was breathing deeply. Another two, and the metamorphosis was complete. He was a cripple no longer!

White Bear slipped toward the door as Night Raven moved through the shadows to Edwina's bed. Crouching beside her in the dim light of the nearby lamp, Night Raven stared down into Edwina's sleeping face. Golden hair, smooth skin, small features tranquilly composed . . .

Night Raven covered her mouth with his hand. Edwina stirred. Her eyes flew open wide. He felt the jolt that shook her.

"Struggle is useless, Edwina."

Her startled response muffled by the hand clamped tight over her mouth, Edwina stared up at Night Raven with disbelief. She was dreaming. She had to be.

Crouched over her, black hair spilling over the broad width of his bare shoulders, Night Raven whispered in the white man's tongue. "Our time together has come full circle, Edwina. I was your prisoner, and now you are mine."

Her momentary disorientation fading, Edwina looked at the chair beside the cot. She panicked when she saw it was empty. She glanced at the door and was startled by the sight of Bobbie standing silently there.

"White Bear awaits my command."

White Bear.

"He came to rescue me."

Incredulity held her motionless.

"Get up!"

Edwina was suddenly fighting him.

"Stop struggling." Night Raven raised a gleaming blade into her line of vision. "You will alert the guard and cause his death as well as your own."

Edwina went still as Night Raven drew her upright with unexpected strength. He clamped an arm around her waist and pulled her back against him. With his knife pressed to her side, he dragged her along with him toward the door.

Bobbie looked up at Night Raven. She saw

him nod at Night Raven's signal, then call out, "Anderson, Miss Keene wants you."

Night Raven drew her back as the door opened. She saw no more than a glimpse of Anderson's shadow before Night Raven struck him a stunning blow.

"You killed him!"

Night Raven made no response. Pressing the knife more sharply against her, he all but lifted her from her feet as he moved her out into the shadows of the fort yard.

Bobbie motioned them forward. "This way, Night Raven!"

Her breath coming in deep gasps, her feet barely touching the ground, Edwina was swept along by Night Raven's strong arm as Bobbie's pale-haired figure led the way toward the dark rear of the fort yard. She heard the pride in Bobbie's voice as he halted at the wall and turned back toward them.

"We can get over the wall here. I hid a ladder and a rope. Nobody saw me take them."

Bobbie . . . who was White Bear.

Mounting the ladder as soon as it was in place, Bobbie climbed ahead of them and motioned them up. She hesitated, and Night Raven spoke softly against her ear.

"You will climb, Edwina, if you value your life."

Edwina mounted the ladder, with Night

147

Raven at her back. She paused behind Bobbie as the boy looped the rope over the log wall, dropped it into the darkness beyond, and turned back to whisper, "I did just what you told me to do, Night Raven. Everythin's ready."

Behind her, Night Raven uttered a soft call that sounded so much like a night bird that Edwina turned spontaneously toward him. He was staring into the darkness below them. He called again, and Edwina's heart jumped as a response came from the shadows.

Night Raven's chest was pressed tight to her back. It heaved with growing excitement as a figure materialized out of the shadows. He ordered, "Go down the rope, White Bear."

Bobbie slid down the rope and dropped off into the darkness. Edwina turned back toward Night Raven again to see him gesturing to the figure below them with Indian signs that she did not comprehend. Her heart jumped when Night Raven spoke again.

"Silence will save your life."

Scooping her off the ladder unexpectedly, Night Raven held her over the wall and dropped her into the darkness below. Gasping as strong arms broke her fall, Edwina stood on wobbling legs as Night Raven descended the rope behind her.

Whisked into the darkness with Night Raven's imprisoning arm again clamped around her waist, Edwina was hardly able to comprehend the dizzying progress of events as they raced to a nearby wooded patch and Night Raven tossed her up onto a waiting horse.

Mounting behind her, his powerful body flush against her back, Night Raven urged his mount forward into the night.

Chapter Six

"She can't be gone! Did they search the fort?" Margaret's voice trembled. "That Injun couldn't have forced Edwina *and* the boy to go with him! He was wounded . . . weak!"

His fair skin colorless, Craig gripped Margaret's shoulder, speaking softly. "Sit down, dear. Don't get excited. That's the last thing Edwina would want."

"The last thing Edwina would want is to be kidnapped by that savage!" Margaret shuddered. "Maybe she's still in the fort somewhere—tied up or somethin'—her and the boy."

Gently coaxing his wife to sit on the side of the bed, Craig was more shaken than he chose to reveal. He had awakened that morning to a nightmare. The alarm had sounded as he emerged from his quarters just before daybreak—when Corporal Lee went to relieve Anderson at Edwina's door and found Anderson unconscious; Night Raven, Edwina, and the boy were gone.

Locke had been enraged when a ladder and an escape rope were discovered at the rear wall, along with footprints that led into the wooded copse beyond. The footprints were revealing—moccasin prints, a woman's, and a child's. Locke had immediately dispatched patrols.

Craig shuddered. But even in the face of that evidence, he had refused to believe that Edwina was gone. As the patrols set out, he had conducted an extensive search of the fort, exploring every possible place where Edwina and the boy could have been confined. He had only been fooling himself. Night Raven had kidnapped them.

He had raced to Margaret's side then, grateful to discover that she was just awakening and had missed the worst of the confusion. But Margaret's anxiety was none the less for being belated.

"They're gone, Margaret—Edwina and the boy. There's no doubt about that now. Night Raven took them both, but he won't get far. Locke has two patrols out chasing them. They can't possibly escape."

"Why did he take them, Craig? It would have been easier for him to escape without them. What does he intend to do with them?"

"He won't have a chance to do anything. We'll find them first."

Margaret's plain face was etched with fear. Her breathing was uneven, and Craig's concern deepened. "Margaret, please . . . if Edwina was here now, she'd tell you to lie down and rest."

"She's not here, Craig. That Injun's got her, and it's my fault! Everythin' that has happened to her here's been my fault, because I'm the one who asked her to come to this fort in the first place."

"If you hadn't asked Edwina to come when you were sick, she would never have forgiven you."

"But—"

"Friendship goes both ways. Darling"— Craig stared at his wife's guilt-stricken expression—"rest, please. That's what Edwina would want, and it's what I want, too. I'll take care of everything else. I'll get her back."

Pressing Margaret backward against the bed, Craig pulled the coverlet up over her. He whispered, "You do your part by taking care of yourself until Edwina returns, and I'll do mine."

Craig brushed away the tears that trailed from the corners of his wife's eyes. He touched her trembling lips with his. "I'll get her back, I promise."

The light of day had fully dawned as they moved steadily forward. Uncertain how long or how far they had ridden, Edwina knew only that she ached from weariness. The incredulity with which she had awakened had not yet fully dissipated. Yet the hard male body supporting her as she rode was all too real, as was the arm clamped cruelly tight around her waist.

Night Raven's powerful muscles moved against her back in a play that was somehow sensual, as was his warm breath against her cheek, and the occasional brush of Night Raven's chin against her temple.

A chill unrelated to the damp morning air shook Edwina, and Night Raven's arm tightened with effortless power. The irrefutable truth could no longer be denied. The impossible had become reality. So close to death only a few days earlier, Night Raven now showed no signs of his previous debility. He had sustained their relentless pace without a sign of weakening, seeming to grow stronger with each hour that elapsed. She was at a loss to explain it. Years of treating the sick and wounded at her father's side, and her own personal experience since his death, told her it was impossible.

Human will stronger than circumstance . . .

A maxim her father had once used returned unexpectedly to Edwina's mind. She remembered his saying that he believed a man could overcome any circumstance if the motivation was right.

Edwina's heart pounded. She knew what Night Raven's motivation was. It was hatred. She had seen it in his eyes each time he looked at her. She had heard it in his deep voice the first time he spoke her name. She sensed it now in the possessive grip that declared her a prisoner he would yield to no one.

Battling the part of her still unwilling to accept that harsh reality, Edwina stared at the horsemen who rode ahead of them. She knew little about the Sioux who lived in the area, but she recognized at a glance the authoritative manner of the Indian referred to as Jumping Bull. Though older than Night Raven, the warrior's power had not been compromised by time. His arms had broken her fall without strain when Night Raven dropped her from the wall, and it was he who led their relentless escape.

Behind Jumping Bull, Bobbie rode without complaint, and a sense of betrayal twisted tight inside her. Fair-haired Bobbie, who had so easily deceived them all . . .

Night Raven's mount stumbled unexpectedly. She heard his low grunt as they were jerked forward, and she knew that if it was not for the power of Night Raven's guiding hand, the animal might have lost its footing. Jumping Bull turned back toward them abruptly, then reined his mount to a halt. Edwina saw the concern in his face as Night Raven and Bobbie followed suit, a concern that was evident in his voice as he addressed Night Raven in their native tongue.

Resisting the urge to look back at Night Raven, Edwina heard his brusque reply. Obviously objecting to whatever Jumping Bull suggested, he tightened his arm around her waist.

Riding up beside them as the conversation continued, Bobbie whispered, "Don't worry, Miss Keene. Jumping Bull's not mad at you."

Edwina looked sharply at the boy. There was no sign of remorse in his eyes for the deception he had practiced. Instead, he continued easily, "He's just worryin' about Night Raven because he—"

"White Bear!"

The harshness of Night Raven's tone halted Bobbie's whispered reassurance. Night Raven spoke sharply to the boy in rapid Sioux, and Bobbie flushed. Turning his mount, Bobbie separated himself from her without a word.

Their escape resumed abruptly. Unable to restrain herself a moment longer, Edwina looked up at Night Raven. His features were stiffly set, as if carved in stone.

* * *

Standing at the lookout post, a spyglass to his eye, Major Locke scanned the sunswept afternoon landscape for a sign of the returning patrols. Two patrols had been out since daybreak. Two full patrols chasing an Indian, a woman, and a boy who could not possibly be traveling very fast, considering the hindrance of Night Raven's wound and the fact that the latter two were hostages. Yet there was no sign of either patrol's triumphant return.

Locke's lean frame twitched. This was Edwina Keene's fault—all of it—the entire debacle to which he had awakened at dawn and which still continued.

Frustrated beyond measure, Locke lowered the spyglass from his eye and jabbed it in the direction of the soldier beside him. "Keep looking, and make sure I'm notified the moment you see something!"

Stepping down into the fort yard, Locke continued his silent railing. He had been right about that wily Sioux bastard all along. He never should have listened to Edwina Keene. For all her bold claims of being a doctor, she had been no more competent to assess that savage's degree of debility than the fort blacksmith.

Locke sneered. The prisoner was weak, so weak that he might not live the night . . . the prisoner had lost so much blood that he couldn't possibly attempt an escape. To the last, she had battled him, protesting Night Raven's incarceration in the cell where his escape could have been avoided—where the savage would now be confined if not for the miscalculation of one day.

A nervous tic appeared in Locke's cheek as he crossed the fort yard, passing a gathering of uneasy residents. His men avoided his eye, but Bertha Charles, her oversize frame unmistakable among the group of women watching him with open disapproval, made no attempt to hide her feelings. But he cared little what that cow of a woman thought—or what any of them thought!

Turning toward his office, Locke did not return the salute of the guard on duty as he pushed open the door and slammed it closed behind him. Foremost in his mind was the report he had dispatched to Washington two days earlier, requesting that he be made personally responsible for Night Raven until that savage was delivered for trial.

Striding toward the window, Locke stared out blindly, his chest heaving. What had begun as his passage to glory had deteriorated into a ticket to disgrace. But he would not submit to defeat!

His raging thoughts halted as a red-haired military figure strode into his line of vision in the fort yard. Locke growled with true antipathy. Captain Craig Rice was the man who had summoned the obnoxious Miss Keene to Fort

157

John Carter. Rice would not go unrewarded. They would all pay—Edwina Keene, Captain Rice, *and* Night Raven. He would not be satisfied until that murdering Sioux dangled at the end of a rope for all to see!

Striding toward the door, Locke jerked it open and commanded, "Have the captain of the guard report to me immediately."

Yes . . . they'd pay.

The sun was past its zenith. His mount moved steadily as Night Raven held Edwina against him in a relentless grip. Her heart pounded against the arm he clasped around her ribs as he perused the surrounding landscape with growing satisfaction. They had seen no sign of the bluecoat patrol that he was certain had been dispatched at dawn. The path Jumping Bull had chosen in their flight had been filled with diversion. Few were skilled enough to follow their trail, and the bluecoats were not among that number. Pursuit was no longer a threat.

Night Raven breathed deeply against the pain in his chest and the weakness assailing him. He would not submit to either. Nor would he submit to the scent of Edwina's hair as it teased his nostrils, or the tantalizing brush of her rounded breasts against his arm, or the female warmth pressed intimately against his male heat. Instead, he accepted the challenge, boldly adjusting Edwina more firmly against him as their journey continued.

Scrutinizing Jumping Bull's stalwart figure ahead of them, Night Raven saw no sign of fatigue, but a few feet behind, White Bear's shoulders had begun to slump and his head to droop. The boy was growing tired.

The pain in his chest surged deeper and Night Raven suppressed a grunt of pain. As if sensing his thoughts, Jumping Bull looked back at him, then reined in his mount. Preparing himself as Jumping Bull turned his horse toward him, Night Raven maintained an impassive facade. Jumping Bull had paused earlier in concern for his welfare. He had met that concern with anger, refusing to rest, and the journey had continued.

An unexpected tremor shook Edwina as Jumping Bull approached—her first sign of fear. Startled by a sudden surge of protectiveness, Night Raven listened as Jumping Bull addressed him in their native tongue.

"The bluecoats do not follow. They have lost our trail. White Bear tires." He motioned with his chin toward the nearby stream that rippled in the midday sun. "We will pause here."

"I'm not tired, Jumpin' Bull!"

The boy denied his weariness, but a glance from Jumping Bull silenced him, even as pride flooded Night Raven at the boy's courage.

The unexpected grumbling of Edwina's

stomach sounded in the silence and she stiffened. She was hungry, as was he. It would be well for their party to stop to tend to their personal needs, so they would arrive at the camp with their full strength.

Nodding in consent, Night Raven dismounted. Unwilling to acknowledge the unexpected pain that ripped through his chest as he did, he paused only briefly for a stabilizing breath before swinging Edwina down from the horse. He saw the manner in which her gaze jumped to the bandage that still circled his chest and noted for the first time the fresh bloodstain that marked it. He responded succinctly.

"It is nothing."

Edwina's eyes flashed contempt. "Another doctor."

Night Raven snapped, "Your mistake was to judge the effect of my wound by white man's standards. For that reason, you are now my captive."

"I'm your captive because of the Sioux spy who was so generously allowed into the fort." Edwina glanced sharply at Bobbie. "Otherwise, you'd be in that cell in the fort yard right now, without a chance of escape."

"White Bear succeeded only because you erred."

Edwina's eyes challenged him. "I made a mistake underestimatin' your stamina, but you *bleed* just like a white man bleeds, and I'm a good enough doctor to know that your wound's broken open again. You won't last much longer if it keeps bleedin' at that rate."

"My wound heals!"

"It *was* healin'."

Grasping her arms unexpectedly, Night Raven held Edwina's face up to his as he rasped, "You seek to undermine me, Edwina, but you cannot. I recognized you the moment I saw you. I know the end you seek, but you will fail!"

Edwina was quaking visibly when he released her. He realized belatedly that it was anger rather than fear that shook her. "I don't know what you're talkin' about, but I *do* know you're tryin' to frighten me," she responded heatedly. "I know now that you understood me when I said this to you the first time, but I'll say it again anyway. You're wastin' your time. You don't scare me!"

Night Raven reached out boldly and placed his hand against her breast. He sneered. "The rapid beat of your heart betrays you."

Thrusting away his hand, Edwina spat, "My heart doesn't betray me. It never has, and it never will."

Pain sliced unexpectedly through his chest and Night Raven clenched his teeth tightly shut. Recognizing his pain, Edwina snapped, "Yeah . . . you're healin', all right."

Acutely aware that pain was not his true enemy, Night Raven ordered, "Go to the stream while time remains." His voice took on a warning note. "But take care. You will be watched."

Observing as Edwina turned away without response, Night Raven staggered as he was rocked by another jolt of pain. Grateful that Edwina had not seen his fleeting debility, he briefly followed her departing figure with his gaze, then turned away.

"Sir, you wanted to see me?"

Barely able to maintain a civil tone, Craig stared at Major Locke, his jaw tight. He had been examining the site where Night Raven had gone over the fort wall when he was approached by Corporals Murray and Pitts. Startled when he was informed that he was to be escorted back to Major Locke's office under guard, he had turned abruptly from his findings and proceeded ahead of them. He had arrived at the office hardly able to restrain his indignation. But indignation became silent fury as Locke dismissed the guards and waited until the door closed behind them to sneer, "Yes, I wanted to see you, Captain Craig. I wanted to waste no time in informing you that I hold you fully accountable for the fiasco in this fort."

"I don't know what you mean, sir."

"You know what I mean, all right." His

expression suddenly rabid, Locke approached him hotly. "Night Raven's escape is your fault!"

"Mine?"

"You're the person who brought Miss Edwina Keene into this fort. You're the person responsible for the resistance I encountered from fort residents and personnel alike after her arrival. You were responsible for the decision to keep Night Raven in Miss Keene's quarters until he was well enough to be returned to his cell, and you're also responsible for suggesting that we delay his incarceration until that cell was cleaned up enough to be suitable for Miss Keene's visits. By doing so, you afforded Night Raven an opportunity to escape, and I intend to make that clear to Washington in my report."

"Sir, *you're* the commander of this fort."

"Meaning the responsibility is mine? Oh, no, you won't get away that easily. Another point"—spittle sprayed from Locke's mouth as he continued emphatically—"I also intend to report to Washington that I believe Miss Keene was in league with Night Raven in planning his escape."

"That's crazy!"

"Is it?" Locke was shuddering. "How else could a man as critically wounded as Night Raven was supposed to be free himself from bonds that were tested each morning by my own guards, and make his way across an unfamiliar fort to affect an escape with two hostages?"

"It wouldn't be difficult . . . if there was a spy in the fort."

"A spy!" Locke laughed aloud. "You're grasping at straws, captain."

"No, sir. I was about to make my report when the guards caught up with me."

"Your report?"

"I went back to Night Raven's departure point at the rear wall to examine it more closely, and things didn't add up. The second set of Indian moccasin prints was only *outside* the wall. The Indian who helped Night Raven escape never entered the fort grounds. Also, Night Raven used a ladder and a rope from the stable in his escape, yet he had no familiarity with the fort and wouldn't have been able to search them out and move them to the rear wall in the middle of the night without alerting the guard."

"That's where Miss Keene came in."

"Sir, Miss Keene hasn't been seen anywhere near the stable since she arrived. Somebody would have seen her if she went there during the day, and with a guard at her door, she would've been seen if she left her quarters at night."

"You're saying—"

"I'm saying Edwina wasn't the spy."

"The *spy* was some mysterious person who is

now still wandering the fort, is that what you've deduced, Captain?"

"No, sir. I'm saying that Bobbie Ray was the spy."

"Bobbie Ray—the child?"

"Sir, Bobbie Ray spent time in the stable the day before Night Raven's escape. The blacksmith said he figured the boy was at a loss for something to do, so he gave him free access and let him stay when he left for dinner."

"That doesn't mean—"

"Sergeant Anderson said he heard the boy begging Edwina to let him sleep in her quarters last night. Anderson said she wanted to send him back to Mrs. Sinclair, but Bobbie played on her sympathies and she finally relented."

Locke's expression tightened.

"Sergeant Anderson also said Bobbie was the one who called him into the room when Night Raven escaped. He said he glimpsed Bobbie inside the room just before he was struck on the head, and the boy stood free and unencumbered." Craig paused. "If Bobbie was a hostage, it wouldn't have made sense to chance letting him call Anderson. Edwina would've done it." Craig paused again, continuing, "You were right when you said Night Raven wouldn't have been able to handle *two* hostages. He didn't have two. Edwina was his only hostage."

"Don't think that this will get you off lightly, Captain, even if you're right. In case you've forgotten, you took *personal responsibility* when you rode out to pick up that turncoat!"

"Yes, sir, but it's not that personal responsibility I'm concerned about." Craig paused. His pale skin heated revealingly. "Edwina came here because Margaret and I asked her to come. It's my responsibility to get her back, and I'm going to do it."

"Really?"

"Yes, sir."

"All right." Locke's small smile was caustic. "Then I'll go a step farther in that regard. I'll make it your personal responsibility to find Miss Keene *and* Night Raven. If you fail, you will suffer the consequences."

Locke paused to observe Craig's reaction to his statement. When Craig's expression remained too stoic for him to obtain the satisfaction he sought, Locke added with true antipathy, "If you've become attached to your commission, Captain, I would strongly suggest that you do *not* fail."

"Yes, sir."

"You're dismissed."

"Are you mad at me because I talked to Miss Keene, Night Raven?"

Seated on a fallen tree where he was attempting to rest before resuming their flight, Night Raven did not immediately respond to White Bear's inquiry. His physical discomfort was growing. Edwina remained at the stream nearby, and he had accepted the dried beef that Jumping Bull gave him, but one bite and his stomach had rebelled. Despite his denial, he knew that Edwina was correct in her assessment. He was weakening.

The uneasiness of that knowledge tightened the frown that Night Raven turned toward White Bear. The boy's eyes shone with a misting of tears he ferociously withheld, yet Night Raven held the boy's gaze without smiling.

"The woman is my captive. No one speaks to her without my permission."

White Bear's expression grew pained. "But she was afraid when she saw Jumpin' Bull ridin' back toward you, and she was tryin' so hard not to show it. I didn't want her to be scared."

Night Raven observed the concern in White Bear's gaze. He remembered discovering the boy in the tall grass many moons earlier. The boy was ill from the sun and he was frightened. He recalled reading in the boy's expression the same loss and uncertainty that he had suffered at that same age, when he lost Morning Sun and his brother in the bluecoat raid. His heart was touched in a way it had never been touched before. He had cared for the boy, then brought him back to their village. The closeness between them remained. It deepened when the boy opened his young heart to him and his people in a way that made him one with the Sioux.

Night Raven's gaze lingered on White Bear's earnest expression. He had sensed from the beginning that the boy's slender proportions and pale skin belied the brave heart that beat within him. When the boy had entered the fort to rescue him at the expense of his own comfort and safety, he had proved himself worthy of the name he had accepted so proudly, and of the trust placed in him by Jumping Bull. Night Raven knew that if not for White Bear's valiant efforts, he would indeed be lying in the blue-coat cell with no hope of escape, as Edwina had reminded him earlier.

All the same, much depended on the intimate encounter that was yet to come between Edwina Keene and him. He could not explain his actions and decisions to a child.

Night Raven's response to the boy was curt and brief. "The woman is my captive. Her fate is mine to decide."

Unwilling to reveal to the boy the weakness suddenly sweeping him, Night Raven turned away. He forced from his mind the slow shuffle of White Bear's footsteps as the boy departed, and then raised the dried beef resolutely to his lips.

Crouching beside the stream, Edwina peered back through the foliage toward the shaded clearing where Night Raven and Jumping Bull sat, silently eating. Bobbie sat apart from them, appearing disheartened as he chewed without enthusiasm. All seemed engrossed in their own thoughts. The time would never be more opportune.

A warm afternoon breeze rustled through the leaves as Edwina glanced at the horses grazing in the sun a little distance away. She made a swift decision. Grateful for the soft shushing of the wind that disguised any sound of her progress, she moved quietly and carefully from one bush to the next. She noted that Night Raven seemed particularly engrossed in his thoughts as she crept to the side of the great chestnut stallion that Night Raven and she had ridden. Depending on the animal's familiarity with her scent, she stood up slowly beside him, speaking softly as she grasped his reins.

The horse whinnied loudly and a jolt of fear rocked Edwina. Pulling herself up onto the animal's back, she glanced behind her in time to see Night Raven and Jumping Bull leap to their feet.

Digging her heels into her mount's sides, Edwina jolted him into a wild leap forward. Unconscious of the wind that battered her face or the danger of the uneven terrain that the animal covered in long, even strides, she rode recklessly. Her confidence growing as the earth flew beneath her mount's hooves, Edwina gasped aloud as the stallion stumbled unexpectedly, then regained his footing. Whipping him on, she refused to look back, despite the sound of hoofbeats drumming behind her. The pounding hooves were drawing steadily nearer!

With a panicked cry, Edwina whipped her horse harder, but the sound had barely left her throat when she was swung from the saddle in a grip that left her breathless. Suspended by a powerful arm from which there was no escape, Edwina hung helplessly in midair as Night Raven dragged his mount to a halt. She glanced upward at his furious expression just before he dropped her abruptly to the ground.

Drawing herself to her feet as Night Raven dismounted, Edwina faced him, breathing hard. His gold eyes blazed into hers and she saw the furious twitch of his cheek as he grated in a voice deep with menace, "You have erred again, Edwina."

"What are you doing, Margaret?"

Margaret turned abruptly toward the sound of Craig's voice behind her. She had no clear response to that question. Dismissing Craig's request that she rest, she had left their quarters a few minutes earlier, somehow driven to Edwina's room, needing to see . . . somehow hoping . . .

But whatever she had hoped for had not materialized. Instead, she had entered Edwina's quarters to see a confusion of upset furniture, beds that lay empty and abandoned, and freshly cut rope ties lying on the floor.

Edwina was gone.

Her voice a forlorn sound in the silence, Margaret forced her greatest fear into words.

"Will I ever see her again, Craig?"

"Of course you will!"

But Craig's swift response had a hollow sound, affording her little comfort as her husband slipped his arms around her and drew her close. The babe inside her leaped at the contact of its father's warmth, and an unconscious sob escaped Margaret's lips.

"Don't cry, Margaret. I'll get Edwina back for you. I've already promised you that, haven't I?"

Craig clutched her closer, but the deep desolation dragging at Margaret's heart remained. Dear Craig . . . she loved him so much. She had loved him from the first moment she saw him, when he arrived on the frontier fresh from the East, his uniform meticulous and his red hair blazing in the sun—but he had hardly looked at her. He had had eyes only for Edwina. It was a source of true amazement to her that Edwina never seemed to realize how Craig felt about her.

Margaret clutched Craig tighter. She knew the truth. Craig had turned to her hoping to salve the ache of his unrequited love for

Edwina, but she hadn't cared. She had been grateful for any measure of affection he gave her, and in the end, Craig grew to love her as well. Edwina had been delighted when they announced their betrothal—Edwina, her beautiful friend, whose place in Craig's heart she knew she would never truly fill.

Margaret's eyes filled to overflowing. But she loved Craig, and she loved Edwina. She was happy when they were all together, and she knew Craig was, too—but that reality was a double-edged blade that sliced deep. How could she tell Craig that her own suffering was increased a hundredfold by the knowledge that he had loved Edwina and lost—and because she knew his torment was even greater now that he had lost Edwina again?

She couldn't.

Instead, Margaret drew back and looked up into her husband's clear brown eyes and said, "I love you, Craig. I know Edwina loves you, too, and we'll all be together again."

And when Craig slipped his arm around her and drew her out again into the fort yard, Margaret wished with all her heart that the confidence she had expressed was real.

She ached.

Edwina's head throbbed and her vision was blurred as she watched the world bobbing below her. Dust rose from the steady progress of the mount on which she rode, but the world was upside down.

She was riding thrown over a horse's back like so much baggage, with her hands bound behind her.

Not for the first time, indignity fused with fury, and Edwina demanded, "Untie me!"

No response.

Edwina stared at Night Raven. She struggled to clear her vision, suppressing a groan as the horse stumbled, jarring her bruised ribs where they bumped against its back. She was sore, and she hurt all over.

"Let me loose, dammit!" she shouted. "I won't be carried like a sack of—"

"Silence!" Night Raven glowered down at her. "You have earned the entrance you make into camp."

Night Raven's response halted Edwina's protests abruptly. Turning to look ahead of them, she saw an Indian camp where a crowd was rapidly gathering at their approach. She heard an occasional welcome call, but the appearance of most was sober.

Her humiliation was matched only by the fear rapidly expanding within her, for Edwina saw something else, as well, on the faces of the waiting crowd.

Hatred.

Despising the cowardice that momentarily overwhelmed her, Edwina closed her eyes.

* * *

"Jumping Bull returns!"

Running Deer froze as Trailing Mist's joyful voice resounded outside her tipi. Standing abruptly, she smoothed her palm over her hair and straightened her spine, then raised the entrance flap to see for herself the truth of the woman's exclamation.

Outside, Running Deer saw Winter Flower and Trailing Mist running toward the approaching horsemen. She sneered contemptuously at their ungainly strides. They were old and awkward in their excitement.

Running Deer's thoughts halted abruptly as the horsemen drew clearer. Jumping Bull led the procession. Behind him rode the boy whose white skin so offended her, despite his acceptance by the camp, and behind the boy—

Shock jolted through Running Deer. It was Night Raven, alive and well!

Running Deer struggled to control a choking rage. The old witch had been correct in her prediction. If she survived, Seeing Woman would be heaped with praise now that her "vision" had proved true.

Hatred twisted tight inside Running Deer as her gaze remained fixed on the third figure in the approaching column. She knew what the reaction to Night Raven's return would be. Welcome and honor would be heaped upon him— again—praise that Night Raven wore with the comfort of his own skin. She had once believed that she would share his glory. Refusing her many suitors, she had sought his favor openly, and when he failed to respond, she had sought him out in secret, in a more intimate way. Night Raven did not refuse her offer. She recalled the heat of his strong body warming hers, and she remembered her feeling of triumph when he shuddered to completion within her.

But her triumph was short-lived. When she awakened, Night Raven was gone, and she discovered that she had silently joined the many others before her who were left with nothing more than the memory of a night he had chosen to forget.

Running Deer seethed. But unlike the others, she did not revere the memory, hoping for more. Instead, she had crushed it, nurturing instead her desire for vengeance.

Running Deer forced a smile. She would greet Jumping Bull warmly. She would appeal to him subtly when the jubilation of his return waned, in ways certain to arouse his male hunger. She would yet have his child, and that child would yet supplant Night Raven in Jumping Bull's heart. She would also make sure Seeing Woman met an end that would slice at Night Raven's cold and empty heart, so he suffered as she was made to suffer.

* * *

"What do you mean, you lost the trail?" Major Locke stared at Lieutenant Ford, incredulous. The burly officer's hatred of the Sioux had always assured success in Ford's endeavors against them. He had been certain this occasion would be no different. Instead, Ford's patrol, dispatched at dawn, had returned in late afternoon with nothing to report but failure.

Locke stared at Ford in continued astonishment. He repeated, "You lost the trail? How?"

"I don't know how, sir." Ford's thick features dragged into a scowl. "The terrain was rough. Those Injuns must've backtracked a couple of times. All I know for sure is that the tracks got so confused that we were runnin' around in circles."

"Where's Johnson's patrol?"

"He's still out there, sir. We met up a couple of times . . . crisscrossin' each other."

"But Johnson hasn't given up!"

"He's comin' in right behind us, sir. He had to stop because of problems with the horses."

"You failed, Lieutenant."

"Yes, sir."

"But you'll go out again at dawn tomorrow."

"Yes, sir."

"You will *find* that trail you lost today, and you will bring Night Raven back here to meet the justice he deserves."

"Yes, sir!"

"Or you will suffer the consequences."

Ford's square jaw clenched.

"That's all, Lieutenant."

Hardly aware that he was alone again in his silent office, Locke nodded. Yes, they'd get that Sioux bastard tomorrow.

Struggling to hold himself erect, Night Raven searched the familiar faces of the welcoming crowd as their party approached the Sioux camp. He saw two female figures moving quickly toward them. Trailing Mist and Winter Flower hastened to welcome Jumping Bull home. At the rear of the crowd he saw Running Deer approaching without apparent haste. He scowled at the reminder of the difficult burden Jumping Bull had assumed for the sake of a friend.

Dismissing that thought, Night Raven searched the faces of the gathering more closely. He saw Dawn Woman, her smile bright as she sought his eye. He saw Flower Dancer, Walking Sun, and Smiling Bird, those who had sought his favor and whose faces had paled in the light of the golden-haired image that had replaced them. His heart cold, he dismissed them.

He saw Many Faces and Singing Bird greet White Bear as the boy dismounted. Their relief at his return was obvious.

His attention was caught next by Lone Dog. The aged shaman stood apart from the crowd, and Night Raven dismounted near him, at the edge of the camp. He automatically acknowledged those who approached him as he pulled Edwina from his horse and stood her on her feet. He noted her momentary instability and supported her with a firm hand on her arm, then urged her forward. With sharp glances and a few curt words of warning, he protected her from the epithets and blows of those who had suffered from the camp's most recent encounter with the bluecoats. Determinedly, he made his way to Lone Dog's side.

When Night Raven halted beside the shaman, Lone Dog said, "Seeing Woman lies in my tipi. She fell and struck her head, and she lingers in a world where the healing smoke does not touch her."

Appearing beside him unexpectedly, White Bear spoke up softly. "I'll take Miss Keene to your tipi so you can visit Seeing Woman, Night Raven."

Night Raven accepted the boy's offer with a nod, admonishing in the Sioux tongue, "Keep her from those who would heap their vengeance upon her. Do so by telling all who approach that this woman is mine!"

Relinquishing Edwina's arm abruptly, Night Raven forced himself to walk without showing any sign of weakness as he turned to follow Lone Dog.

* * *

"Come this way, Miss Keene."

Startled when Night Raven abruptly abandoned her, Edwina surveyed the women slowly encircling her. Fear unlike any she had ever known set her to trembling. She twisted her bound hands in a futile effort to free herself. Terror choked her throat as she took a revealing backward step. The women picked up stones scattered on the ground around them.

Stepping in front of her, Bobbie spoke out boldly in the Sioux tongue. His words were strong as he stared at the women, backing them down one by one. Edwina's gaze halted on a young woman with smooth skin and small, perfect features as she worked her way through the gathering. She saw the malice in the woman's dark eyes when she picked up a stone, ignoring Bobbie's obvious warnings to the contrary. She steeled herself, seeing in the expressions of the women behind her that they, too, would attack once the first stone was thrown.

Refusing to close her eyes, unwilling to reveal her fear, Edwina faced the woman boldly despite the shuddering she was unable to control. She saw the cruel twist of the woman's lips as she raised her arm.

Stepping up beside the woman abruptly, Jumping Bull caught her hand. Edwina saw his rage as he thrust the woman's arm back to her side, and the fury the woman sought to conceal the moment before she turned and moved quickly back through the rapidly dispersing crowd.

Shuddering, uncertain if her wobbling legs would hold her, Edwina wavered, then looked down as Bobbie's small hand gripped her arm.

"It's all right, Miss Keene." Bobbie's small smile was meant to encourage her, but it was shaky as he continued, "No one will try to hurt you now." He pulled her forward. "Come on. I'll take you where you'll be safe."

Her throat tight, Edwina followed.

"I tire of your ways, Running Deer!"

Running Deer fell to her knees as Jumping Bull thrust her into her tipi and dropped the flap closed behind them. Running Deer cowered under Jumping Bull's ire as he towered over her. Her face averted from him, she listened as he addressed her again in a voice that seemed to shake the hide walls surrounding them.

"Black Dog was a brave warrior. You are of his noble blood. I took you to wife believing that one day the goodness within you would grow to match the beauty without, but the wait has been endless and bitter. My patience falters. I do not wish to darken the memory of my brave friend by declaring that one of his blood has lost my favor, but the time is fast approaching."

Looking up, Running Deer stared at Jumping Bull with stark incredulity. To be cast aside by this great chief! To be so marked, forever!

"You do well to concern yourself with the fate that awaits you." Jumping Bull leaned over Running Deer, so close that she felt his breath on her cheek and the burning sting of his glare as he rasped, "Whatever dark memories you seek to avenge, you would do well to remember that they were better cast aside when I took you to wife."

"I hold no one above you, Jumping Bull." Running Deer's voice quavered. "I seek to please no one but you!"

"The stone in your hand was not meant to please me."

"I was angry at the spilled blood of our people when I saw the woman's white skin!"

"The woman belongs to Night Raven. An assault on what is his is an assault on me as well."

"I sought only to welcome you home, not to anger you."

Jumping Bull's eyes pinned her. "Your words appease, but your actions defy."

Running Deer's tears fell. Averting her gaze, she whispered, "I will anger you no more."

Drawing back abruptly, Jumping Bull remained towering over her for silent moments. Then Running Deer heard the entrance flap fall closed behind him.

Running Deer drew herself to her feet. Still shuddering, she raised a hand to her hair and smoothed the heavy strands, then wiped the tears from her cheeks. She had been a fool. She had caused her husband to openly rebuke her. She would not make that same mistake again. There were other ways to achieve her end.

The healing smoke of Lone Dog's tipi filled Night Raven's lungs as he entered. His gaze darted to the pallet across the fire where Seeing Woman lay, and his heart faltered. She lay motionless, her features without expression, her breathing faint, and he kneeled beside her.

"Seeing Woman..." Night Raven touched the braided gray of her hair. The numbness within deepened when she made no response. This woman who had been as a mother to him... He saw the bruise that darkened her temple and looked up at Lone Dog.

"How did this occur?"

"Seeing Woman emerged from her tipi in the early morning and stumbled in the darkness."

"Seeing Woman has befriended the darkness that encloses her. She would not falter in it!"

"The darkness betrayed her."

Night Raven touched Seeing Woman's hand. He spoke her name again. Her silence sliced at his heart as he offered, "Perhaps she rests until the time is right to awaken."

"She awaits the right word to be spoken."

Night Raven's head jerked up toward the shaman. "If you know this word, tell me, and I will speak it."

When Lone Dog made no reply, Night Raven rose to his feet with a heavy heart. He felt a rush of blood from the bandage on his chest. He wiped at the blood that trailed from it and brushed it away.

"Your wound weeps."

"It is nothing."

Not waiting for Lone Dog's reply, Night Raven abruptly departed.

"Are you mad at me, too, Miss Keene?"

Seated on a pallet in the tipi where Bobbie had delivered her from the angry women of the camp, Edwina allowed her eyes to close briefly. She was still trembling. Her hands were still bound and she could neither brush away the hair that clung annoyingly to her cheek, straighten her aching arms, nor rub her bruised ribs. She was disheveled, miserable, and hungry; and she was a captive in a Sioux camp where many had suffered greatly at the hands of white soldiers only a few days previously. The women would have stoned her to death without the blink of an eye if not for the intervention of the Sioux chief, who bore her no true goodwill. All this had come about because of the boy who looked up at her now with an expression of innocence and asked sincerely if she was mad at him.

Edwina stared at him in stony silence, then grated, "What's your real name?"

Bobbie blinked, then frowned. "My name's Bobbie Ray, like I said, but nobody here calls me that because Night Raven gave me a Sioux name. He calls me White Bear."

"What do you want me to call you?"

Bobbie paused, still frowning. "My name's White Bear."

Bobbie's response tightened the knot within her as Edwina replied, "You're an Injun now, is that it?"

"No, I ain't changed the color of my skin— but my pa's dead, and I'm a part of Night Raven's family now."

"Your pa's dead?"

"I didn't lie, you know. Everythin' I said in the fort about my pa was true, except I left out the part about Night Raven findin' me . . . and about him findin' what was left of my pa later on."

"Your pa was killed by the Injuns."

"No! My pa fell from his horse!"

"I thought you said your pa was strong and a good horseman."

"He was."

"Well?"

184

"Night Raven said he found my pa and his horse dead."

"How do you know he told you the truth?"

"I know because Night Raven don't lie—not for nobody!"

Edwina's jaw tightened. She responded abruptly. "Yes, I am mad at you."

"Don't be." Bobbie's eyes grew moist. "I had to help get Night Raven out of that fort. They were goin' to kill him!"

"He killed a lot of soldiers!"

"The soldiers killed a lot of Sioux!"

"How can you take Night Raven's part against your own people?"

"These *are* my people, Miss Keene."

"Bobbie!" Edwina's incredulity expanded. "You saw how those women acted toward me."

"That's because the soldiers killed so many of their husbands. They've been mournin', and they ain't thinkin' right."

"White women wouldn't try to stone their enemies!"

Bobbie's small face twitched. "Mrs. Sinclair said she wanted to see Night Raven hangin' from the highest tree. She said she'd be happy to fix the rope if she could."

"She didn't mean that!"

"I asked her. She said she did."

"Bobbie . . ."

"My name's White Bear."

"You don't want me to be angry with you, is that it?"

"That's right."

"But you're goin' to let Night Raven mistreat me."

"He won't mistreat you."

"He took me from the fort with a knife at my ribs. He tied me up and brought me here hanging over his saddle like a sack of potatoes!"

"I don't know why he took you from the fort." Bobbie appeared momentarily puzzled. "Except maybe he thinks he can exchange you for somebody else the soldiers are holdin'." Bobbie paused. "The rest was your fault. You shouldn't have made him mad."

"I'm a doctor, Bobbie... White Bear. I'm needed back at the fort. Mrs. Rice is goin' to have a baby, and she's dependin' on me."

"Laughin' Water had a baby all by herself. She didn't need no doctor."

"Mrs. Rice needs *me*."

Bobbie hesitated. "Well, maybe you should tell Night Raven that, and maybe he'll let you go."

"Bobbie..." Edwina looked directly into Bobbie's eyes. "You helped Night Raven escape because you knew he shouldn't be a prisoner at the fort. Well, I shouldn't be a prisoner here, either."

"Night Raven thinks you should, or he wouldn't have taken you along. If he wasn't sure you should be here, he would've let you go when you caused him so much trouble."

"Did you ever think that maybe Night Raven wants to take revenge on me for what the soldiers did a few days ago?"

"If that's what he wanted, he wouldn't have told me to tell anybody who tried to hurt you that they would answer to him if they did."

"Is. . . . is that what he said?"

"And Night Raven always means what he says. That's why them women backed off like they did."

"Not that last woman!"

"Oh, her . . ." Bobbie shook his head. "Night Raven don't like Runnin' Deer and he don't pay no attention to her. She don't like that, even if she *is* Jumpin' Bull's wife."

"Jumpin' Bull? He's old enough to be her father."

"Yeah, well, he has two other wives he likes better than her. She's pretty, but she ain't nice." Bobbie paused. "But Runnin' Deer ain't as pretty as you are, Miss Keene."

Edwina looked at Bobbie, her amazement deepening. A little boy in so many ways, yet—

"My hands hurt, Bobbie. Please untie them."

"I can't. Night Raven would get mad."

"They hurt a lot."

"Not as much as Night Raven's hurtin', Miss Keene. And he's bleedin' again, pretty bad, too."

187

"He says it's nothin'."

"That's 'cause he's so brave and he won't give in to pain or feelin' weak. He taught me how to do that. I'm goin' to be a brave warrior like him some day."

"Are you goin' to fight the soldiers like the Injuns do, too?"

"Well . . ." Appearing to consider the question seriously, Bobbie replied, "If the soldiers keep tryin' to hurt the Sioux and chase them from their land, I guess I won't have no choice when I grow up."

Edwina glanced around her. It was getting darker. The sun would soon set on what could possibly be the last day of her life. She had no idea what the night would bring, yet she sat conversing with a boy who was trying to assure her that the danger was all in her imagination. She had to get away!

Forcing a smile, Edwina repeated, "My hands hurt, Bobbie. Please untie me."

"I can't, Miss Keene."

"Please."

The flap of the tipi slapped open with a startling crack of leather. Standing in the entrance, anger reverberating in his every word, Night Raven replied, "No, Edwina, White Bear will not untie you."

Entering, Night Raven towered over her. The russet tone of his cheek had noticeably paled, and the bandage across his chest was soaked with blood, but the realization that he must be near collapse did nothing to still the ragged pounding of Edwina's heart.

"You waste your time!" he spat. "White Bear is a child, but his mind is bright. He will not be confused by a smile that is intended to deceive, or words intended to evoke pity, and he will not turn against me."

"You've twisted his mind."

"White Bear thinks clearly . . . as do I."

Turning toward Bobbie abruptly, Night Raven spoke more softly. "Singing Bird and Many Faces await you. You have done well this day. It is time to return to your tipi."

Bobbie stood up slowly, without response. Panic invaded Edwina's senses as he started toward the exit. She held her breath when Bobbie turned back toward Night Raven abruptly and said, "Miss Keene thinks you're goin' to hurt her. I tried to tell her you wouldn't, but she doesn't believe me."

Not waiting for a reply, Bobbie left abruptly. Edwina withheld a gasp as Night Raven crouched beside her and whispered, "And now, Edwina, we are alone."

Trailing Mist stirred the great cooking pot over the fire, then glanced back at Jumping Bull's tipi. The sun was gradually setting in a sky that was bright with color. The day was fading, but the excitement of Jumping Bull's return had not yet settled. Nor had the whispers that abounded after Jumping Bull's open admonishment of Running Deer.

Trailing Mist shivered, her weathered cheek creasing with concern. She remembered the day when Jumping Bull announced that he was to take a third wife. Her heart had squeezed tight as she searched her husband's face. She was his first wife. When Jumping Bull took Winter Flower to wife, she did not allow herself to feel pain. It was the way of all great chiefs, and she accepted it. She remained the favored wife; although Winter Flower was good and faithful, Jumping Bull knew that the love of Trailing Mist would never fail him. Yet at the announcement of a new wife, she had held her breath.

When Jumping Bull named Running Deer as his new wife, she had been relieved. She had seen no threat in Running Deer's youth, despite the young woman's contempt for her age. Instead, she had silently berated herself for her foolishness in believing for a moment that Jumping Bull might surrender to the silent love he cherished—the love that could never be.

Trailing Mist raised her chin proudly. Jumping Bull's love for Seeing Woman—the wife of his friend—had mattered little to her when he took her to wife. So great a chief was he, so true was her admiration of Jumping Bull, that she proudly shared his tipi. Through the years, she had consoled herself that she filled Jumping Bull's arms as Seeing Woman never would, and with the knowledge that she alone was able to assuage Jumping Bull's need each time the ache in his heart became more than he could bear.

Nor did she fear Seeing Woman. In Seeing Woman, she saw a sister of the spirit, one who remained as true to her husband as she. And if she had learned over the years that Seeing Woman returned Jumping Bull's love in many ways, she knew Seeing Woman's love would remain chaste, and her admiration grew.

Running Deer did not share those feelings—but Running Deer was young and a fool. She had sought to warn Running Deer that she risked all by turning against Seeing Woman, but Running Deer had dismissed her with contempt, refusing to acknowledge the danger of the path she traveled.

The sound behind her halted Trailing Mist's thoughts. She started as Running Deer stepped up beside her—as if out of the shadows of her mind.

Running Deer spoke haltingly, her eyes downcast.

"I . . . I have angered Jumping Bull. I caused him to rebuke me, and now the camp talks of the rift between us. I have acted foolishly and I seek to please him. You cook Jumping Bull's favorite food. I would take it to our husband this night so he will see I wish to serve him and end the harshness between us."

Trailing Mist considered Running Deer's sincere expression. It did not escape her that a trace of tears still remained on Running Deer's cheeks. She suspected that they were left to impress, but she saw in the woman's youthful face a fleeting glimpse of Black Dog, who was a brave and noble warrior, and her heart softened. Reaching over, Trailing Mist filled a nearby bowl and offered it to her.

Pausing before she released it, Trailing Mist warned, "Speak sincerely and softly. Jumping Bull has just returned from Lone Dog's tipi, where he visited Seeing Woman. His heart is heavy."

Running Deer accepted the bowl with proper acknowledgment, her gaze still lowered. Trailing Mist watched as the younger woman approached Jumping Bull's tipi. She sighed as Running Deer paused at the entrance, knowing that Jumping Bull's shoulders were bowed under the weight Running Deer had placed upon them.

Running Deer lifted the flap of Jumping Bull's tipi and stepped inside. Her gaze remaining fixed on the point where the younger woman had disappeared from her sight, Trailing Mist hoped desperately that Running Deer would relieve that weight, and yet—

* * *

Outraged, Night Raven crouched beside Edwina. He had left Lone Dog's tipi abruptly, aware that his strength was close to failing. His head was light, his breathing difficult, and his step unsteady when he approached his tipi, but the conversation he overheard within had bolstered his waning strength with fury.

Edwina sat unmoving before him and Night Raven studied her, sensing the fear that she concealed. The sunset filtered through the smoke hole above them in brilliant shades of red and orange, but its splendor paled in comparison with the smooth texture of Edwina's skin and the spirals of brilliant gold that edged her cheek. Lashes similarly tipped with gold brushed her delicate brows, framing glorious eyes that moments earlier had pleaded with White Bear—a plea calculated to turn the boy against him.

Yet her beauty called out to him, drawing him in.

Night Raven studied her closer still. The fair skin that drew his eye was stained from travel, the golden spirals of hair glittering in the light were disheveled, the glorious eyes that spoke her emotions so clearly showed signs of strain that were also reflected in the tightness of her lips and in the effort she expended to hold her head high. He reached out to brush back her hair, but she jerked away from his touch.

Beautiful . . . but his enemy.

193

Night Raven whispered, "You asked White Bear to untie you. Would you like me to untie you, Edwina?"

Edwina did not reply.

"You have but to ask."

"You want me to beg."

Ignoring her response, Night Raven pressed, "What else would you like? You are hungry."

"No, I'm not."

"You are weary."

"No more tired than you."

The lines were clearly drawn.

Night Raven stood up abruptly and pulled Edwina to her feet beside him. "You want something that I want as well."

Holding her arm in an unrelenting grip, Night Raven led Edwina out of the tipi toward a well-used path nearby. He felt her resistance as the path wound down from the camp, as the shadows deepened and the sounds of the camp behind them faded, to be replaced by the chirping of night creatures in the grasses surrounding them. Drawing her out into the open at last, he noted Edwina's confusion when she saw a pool glimmering with the bright pink and gold of the setting sun. He saw her uncertainty when he stripped the leather ties from her wrists.

Aware that his strength was never closer to failing, Night Raven unfastened his breechcloth. Dropping it to the ground without a thought for his nakedness, he walked into the pool. The cool water jolted him. A shiver shook him as he walked deeper, as the water lifted the travails of the day from his body, stripping the pain from his chest and easing muscles cramped from days of inactivity—inactivity that had ended abruptly in a tense and prolonged race for freedom.

Submerged to his chest, Night Raven worked at the bloody bandage. Finally freeing himself, he stripped it away and threw it toward the bank, wincing as the water met the open wound.

Night Raven submerged himself abruptly and remained under water, holding his breath until his lungs were bursting and his mind was free of the last, dim shadows of his weakness. Bursting to the surface again, he breathed deeply, revived.

Night Raven turned to see Edwina's gaze fixed on him. Her beauty summoned him more clearly than words. Her silence fed his need. He walked toward her.

He had been submerged in the pond too long. Gripped by an unexpected sense of desperation, Edwina had been about to run into the water when Night Raven burst through the surface of the pond in a glittering shower. He stood momentarily silhouetted against a sky emblazoned with color, water trailing in glimmering streams down the muscular width of his chest from hair lying in dark spirals against his shoulders. He started toward her abruptly.

Edwina took a backward step, but she was somehow unable to retreat any farther. Standing beside her at last, Night Raven displayed no discomfort at his naked state. The raw virility he exuded set Edwina to trembling as he stroked a wisp of hair from her cheek with his damp hand. "I wish to share my pleasure with you, Edwina."

Grasping her arm, Night Raven attempted to draw her toward the water, but she pulled back.

He met her gaze boldly. "Clean or unclean. Afraid or fearless."

Edwina stiffened at Night Raven's direct challenge. She was dirty, uncomfortable, and her body ached—and she'd be damned if she'd let this enigmatic Sioux back her down!

Raising her chin, Edwina reached for the buttons at the back of her dress. Her dress and petticoat were lying in a circle around her feet when she walked to the water's edge in her chemise. Refusing to consider Night Raven's reaction to her maidenly modesty when she was certain he had seen many women as naked as he was now, she stepped into the water. She caught her breath at the coolness of the water. Another few steps and she breathed deeply. Submerging herself moments later, she reveled in the sense of triumph over fear, and the accompanying sense of freedom that the water evoked.

But she wasn't free.

Coming back to the surface, Edwina felt the harsh slap of reality when she saw Night Raven standing in the water a few feet from her. He startled her by saying, "It is time to leave."

"But—"

"We leave . . . now."

Confounded, Edwina walked back toward the bank. Grabbing up her clothes as he pulled on his breechcloth, she yanked her dress down over her wet body and then started back up the path. Night Raven's hand closed on her arm as they neared the camp. He tightened his grip as he ushered her through the maze of smoldering campfires and, lifting the flap of his tipi, thrust her inside.

Turning back toward him with an angry retort, Edwina saw that Night Raven stood stiffly in the entrance, blood streaming from the wound on his chest. It was open and raw, obviously causing him great pain.

Edwina averted her face deliberately. It was what he deserved.

When she turned back toward him, Night Raven was inside the tipi, his face drained of color. But his obviously weakened state did not diminish the anger that flashed in his eyes.

"Sit down, dammit!" she ordered.

Night Raven remained standing.

"If you want to bleed to death, that's all right with me, but I'm not goin' to stand here and watch without a fight. I've spent too much time workin' on that wound to ignore what's happenin' now."

"The wound is nothing."

Blood dripped onto the ground at Night Raven's feet and Edwina's forbearance snapped. Snatching up her petticoat, she ripped ragged strips from the skirt and turned back toward Night Raven to grate, "You can say what you want about Sioux endurance, but one thing I do know is that *any* man can bleed dry."

His gaze unreadable, Night Raven sat abruptly. Sensing that his reaction was more out of physical necessity than compliance, Edwina worked industriously at the wound, silently reasoning that the situation was much the same with her. Necessity—she needed to keep Night Raven alive and well. She had already seen what would happen to her in this camp without his protection.

Unable to ignore an inner voice mercilessly retorting that her fate was similarly uncertain *with* his protection, Edwina forced herself to continue her ministrations.

Jumping Bull looked up as Running Deer entered his tipi. Reclining on his pallet, he watched as she approached him, feeling his anger simmer anew.

Running Deer kneeled beside his pallet. She raised her great eyes to his as she whispered, "I bring food from Trailing Mist's campfire, to warm your body and your heart."

"Put it down."

Running Deer blinked at the harshness of Jumping Bull's tone. She placed the bowl beside the fire, but her attempt to retreat was halted as Jumping Bull spoke again.

"I have come from Lone Dog's tipi, where Seeing Woman lies gravely ill. Lone Dog says you saw her fall."

"She stumbled and struck her head."

"Seeing Woman was steady of foot."

"She misstepped."

"Her step was sure."

"Her step failed her."

"You called for help."

"I feared for her!"

"Because of your affection for Seeing Woman."

"Because of your esteem for her!"

Running Deer felt the bite of Jumping Bull's gaze before he glanced at the bowl she had brought. "You serve me because you wish to please me."

"Because I regret that I have angered you."

"You wish to regain my favor."

"I wish to erase your displeasure toward me."

Jumping Bull's eyes swept her body intimately. "You come to tell me you will do my bidding gladly."

Running Deer's heart skipped a beat as she saw victory near. "Yes. I submit to your will, my husband."

"I would have you perform duties in my name." Jumping Bull watched her reactions closely. "You will serve the needs of Night Raven's tipi while he remains injured."

Triumph faded to a humiliation that flushed Running Deer's skin hotly. She responded with a nod.

"And you will serve the needs of his captive as he directs."

Running Deer's composure snapped. "You would have the wife of a chief serve a captive?"

"I would have my wife obey me!"

Running Deer's lips pressed tight.

"You will put aside all other duties until Night Raven dismisses you."

Rage shuddered through her.

"And you will tell him I have declared you his servant until he says the word."

Running Deer stood up. "I will do this to please you."

As Running Deer emerged from the tipi, she added with silent determination—*and when I have turned away your anger, my vengeance will begin.*

* * *

"Come to bed, Craig. It's late."

His attention drawn from the map spread across the desk in front of him, Craig turned toward Margaret with a frown. He glanced at the window to see that twilight had long since faded into night.

He had been perusing these same maps for hours while Margaret had maintained her silence, enveloped in her own thoughts. But exhaustion now lined Margaret's freckled cheeks, and her eyes were weary. She could remain awake no longer.

Attempting a smile, Craig responded, "I'm not ready to go to bed yet. Try to sleep, darling. I'll lower the lamp so the light won't disturb you."

"The light doesn't disturb me. I was just thinkin' about Edwina." Margaret's voice trailed off.

"You've done enough worrying today. It's time for you to get some sleep."

Margaret fought her heavy eyelids as she asked, "What are you doin' that's takin' so much time?"

"I'm studying the most recent maps of this area. They're not totally accurate, but they give a general idea of the territory. I've marked the places that Johnson and Ford claimed to have covered today. I'm trying to establish the most likely location of the Sioux camp. I've eliminated a few areas, but that still leaves a lot of country to cover."

"Major Locke's angry. The talk is that he blames you for everythin' that's happened."

Craig turned sharply toward her. "What talk is that?"

"You know . . . Bertha Charles and Emily Sinclair."

"Those two . . ."

"Is it true? Is that what Major Locke said when he called you to his office?"

"Locke's trying to pass the blame off on anybody who'll sit still for it. But I won't sit still for it, Margaret, so don't worry. I'm going to find Edwina and bring her back. I'm going to get Night Raven, too."

"I don't want you to feel you have to bring that Injun killer in, Craig! I don't want you to risk your life just because you feel you have to prove somethin' to Major Locke!"

"Whatever I do, you can rest assured it won't be for Locke's sake."

"Craig, please."

"Go to sleep, darling. Johnson and Ford are taking patrols out at daybreak, and I'm going along—but I'm making sure I go prepared."

"Promise me . . ." Margaret had pulled herself to a seated position in bed. Her brown eyes were wide and dark against her pale face as she rasped, "Promise me you won't take any unnecessary chances . . . that you won't do anythin' without makin' sure you have enough men behind you."

Pushing back his chair, Craig walked to the side of the bed. He sat abruptly and drew Margaret into his arms. Her brown hair was sweet under his chin as he held her quaking body close. How could he help but love her?

"I'll be careful. And I'll bring Edwina home."

"Oh, Craig, it's so dark out there." Margaret's trembling increased. "Where do you think Edwina is now?"

"I don't know, darling." Craig drew her closer. "I don't know."

She lured him to her when he was weak. She assaulted his mind with her beauty. She bathed him with concern and sought to confuse him with gentle ministrations.

Night Raven struggled against his rambling thoughts as Edwina kneeled beside him, looking up from the bandage she had secured around his chest. She had seen the blood that flowed, but she did not know that his weakness was quickly slipping beyond his control. As wise as she claimed to be, she had not realized that he had been forced to surrender to that weakness at the pool, when the strength he had felt returning moments earlier had fled as quickly as it had come.

A hot flush surged in Night Raven's chest,

interrupting his thoughts, and he knew without a glance that a new flow of blood seeped from his wound. That knowledge was confirmed by Edwina's sudden frown as she glanced at the bandage and reached behind her to wad several pieces of the ripped cloth in her hand.

"Your wound's bleedin' again. It should be cauterized, but—" She glanced up at him, as if canceling that thought, adding, "Pressure should stop it, but it's goin' to hurt. It would be better if you'd lie down."

Night Raven made no move to comply.

Her mouth twitching with annoyance, Edwina pressed the wad against his wound, and Night Raven gritted his teeth against the pain.

The bleeding continued.

"I can't get enough pressure on the wound at this angle. I'm not doin' any good this way."

Forcing aside his light-headedness, Night Raven grasped Edwina's arms. Fear flashed in her eyes as he lifted her with the last of his remaining strength and situated her between his spread thighs, positioning her so she could exert the pressure she sought. The pain stole his breath away as Edwina pressed the wad against his wound with a trembling hand, and his body quaked violently.

"Lie down, dammit!"

He would not submit to her command.

Tightening his thighs around Edwina's waist, establishing his mastery over her even as his weakness increased, Night Raven refused to allow her dominion in any way. This woman was his torment and his challenge, but she was also his prisoner, and so she would remain.

A sound outside the tipi turned Night Raven's head toward the entrance as a voice declared, "It is I . . . Running Deer. I ask permission to enter."

Night Raven frowned.

"Jumping Bull sends food for your tipi."

Brushing Edwina's hand away from his wound, he held it fast beside him as he responded, "Enter."

Running Deer entered. Her step faltered at the sight of Edwina kneeling between his thighs, and Night Raven's satisfaction surged. He had not forgotten the night when Running Deer had come to his sleeping blanket. He had known she did so only to increase her own importance, but he had accepted what she offered him. In the moments they were together, his thoughts were confirmed, and he'd cast the memory of the night aside, as was fitting of the encounter.

But Running Deer would not be so easily forgotten. In the time since, he had felt the heat of her enmity as it grew. He had noted her many unkindnesses. He knew her bitterness extended to all that was his, and he had seen her jealousy of Seeing Woman for the affection Jumping Bull bore her.

Drawing Edwina closer, Night Raven looked at the bowls Running Deer carried. He watched as Running Deer placed them by the fire and said, "Jumping Bull asks me to serve the needs of your tipi until you are well."

"I *am* well."

"Jumping Bull wishes to have me meet all your daily needs until my services are no longer required."

"I have a woman to serve me, and she serves me well . . . in every way . . . but you may tell Jumping Bull that I will accept the food from his campfire until my woman has learned to provide that comfort with ease."

Night Raven saw the tight twist of Running Deer's lips. Glancing with pure antipathy at Edwina, she nodded her compliance and left without a word.

After watching the flap close behind her, Night Raven turned back to Edwina.

"I'm not your woman!"

His gaze intent on her face, Night Raven slipped his hand to her shoulder. She remained rigid as he cupped her chin with his palm, whispering, "Your fate is in my hands, Edwina."

Edwina shuddered. Her face flamed, but she made no attempt to withdraw from him. Glancing down at his wound, he saw that the bleeding had stopped, but he was weak and unfit to meet the intimate challenge of the moment.

Edwina blinked when he released her abruptly.

Patience.

Another day.

Night Raven picked up the bowl beside the fire and started to eat.

Jumping Bull stood outside Lone Dog's tipi, his great shoulders slumped. He had seen Running Deer make her way to Night Raven's tipi with bowls of food as he'd instructed. He had watched, noting her exit a few minutes later. Running Deer's posture was rigid and her expression frozen.

Jumping Bull's powerful frame shuddered with the weight of suspicions growing ever stronger. Were he certain they were true, Running Deer's punishment would far outweigh the humiliation he had forced on her that night.

Pausing, somehow unwilling to enter Lone Dog's tipi, Jumping Bull heard the aged shaman's droning song of healing. He saw the scented smoke that rose in thickening swirls of white against the dark sky. He watched as they were consumed by the night, like the many dreams he had held in his heart.

But he was not ready to completely surrender those dreams. He had never touched his lips to Seeing Woman's lips, or felt the joy of their bodies joining, but his heart claimed hers as it did no other. He was a great chief, and a brave and skillful warrior. All admired him and sought his counsel, yet deep within him was the knowledge that the joy of each new sunrise would be lost to him without Seeing Woman's presence beside him.

Jumping Bull raised a weary hand to his face. Lone Dog's chanting ended, and he lifted the flap and entered. His gaze halted on Seeing Woman's still face. Behind him, Lone Dog slipped silently away as Jumping Bull kneeled beside her.

Grasping her hand, his heart weeping as he could not, Jumping Bull urged, "Awaken, Seeing Woman. I await the sound of your voice speaking my name."

When there was no response, Jumping Bull continued more softly, "Time stretches empty and long in your silence. I would have you open your eyes, and hear me when I say that I eagerly await the next sunrise we will face together. I would have you heed my words while I tell of a vision I cherish in my heart—of a time fast approaching when age will overcome me, and my life will wind to its end. In that vision I see you standing beside me, your presence healing all and bringing the joy that you alone can bring. Do not disappoint me,

Seeing Woman. I, who know no fear in the face of the enemy, shudder at the thought of those endless days spent without you."

Jumping Bull's deep voice was hoarse with the emotion that quaked within him as he whispered, "Awaken, Seeing Woman. Hear my call."

Jumping Bull waited.

Lowering his head when Seeing Woman remained unmoving, he drew himself to his feet. His heart a dead weight within him, he left without looking back.

Margaret awakened with a start. She glanced at the dark sky beyond the window, then looked at the clock on the wall and closed her eyes. She had slept only a few minutes.

"Margaret, are you all right?"

Anxious, Craig raised himself on his elbow where he lay beside her, and Margaret hastened to reassure him. "I'm fine. It's just that it's so dark. Craig . . . will mornin' never come?"

"Morning will come. Close your eyes and get some sleep."

"I love you, Craig."

"I love you, too, dear."

"We both love her, too, don't we?"

"Yes . . . we do."

It was dark. The camp was silent. Night Raven had emptied his bowl and set it aside. Watching him from the corner of her eye, Edwina had done the same. She waited as he rose and walked to the sleeping bench where she sat.

Edwina assessed Night Raven intently. His color had improved, but his eyes were heavy and his step unsteady. He was at the point of collapse.

"You study me, Edwina. You see frailty in my demeanor, and you see an opportunity to escape."

"No! I . . . I—"

"You lie poorly."

Edwina struggled not to react.

"I give you a choice, Edwina. You may sleep alone, with your hands and ankles bound, or you may sleep beside me, with only my arms to prevent your escape."

Edwina opened her mouth to speak a haughty reply, but Night Raven halted her.

"Consider, Edwina. You have no chance of escape if you lie bound through the night, but my arms are not as unyielding as leather ties. My arms may loosen during the night. I may fall into a deep sleep and be unable to awaken if you slip free of me. If you are silent, you may reach the horses and make your escape while the camp sleeps, and your ordeal will be over."

"You're mocking me."

"I give you a choice this night."

"Why?"

"Because you are worthy."

"Worthy . . ."

"This is but the first of our encounters."

He was testing her. He was offering her a choice . . . a chance of escape if she was brave enough to take it. She didn't understand him or the way he thought, but—

Edwina raised her chin and linked her gaze with his. "I don't like bein' bound, especially with leather ties."

Responding wordlessly to her reply, Night Raven lay down beside her. Turning to her side away from him, Edwina forced her eyes closed. Her heart began a slow pounding as Night Raven curved his powerful body against her back and slipped his arm around her. She silently cursed the shudder that rocked her as his male heat pressed tightly against her.

Night Raven's grip tightened. She felt his chin against her hair and his warm breath against her cheek as he whispered, "My arms may loosen and my sleep may deepen . . . but you will not escape me."

Night Raven's words infused Edwina with sudden rage. He was so sure—but he was wrong. She *would* escape him. If not tonight, then tomorrow, or the day after. Of that she was certain.

Chapter Seven

The sound of their horses' hooves was muted
by the birdsong of impending dawn. The patrol
had mounted and been underway while stars
were still bright in the night sky. Craig glanced
beside him. Riding in the lead, Lieutenant Ford
sat his mount stiffly, his thick features sullen. A
quick look behind him revealed that the mood
of the men appeared similarly morose, and
Craig's suspicions were confirmed. Though
Lieutenant Ford was in command of the men,
he still resented Craig's presence. His resentment affected the men. Craig addressed the
burly officer beside him cautiously.

"Has Major Locke clarified this mission to
your satisfaction?"

Ford glanced at him sharply. "What's there to clarify? We're in pursuit of Night Raven and the prisoners. We're to bring the prisoners back alive, and to bring Night Raven back any way we can."

"Which means?"

"It means I'm not an Injun lover like some people at this fort, Captain!"

Craig's color mounted. "Explain that remark, Lieutenant."

Ford turned fully toward him. "The major told me that there's a rumor goin' around that Night Raven got away with the help of a spy. To my mind, there's only one person that spy could be."

"Name him."

"Name *her*, you mean. It's Edwina Keene, that's who!"

"You're a damned fool!"

Ford cursed under his breath.

"Would you care to repeat that aloud, Lieutenant?"

"Funny you should call me a damned fool, *sir*, when that's the name the people of the fort are puttin' to you!"

"I doubt that."

"Ask any one of them. Go ahead! Nobody's believin' that story about that kid bein' the spy . . . and if it isn't him, it can't be anybody else but Edwina Keene."

"You see what you want to see, Lieutenant."

"Funny, I was thinkin' the same thing about you, Captain."

"Don't let your lust for blood muddle your brain, Lieutenant."

Ford sneered. "Talk is, it ain't your brain that's causin' you the problem."

A blood-red fury turned Craig sharply toward the burly lieutenant. "Take that back, Ford, or I'll drag you from that horse right now and beat an apology out of you!"

"You do that, *sir.*"

Craig lunged toward him.

Ford's eyes widened almost comically as he called out, "Wait a minute!"

Shuddering with tenuous control, Craig rasped, "I'm waiting."

"I'm sorry. I was talkin' out of turn." Ford glanced behind him. Lowering his voice, he spat, "But whether you want to believe it or not, I'm only repeatin'—"

"I'm not interested in fort gossip! I'm here for one thing only. Major Locke has made me personally responsible for the return of the boy, Edwina, *and* Night Raven—a responsibility I gladly accepted because my wife and I are responsible for Doctor Keene's presence at the fort. So let me tell you this: I intend to recapture Night Raven, and I also intend to bring the captives back to the fort unharmed. I'll do that with or without the help of you and this patrol—but what I will not abide is any more of your innuendo—no matter what source you claim. Is that understood, Lieutenant?"

Silence.

"Is that understood?"

"Yes, sir!"

Allowing his stare to linger on Ford's tight-lipped expression, Craig then turned his attention back to the trail ahead and a perusal of the gradually lightening horizon.

Night Raven heard again the sound of fluttering wings. The sound grew louder as a familiar rainswept battlefield littered with the bodies of his enemy materialized. The raven returned to circle with harsh, mocking calls. He watched as the raven flew lower, knowing what would soon come. The time of retribution approached as the raven alighted on a motionless, blue-coated form.

The raven turned to look at him—confirming that the eye of the raven was his own.

Night Raven held his breath as the moment of final vengeance arrived. But his frustration soared when the raven again refused to feast on the flesh of his enemy, choosing instead to spread out his wings to shield the wounded soldier from the falling rain.

Night Raven awakened with a jolt to the silent darkness of his tipi. He turned to the woman beside him, knowing the assault of the vision was not yet complete. Its power still gripped him as he looked down at the woman who lay in the curve of his arm. He saw hair of shimmering gold . . . delicate features . . . fragile lids closed over eyes he knew to be a brilliant blue, eyes that threatened him with more true power than the arm of a warrior. But the woman he beheld was not a fantasy. Instead, he saw the living, breathing, flesh-and-blood embodiment of the illusion that had haunted him.

Edwina.

Night Raven steeled himself against a myriad of emotions. No, he would not become the weak, confused creature of his dream. He would not allow this woman to defeat him! Nor would he succumb to the pulsing hunger she evoked within him.

Night Raven looked upward at the first pale pillar of dawn slanting through the smoke hole above. The throbbing need within clamored for release, and he told himself that this first dawn when he awakened with Edwina in his arms would be the most difficult of many tests.

Throwing back the blanket, Night Raven forced himself to remain aloof as Edwina stirred, as her eyes opened and she looked up at him. Struggling to deny her allure, he stood up and addressed her in a voice devoid of emotion.

"The day begins. Jumping Bull has bid Running Deer to see to your needs. She will obey him. You will be safe when she walks beside you in the camp, but without her, you will not." He paused. "You cannot escape."

Thrusting aside a sudden need to stroke the strain from Edwina's cheek, Night Raven held himself remote.

Not yet.

His first few steps away from her were more difficult than any he had ever taken.

"I'd watch what I said, if I were you, Bertha!"

Margaret was trembling. The day had not yet begun when Craig left the fort with Lieutenant Ford's patrol. She had watched from the window as the fort gates opened and the men rode through, and she had been powerless to halt the tears that followed. She had forced herself to stop crying when the babe within her stirred restlessly, and she had gone outside to walk away her tension. She had been stopped only minutes later by Bertha Charles, who now blocked her path.

Her hand on her stomach, Margaret tried to soothe the babe's squirming.

"You're a fool, Margaret Rice, allowing your husband to assume personal responsibility for Edwina Keene's welfare! She got what she deserved. As a matter of fact, talk is that she—"

"Talk?" Margaret's eyes opened wide. "Talk that you initiated! Bertha Charles, you were jealous of Edwina from the moment she

217

entered this fort! Unfortunately, I've seen that reaction to Edwina's beauty too often to be surprised by it, but your ingratitude amazes me! You conveniently choose to forget that Edwina worked day and night takin' care of you and the others when you were all afflicted with the fever. If not for her—"

"That's in the past. The present is what concerns all of us now, and the talk is—"

"I'm not interested in gossip! If I were you, I'd be doin' somethin' worthwhile instead of wastin' my time gossipin'—somethin' like takin' care of the wounded, who are probably sufferin' without Edwina's attentions."

"The talk is—"

"Bertha Charles"—Margaret tightened her fists and growled through gritted teeth—"get away from me."

"The talk is—"

"Corporal Lee!" Turning toward the trooper who stood guard at the fort gate nearby, and who had watched much of the exchange in silence, Margaret snapped, "This woman is harrassin' me! She's a threat to my health in my condition! Please ask her to get out of my way!"

Bertha's expression grew haughty. "Well, I never!"

"Ma'am . . ." Corporal Lee looked up at the towering Bertha Charles. His expression showed no sign of amusement as he said,

"Please move on or I'll be forced to report this situation to Major Locke."

"Well, I *never!*"

Watching as Bertha lumbered off in a snit, Margaret turned back toward the frowning Corporal Lee.

"Thank you, Corporal."

"Are you all right, ma'am?"

"I'm fine . . . now."

Corporal Lee moved a step closer. "I never did like that woman. She never has a good thing to say about nobody." He leaned toward her confidentially. "Sometimes . . . well, she puts me in mind of a cow with those big . . . shoulders of hers."

"Corporal!"

"I didn't mean to offend you, ma'am!"

Margaret struggled to hide her smile. "Bertha offends me. You don't. Thanks again. I'll be sure to tell my husband how you came to my rescue."

"Seeing Woman . . . hear me."

Lone Dog's tipi was lit by a smoldering fire still bearing the scent of the healing smoke that filtered upward. Unmindful of the deep creases of concern on Lone Dog's wizened face, Night Raven knelt beside the sleeping bench. Seeing Woman's features were motionless, as if made of stone. It occurred to him as he perused her face that her appearance was

219

somehow strange, almost as if she was another person without the animation of her smile and the warmth that usually shone through her sightless eyes.

Sorrow clenched tight within Night Raven as he repeated, "Seeing Woman . . . hear me. I have returned, and I await your smile. My heart is heavy with concern. You sleep, but the time has come for you to awaken." Unconsciously stroking the bruise that darkened her temple, Night Raven whispered, "Your spirit is hale, and your body strong. Do not submit to this injury that would take you from those who esteem you. Wake up, Seeing Woman. Hear me now!"

His heart sinking, Night Raven drew himself slowly to his feet. Turning at the sound of movement behind him, he met Lone Dog's grave expression.

"Seeing Woman's breathing slows, and her spirit weakens." Lone Dog's voice grew strained. "Her life drifts rapidly from her."

"The healing smoke—"

"Seeing Woman does not respond. She does not accept food or drink."

"Perhaps from my hand."

Night Raven took the ladle from the pouch hanging nearby. Kneeling again beside her, he raised the living water to Seeing Woman's lips, softly urging her to drink. When she did not respond, Night Raven stood up as the aged shaman repeated, "She awaits the right word to awaken."

Turning toward the old man, Night Raven grated, "I cannot speak a word that is unknown to me."

Lone Dog met his response with silence.

Carrying buckskin garments newly fashioned and sewn, Running Deer walked resentfully toward Night Raven's tipi. Trailing Mist's expression had been bright with pleasure when she placed the garments in her hands and explained that although she had fashioned the clothes for Jumping Bull, the great chief had directed that they be given to Night Raven, to replace the garments he had lost when captured.

Running Deer perused the finely cured skins, the careful stitching, and the decoration Trailing Mist had added with gifted fingers. She spat her distaste upon the ground. Garments worthy of a great chief were not suitable for one who had taken to himself a woman whose capture was certain to draw the bluecoats' ire and bring further hardship upon his people.

Running Deer raised her graceful chin. Night Raven turned his back on the women of his own people. So many lusted for his favor— Dawn Woman foremost of them all—yet he

221

took the pale woman and openly flaunted his possession of her.

Glimpsing Night Raven's unmistakable figure emerging from Lone Dog's tipi, Running Deer halted. Night Raven had doubtless warned his captive of the danger in walking the camp alone. The woman would be inside his tipi, waiting for her.

Running Deer paused to contemplate that thought. So despised was Night Raven's captive, any word spoken against her would be greedily accepted by the women of the camp. It would not be difficult to incite the women to violence against her.

Running Deer reconsidered. No, she could not afford to provoke her husband. She would wait for her satisfaction. Night Raven would tire of this woman as he had all the others, and the stones Jumping Bull had halted the previous day would then find their mark on the woman's white skin.

Her hand closing spasmodically on the buckskins she carried, Running Deer raised the flap of Night Raven's tipi. She would wait, but in the meantime . . .

Craig heard the mutterings of the troopers behind him—mutterings that had grown louder as the morning progressed. He glanced at the lieutenant, aware that Ford heard them as well. The sun had risen, washing all traces of night from the clear sky. They had been out for hours, with only one positive result—the realization that they were riding in circles.

"I think it's time to take a different tack, Lieutenant."

His expression suddenly fierce, Lieutenant Ford turned toward Craig. "You can *think* all you want, Captain, but you're just an observer on this patrol. I'm in charge, and I say what tack we do or don't take!"

"You're acting like a fool, Ford." Craig's patience was rapidly waning. "You're wasting time trying to follow a trail that doesn't exist!"

"Those Injun horses didn't fly! We'll find Night Raven's trail sooner or later."

"Later may be too late!"

"I suppose you know exactly how to find them."

"No, I don't." Craig locked his gaze with Ford's. "What I do have is a plan."

"A plan?"

"A plan for a systematic search based on the most recent maps of the area."

"Everybody knows those maps aren't dependable!"

"Neither is following a trail that is deliberately misleading."

"Let me tell you somethin', Captain." Ford's heavy features drew into a sneer. "I've been fightin' Injuns in this country a lot longer than you have, and there's nothin' *you* have to teach me about it."

"We're riding in circles."

"And that's what we're goin' to keep on doin' until I say otherwise."

"Listen, Lieutenant—"

"No, *you* listen! I've got more Injun scalps to my credit than you'll have if you live to be a hundred, and I'm intendin' to get myself a lot more." Ford's gaze intensified as he rasped, "But I'm goin' to do it *my* way!"

Barely restraining his anger, Craig snapped, "Our orders are to find the captives and bring them home, safe and sound—not take more Indian scalps!"

"Yeah . . . those are our orders."

"And yet you—"

"This is *my* patrol, Captain, and don't forget it!"

Belligerent and unyielding, Ford turned back to face the trail ahead.

Frustrated, knowing he had no recourse, Craig silently cursed the futility that the day was sure to bring.

Night Raven has taken the scalps of many bluecoats, and he will take many more.

Night Raven uses women easily and tires of them quickly.

Night Raven's only goal is the death of the white man.

Night Raven's heart is cold and black, with no place for a woman in it.

Night Raven . . . Night Raven . . . Night Raven . . .

Seated in Night Raven's silent tipi, Edwina fought to subdue the echoes of the malicious diatribe that had spewed from Running Deer's well-shaped lips during their earlier, brief excursion outside the tipi.

Clearly, Running Deer bore Night Raven true malice—malice that would not be banished by Jumping Bull's disapproval. The woman hated Night Raven and all who were associated with him in any way. Running Deer hated *her*, and the danger to her because of the woman's antipathy was real.

Sitting back abruptly on the sleeping bench, Edwina forced herself to admit that much of what Running Deer had said about Night Raven's exploits in battle was probably true. Night Raven's reputation at the fort was legendary. He had killed many soldiers. He would probably kill many more. Eventually, he would tire of tormenting her, and then—

Edwina closed her eyes with a shudder. She needed to escape, but one glance at the camp as she walked through it beside Running Deer had showed that her chances were slim.

The sound of a footstep outside the tipi drew

her attention. "Can I come in, Miss Keene?"

Bobbie.

"Miss Keene?"

"Come in Bobb . . . White Bear."

Bobbie was clad in buckskins that had obviously been tailored to his proportions by a loving hand. Yet he was an incongruous sight with his pale skin, with his raggedly cut, shoulder-length blond hair held in place by a headband adorned with a single feather, and with his light eyes looking up at her in silent supplication. "I need your help, Miss Keene."

A child in so many ways.

Somehow, Edwina could not smile as she responded, "There's very little I can help you with in this camp, Bobbie."

"No, you can help a lot, if you want to."

Edwina remained silent.

"My friend is sick."

"Your friend . . ."

"Seein' Woman fell and hurt herself while I was at the fort. She hasn't woken up yet. Singin' Bird says Lone Dog's been singin' his healin' songs and lightin' medicine smoke, but it ain't done no good. Everybody's feelin' real bad. Night Raven most of all, because she's special to him."

A knot tightened unexpectedly within Edwina as she responded, "This woman is special to Night Raven?"

"Yes. He don't say it to nobody, because he's a

A Special Offer For Leisure Historical Romance Readers Only!

Get Four FREE* Romance Novels

A $21.96 Value!

Thrill to the most sensual, adventure-filled Historical Romances on the market today...

FROM  LEISURE BOOKS

As a home subscriber to the Leisure Historical Romance Book Club, you'll enjoy the best in today's BRAND-NEW Historical Romance fiction. For over twenty-five years, Leisure Books has brought you the award-winning, high-quality authors you know and love to read. Each Leisure Historical Romance will sweep you away to a world of high adventure...and intimate romance. Discover for yourself all the passion and excitement millions of readers thrill to each and every month.

SAVE AT LEAST *$5.00* EACH TIME YOU BUY!

Each month, the Leisure Historical Romance Book Club brings you four brand-new titles from Leisure Books, America's foremost publisher of Historical Romances. EACH PACKAGE WILL SAVE YOU AT LEAST $5.00 FROM THE BOOKSTORE PRICE! And you'll never miss a new title with our convenient home delivery service.

Here's how we do it. Each package will carry a 10-DAY EXAMINATION privilege. At the end of that time, if you decide to keep your books, simply pay the low invoice price of $16.96 ($17.75 US in Canada), no shipping or handling charges added*. HOME DELIVERY IS ALWAYS FREE*. With today's top Historical Romance novels selling for $5.99 and higher, our price SAVES YOU AT LEAST $5.00 with each shipment.

AND YOUR FIRST FOUR-BOOK SHIPMENT IS TOTALLY FREE!

IT'S A BARGAIN YOU CAN'T BEAT! A Super $21.96 Value!

LEISURE BOOKS A Division of Dorchester Publishing Co., Inc.

GET YOUR 4 FREE* BOOKS NOW—
A $21.96 VALUE!

Mail the Free* Book
Certificate
Today!

Get Four Books Totally
F R E E* —
A \$21.96 Value!

(Tear Here and Mail Your FREE* Book Card Today!)

PLEASE RUSH
MY FOUR FREE*
BOOKS TO ME
RIGHT AWAY!

Leisure Historical Romance Book Club
P.O. Box 6613
Edison, NJ 08818-6613

AFFIX
STAMP
HERE

brave warrior and all, but he loves Seein'
Woman a lot. He went to visit her again this
mornin' and I saw him when he left. He was
feelin' real bad."

"If Night Raven is so worried about this . . .
Seein' Woman's health, why didn't he ask me to
help her?"

"He couldn't do that, Miss Keene. You're his
captive!"

"But *you* can ask me."

"You ain't my captive. You're just my friend."

Edwina was incredulous. "I'm your friend?"

"You took good care of me when I was sick,
and you took care of Night Raven, too, so that
makes you my friend."

"Night Raven doesn't seem to feel the same
way about my doctorin' skills as you do."

"Seein' Woman needs your help, Miss
Keene."

Edwina shook her head.

"Please, Miss Keene. Seein' Woman—" Bobbie's words choked off as his eyes filled unexpectedly. He forced himself to continue. "She's
dyin'."

"Whoever that Injun doctor is, he won't like
me lookin' at this woman if he can't cure her,
Bobbie. And the truth is, I probably won't be
able to do anythin' for her, either."

"Just take a look."

"Bobbie . . ."

"Please."

A tear welled up in Bobbie's eye and he brushed it away, but she'd seen it.

Cursing the tightness in her throat that single tear had evoked, Edwina grated, "All right, I'll look at her."

A smile as bright as sunshine broke across Bobbie's small face as he grasped her hand and pulled her forward.

"No, wait!" Despising her cowardice, Edwina withdrew her hand. "You saw what happened yesterday. If I go out there now—"

"I'll be with you, Miss Keene. Nobody will hurt you."

"You said that yesterday."

"There ain't a woman in camp who'll take a chance of makin' Jumpin' Bull as mad at her as he was at Runnin' Deer yesterday."

Edwina still hesitated.

"If you're scared, I'll hold your hand."

Scared?

"Miss Keene . . ."

"All right, let's go."

Allowing Bobbie to drag her forward, Edwina reasoned that Bobbie was doing her a favor, after all. He was giving her a chance to become familiar with the camp, so when the time came—when the time was right—she could make her escape more easily.

Aware of the biting glances cast her way as Bobbie led her across the camp to a tipi where the smell of scented smoke grew strong, Edwina prepared herself.

She was torn by conflicting emotions.

Night Raven don't say it to nobody, but he loves Seein' Woman a lot.

The woman Night Raven loved had been lying near death while he slept with her in his arms.

"She's in here, Miss Keene."

The woman Night Raven loved . . .

"I told Lone Dog I was goin' to ask you to come. We can go right in."

The woman Night Raven loved.

"Come on."

Following Bobbie, Edwina entered Lone Dog's tipi. The swirling smoke within momentarily obscured the aged Indian standing silently a few feet away. Short, exceedingly thin, his long hair streaked with gray and his hollowed cheeks creased with age, he moved into her path. His small eyes were dark pinpoints of light that studied her soberly.

"This is Miss Keene, Lone Dog," Bobbie said. "She's goin' to try to help Seein' Woman."

Uncomfortable under the shaman's scrutiny, Edwina turned her gaze toward the nearby pallet, where a woman lay motionless. She walked closer, then kneeled beside the still figure. Momentarily startled, she saw that the woman's hair was gray, that her features were marked by age and her body matronly. She noted the great purple bruise on the woman's temple that was beginning to yellow.

"What happened to her?" she asked.

"She fell, like I told you. She hit her head."

Edwina looked up at the silent shaman. She turned to Bobbie and said, "Ask him if she's been like this ever since she fell."

Surprising her, Lone Dog responded, "Seeing Woman sleeps. She waits for the right word to awaken."

The right word?

Edwina examined the woman more closely. Her breathing was faint and growing labored. Her heart beat slowly. She could not survive in this condition much longer.

"Has she been able to drink or eat?"

Long Dog shook his head.

Edwina touched the woman's hand. The texture of her skin confirmed the shaman's reply.

"Have you tried to talk to her? Does she show any kind of response?"

"She don't hear nothin', Miss Keene, and she don't say nothin', neither."

A great sadness welled inside Edwina. There was nothing she could do for this woman.

"Try talking to her again, Bobbie."

"No, that's why I brought you here, Miss Keene. Seein' Woman don't hear none of us." Tears again brimmed in Bobbie's eyes. "You talk to her. She's a nice lady. She'd like that."

"Bobbie . . ."

"The boy knows well what he says." Speaking again, Lone Dog pinned her with his gaze. "Speak. Seeing Woman understands your language. She will listen."

Turning back to the unconscious woman, Edwina forced a smile that she hoped was reflected in her voice as she whispered, "Seein' Woman, everybody here wants you to open your eyes. You've been sleepin' too long. It's time to wake up. Bobbie needs you. Your friends need you." Edwina paused. "Night Raven needs you."

Silence.

"Seein' Woman . . ."

The fire popped unexpectedly, and Edwina jumped back as a shower of sparks and a fresh burst of scent filled the room. Embarrassed by her reaction, she turned back to the sleeping bench, then went suddenly still. Was it her imagination, or had the woman's eyelids moved?

"She's movin', Miss Keene! Talk to her again!"

Edwina glanced up at Bobbie, then looked back at the squaw. She addressed her again.

"I know you can hear me, Seein' Woman. Open your eyes. It's time to wake up."

The woman's eyelids moved again.

"Tell her who you are, Miss Keene."

Edwina was at a loss.

"Tell her you came here with Night Raven—from the fort. Tell her you're stayin' with Night Raven so he can protect you."

"Bobbie . . ."

"The boy knows well what to say."

Leaning closer to the woman, Edwina whispered, "My name is Edwina Keene. I came to this camp with Night Raven. He's protectin' me from harm in the camp . . . and I . . . I'm here to help you wake up."

Seeing Woman's eyelids parted. Her lips twitched with a hoarse word.

"She's awake!" Bobbie brushed away tears that were suddenly falling freely. "I knew you could do it, Miss Keene!"

The woman tried to speak, and Edwina motioned toward the water pouch. Holding the ladle to Seeing Woman's lips, Edwina watched as the woman swallowed, convulsively at first, and then more smoothly.

"That's enough for now." Edwina watched the woman closely. Frowning, she waved a hand in front of the woman's eyes. There was no reaction.

"She's blind!"

The woman labored to speak, and Edwina leaned closer. "What are you tryin' to say, Seein' Woman?"

Edwina sat back abruptly as the woman's whispered words became clear. She looked up at the aged shaman, who observed all without comment.

Edging closer, Bobbie asked, "What did she say to you, Miss Keene?"

"She said . . ." Edwina took a shaken breath. "She said she was waitin' for me."

Night Raven returned from the pool. The cool water had again refreshed him. The food Trailing Mist had given him to begin the new day had fed his strength. The wound in his chest no longer bled . . . but his heart was draining dry.

Night Raven glanced at Lone Dog's tipi as he walked back into the camp. Healing smoke continued to rise toward the late-morning sky, but Lone Dog's medicine could not awaken Seeing Woman, and the end was near.

Night Raven approached his tipi. That sad realization had been swept from his mind while Edwina lay in his arms the previous night. Her warm flesh was a balm that allowed no thought but those of her when she lay near.

Night Raven pushed back the flap on his tipi, and his thoughts halted abruptly. The tipi was empty. Glancing quickly around the camp, he saw Running Deer engaged in conversation with another woman. Edwina was not beside her.

Night Raven's heart pounded. He had been a fool to believe Edwina would fear to leave the tipi, and now he paid the price! He would—

His attention was caught by a small figure emerging from Lone Dog's tipi. White Bear motioned urgently for him to approach.

Night Raven covered the distance between them in rapid steps. Responding to White Bear's urging, he stepped into Lone Dog's tipi and stopped short at the sight of Edwina kneeling beside the sleeping bench where Seeing Woman lay.

Seeing Woman's head turned toward him and Night Raven's breath caught in his throat.

"Seein' Woman woke up, Night Raven!" White Bear's youthful voice drummed in his ears as the boy repeated, "She's awake!"

Edwina stood up abruptly as Night Raven kneeled beside Seeing Woman. Aware only of the weak smile that Seeing Woman turned toward him, Night Raven gripped her hand. His throat tight, he whispered, "I welcome your return, Seeing Woman."

"She woke up when Miss Keene spoke to her, Night Raven," White Bear continued. "It was like she was waitin' for Miss Keene to call her!"

Night Raven glanced up at Edwina, his jaw tight, but his gaze softened when he looked back down into Seeing Woman's beloved face. He leaned forward as she attempted to speak. His throat choked tight at her feeble rasp.

"My son."

Momentarily unable to respond, Night Raven nodded, then whispered to her softly before standing up and meeting Edwina's gaze. He turned toward Lone Dog abruptly.

"I leave Seeing Woman in your care."

Gripping Edwina's arm, Night Raven led her from the tipi. He drew her along behind him as they crossed the camp, a single thought in his mind.

The first victory was Edwina's—but it would be her last.

"Seeing Woman has awakened!" Trailing Mist's gulping cry turned Running Deer toward the older woman, who raced to Winter Flower and gasped, "She will live!"

Standing unseen nearby, Running Deer went still as Trailing Mist continued with tears streaking her cheeks. "Night Raven's captive called her name and Seeing Woman opened her eyes!"

Fury shuddered through Running Deer.

"Lone Dog no longer fears for her life. Seeing Woman will be well again!"

The women sobbed their joy as Running Deer walked slowly into the shadows.

"It's a waste of time trying to find Night Raven's trail. The patrol accomplished nothing but the waste of another day."

The sun was setting in brilliant shades of red and gold as Craig's adamant statement reverberated through Major Locke's silent office.

Frustration colored Craig's fair complexion. The patrol that had left with high hopes before dawn that morning had returned frustrated and tense as the sun was setting. His own frustration was compounded by the realization that Lieutenant Ford's personal resentment of him had played a part in his refusal to consider an alternate plan of action in pursuing Night Raven. The knowledge that Ford's resentment was shared by Major Locke, and that Lieutenant Ford had already made a lengthy report to Locke in private, increased Craig's agitation as he awaited Locke's reply.

Deep lines of disapproval were apparent on Locke's bearded face as he responded with cutting sharpness, "Lieutenant Ford informs me that your resistance to his command contributed to his failure in pursuing Night Raven."

"My resistance had nothing to do with the patrol's failure to find Night Raven's trail, sir."

"You admit to your resistance, then."

"I admit to protesting against another wasted day while the captives taken from this fort are exposed to continued danger."

"Lieutenant Ford was in command of the patrol. He's a competent officer."

"If he was truly competent, he'd admit to the failure of his methods and accept an alternate plan that has at least the possibility of succeeding!"

"*Your* alternate plan, of course."

"That's right! I attempted to outline it to Lieutenant Ford, but he—"

"Lieutenant Ford is an accomplished Indian fighter with countless victorious to his credit."

"His most recent 'victory' against the Sioux was no more than the slaughter of an innocent camp of women and children."

"There is no such thing as an innocent Sioux camp."

Refusing to be drawn into that controversy, Craig replied with tight control, "I have an alternate plan that I feel will meet with greater success than Lieutenant Ford's methods of pursuit."

"You do?"

"Yes, sir."

Struggling to ignore Locke's derisive sneer, Craig pressed, "It's obvious that Night Raven's trail grows colder every day, and since the Sioux are far more familiar with this country than we, I believe it behooves us to take another tack."

"Yes, Ford mentioned your alternate tack."

"My plan incorporates the use of maps of the area available to all of us, sir."

"Maps that have already proved to be inaccurate."

"Maps that are only partially inaccurate—but will yet allow us a basis for an organized search."

"That's a waste of time!"

"Which is exactly what our patrols have been doing for the past two days."

"So . . ." His complexion revealing his rapidly escalating agitation, Locke continued. "With your limited experience on the frontier, you feel your plan will be more successful than the instincts of proven Indian fighters."

"My objective isn't to fight Indians, sir. My objective is to find the captives—wherever Night Raven has taken them—and to bring them back unharmed."

Locke stiffened. "I'm afraid I share Lieutenant Ford's view of your outlook. I find it limited and unrealistic."

"Sir, you've assigned me personal responsibility for the return of the captives. I feel that should afford me greater input on the methods to be used."

"I'm not interested in what you feel, Captain."

"Sir, I don't take my responsibility for the captives' return lightly."

"Insinuating that other officers in this fort do?"

"I wish to officially state that my hands were tied when I accompanied Lieutenant Ford's patrol this morning, and that I feel nothing more can be accomplished with his method of pursuit."

"You speak officially . . ."

"Yes, sir."

"Then I suppose I'll have to speak officially,

as well." Drawing his wiry frame up, Major Locke continued stiffly, "Officially, I give you permission to pursue any tack you desire in your effort to find the captives." Pausing, Locke continued with growing derision, "But the life you risk with your unrealistic plan will be your own. I will *not* assign a patrol for you to lead blindly into the wilderness."

"Sir, I've studied the maps."

"And I've told you the maps are inaccurate."

"Sir—"

"I'm done talking, Captain!" Locke's stare grew malevolent. "You have my permission to pursue your plan. Go wherever you want, and take as much time as you wish—but watch your back, because there won't be anyone else to watch it for you."

"Sir—"

"Draw the supplies you need from the quartermaster. You may leave when you're ready . . . preferably tomorrow morning. That's all, Captain."

"Sir, I request your permission to solicit volunteers to accompany me."

"No."

"Several of the men have already asked—"

"No!"

"I'll leave at dawn tomorrow."

The day was drawing to an end when Jumping Bull crouched beside Seeing Woman's sleeping bench at last. He had returned from a solemn journey to the sacred hillside of his youthful vision quest only minutes earlier—to be met with Trailing Mist's joyful announcement that Seeing Woman had awakened. He had rushed to her side, where he now waited.

Unmindful of Lone Dog's departure from the tipi, Jumping Bull stroked her cheek with a trembling hand. He held his breath, hoping for a response to his touch. His heart leaped in his broad chest when Seeing Woman's eyes opened, and her lips parted with a rasping whisper.

"Jumping Bull . . ."

Jumping Bull's heavy features contorted with a sudden surge of emotion he struggled to control. His voice unsteady, he whispered hoarsely, "The days were long and dark while you slept, Seeing Woman. My heart rejoices that you are awake at last."

"My sleep was heavy."

"I feared for you."

"You need not have feared."

"You did not respond to my pleas."

"I would not leave you."

"I despaired when you did not hear me."

"I awaited . . . another voice."

Unexpected jealousy seared Jumping Bull's heart. "Whose voice brought you back when mine could not?"

"Another's."

"Seeing Woman . . ."

Seeing Woman's hand clutched his, then went limp. Her eyes closed.

"Seeing Woman!"

Rigid . . . motionless . . . Jumping Bull stared at Seeing Woman in breathless silence. His heart resumed its beating when he saw the steady rise and fall of her breast.

She was sleeping.

Jumping Bull stood up. He remained looking down at Seeing Woman in tremulous silence as the words she had rasped echoed in his mind.

I would not leave you.

Jumping Bull savored the cherished words deep within him. He allowed their import to linger before he turned away.

The setting sun shone through the smoke hole above Edwina, illuminating Night Raven's tipi with the last, dazzling rays of light, but Edwina took no pleasure in its splendor. Instead, she stared upward in realization that another day in captivity was coming to an end—a captivity that had no end in sight.

Edwina rose from the sleeping bench where she had passed the idle hours in an effort to comprehend the astounding events of the day. Seeing Woman's weak smile returned before her eyes as she paced, and her anxious step paused.

Seeing Woman . . . the woman Night Raven

loved. She had been shaken when Bobbie made that casual declaration. A myriad of mixed emotions had surged to life in the few minutes it had taken for them to cross the camp and enter Lone Dog's tipi. She remembered still the singing sense of relief she'd experienced at first sight of Seeing Woman's mature countenance.

Edwina took a shaky breath. The woman had awakened at her plea when all others failed to move her. The wonder of the moment remained, but it had taken only one glimpse of Night Raven's expression to see that despite his relief, he was not pleased at the part she had played in the squaw's recovery.

Edwina resumed her pacing. Night Raven's fingers on her arm had been talons of steel as he drew her from Lone Dog's tipi and ushered her back to his own. She had not seen him since.

Edwina stiffened. Food to break her morning fast had been delivered with malevolent glances from Running Deer. Bobbie had arrived at midday to take her back to Lone Dog's tipi, where Seeing Woman appeared to be making a steady recovery. Her attempt to persuade Bobbie to take her around the camp had failed. The boy did not dare chance Night Raven's displeasure. The end result had been a long and tedious day that was presently ending with growing anxiety over the night to come.

Familiar footsteps sounded outside the tipi and Edwina went still. She suppressed a gasp when the entrance flap was swept aside abruptly to reveal Night Raven standing in the opening.

Clothed in the buckskins that Running Deer had delivered earlier, Night Raven appeared even larger, more overwhelming than ever as he stepped inside and dropped the flap closed behind him. His gold eyes mesmerized her as he advanced toward her. Halting at her side, he was about to speak when a voice at the entrance inquired, "I may enter?"

Night Raven turned toward the sound of Running Deer's voice. He slipped his arm around Edwina and drew her firmly against his side as he replied, "Enter."

Running Deer halted abruptly at the sight of them. Edwina saw the antipathy in her gaze.

"Lone Dog sends the message that Seeing Woman is well. She eats and drinks, and is regaining strength."

Her mission complete, Running Deer turned away abruptly.

"Running Deer." The young squaw stiffened when Night Raven addressed her. She turned back toward them as he continued coldly, "Do not return to this tipi unless you are summoned."

Edwina resisted the urge to pull herself free of Night Raven's possessive embrace when the squaw's chin jerked, as if she had been struck. Turning toward Night Raven when the flap had closed behind Running Deer, Edwina spat, "I won't let you use me to torment that woman!"

Night Raven's gold eyes held hers, their burning heat somehow chilling as he replied, "How do you expect to stop me, Edwina? You are my captive to use any way I choose."

"No, I'm not!"

His arm a band of steel, Night Raven drew her closer. She saw the unexpected twitch of his lips as his hand slipped into her hair, as he wound his fingers in the heavy strands and drew her near enough that their breaths mingled.

"You may attempt to fight me," he whispered, "but your strength would not match mine. You may cry for help, but no help would be forthcoming. You may scream in protest at my touch . . . but your cries would only stir envy in the hearts of many."

Edwina stiffened. "Of many . . . like Running Deer?"

Regretting her response the moment it left her lips, Edwina felt a new bite in Night Raven's gaze as he responded, "Running Deer is wife to Jumping Bull. She would not betray him. Nor would I."

Dropping his arm from around her, Night Raven said abruptly, "Come, we go to the pool."

"No." Edwina took a spontaneous backward

step as images of the previous night flashed before her mind. "I've already bathed."

Not bothering to respond, Night Raven took her arm and drew her out of the tipi behind him.

Incredulous, Margaret stared at Craig in the shadows of their room. His expression was stiff when he reported the result of his meeting with Major Locke. She had been momentarily unable to reply—but the shock had worn off and her belated response was impassioned.

"I won't let you do it, Craig!"

"I have no choice."

Margaret was aghast at his response. "You do have a choice! Just tell Major Locke that you won't go after Night Raven without the support of a patrol."

"Locke's made it clear that he won't risk a patrol under my leadership."

"Risk a patrol? You're the best officer he has and he knows it, yet he's willing to let you risk your life by denying you the men you need to find that Sioux camp."

"Margaret . . ."

"You know what this is all about, don't you, Craig?"

"Of course I do. Locke resents me, and Edwina and he were at odds from the moment she entered the fort. This is his chance to get rid of us both." Craig's lips tightened. Margaret saw the cold determination in his gaze as he grated, "What Locke doesn't know is that he's making a mistake. I'm going to bring Edwina back, and I'm going to bring back Night Raven, too."

"Craig . . ." Margaret moved closer. She pressed her bulky warmth against her husband, the contact stirring a new wealth of emotion as she rasped, "We both love Edwina . . . but she loves us, too, and I know her well enough to be certain that she wouldn't want you to sacrifice your life trying to rescue her."

Craig stiffened, and Margaret insisted, "You can't do it alone!"

"Yes, I can."

Margaret fought to suppress impending tears. Sliding her hand up to caress her husband's stiff cheek, she whispered, "I don't want to lose you, Craig."

His arms suddenly strong around her, Craig held her tight. Margaret heard the fleeting tremor in his voice as he whispered against her hair, "Don't be afraid, Margaret."

Drawing back just far enough to hold her gaze with his, Craig continued with a new flush of color. "Locke assigned me personal responsibility for Edwina and Night Raven's return. If I fail to get them back, he'll see to it that my career ends here and now, but the truth is, what he does or doesn't intend isn't really influencing me. I just can't"—he took a shaky breath—"I can't abandon Edwina to the hands of that savage! I can't spend the rest of my life wondering where she is . . . what happened to her . . . whether that savage is abusing her or—"

Halting his fervent speech at the sudden paling of his wife's face, Craig moved Margaret to the side of the bed and eased her down. Sitting beside her, he took her hand and raised it to his lips.

"I love you, Margaret."

Margaret's breath came in a gulping sob.

Craig continued hoarsely, "I'd never purposely do anything to hurt or frighten you . . . but I have to do this. I'd be no good to you if I didn't. I wouldn't be able to live with myself, knowing that I had selfishly sacrificed Edwina for our happiness. I couldn't be a husband who was worthy of you, or a father who was deserving of our child. Please, try to understand."

Left without words in the face of Craig's ardent plea, Margaret stared into the warm, brown eyes that held hers so intently. She saw love in those eyes, and she saw honesty, integrity, and *nobility* . . . all the things that Craig was . . . all the things that had drawn her to him. How could she ask him to cast those qualities aside and be a lesser man?

The answer was irrefutable. She could not.

Margaret whispered, "When will you leave, Craig?"

Craig's relieved smile was fleeting. "Tomorrow morning."

"Tomorrow . . ."

"My supplies are already being packed. I'll leave a copy of the route I'm taking with you, just in case." He paused, frowning. "I can't be sure how long I'll be gone, but I don't want you to be concerned if I'm gone a few weeks."

"A few weeks!"

Craig gripped her hand. "I'll be back in time for the baby . . . I promise you that. And Edwina will be with me, to be at your side."

"Craig . . ."

"In the meantime, I've asked Lee, Anderson, and Murray to watch out for you." Craig's smile flickered again. "Corporal Lee's always had a soft spot for you, you know."

"Craig!"

Again sober, Craig drew her closer. Margaret saw the revealing tremor of his lips the moment before he whispered, "I do love you, Margaret . . . more than I ever thought—"

His words were cut short as his mouth covered hers. Margaret quaked at the warmth of Craig's passionate kiss, at the touch of his caressing hands, and at the heat of his naked flesh when it met hers at last—when her body yielded lovingly, eagerly to his.

Edwina stumbled down the familiar trail to the pond as Night Raven dragged her relentlessly forward. The sounds of the camp faded behind them and the chirping of night creatures in the grasses surrounding them grew louder.

A repetition of the previous night.

But the similarity ended with Edwina's assessment of Night Raven. Gone was the instability of his step. His buckskin shirt covered his chest, but she knew that the bleeding had stopped, and that much of his strength had returned.

The thought had her trembling as Night Raven halted at the edge of the pool.

Snatching back her arm, Edwina looked up at Night Raven with a boldness that did not match the quivering deep inside. "I told you, I've already bathed."

"What makes you think I brought you here to bathe, Edwina?"

The piercing gold of his eyes held hers for long moments before Night Raven abruptly pulled his buckskin shirt from his shoulders. Her gaze flew to his chest. As she'd suspected, the wound was dry and healing, and she silently cursed. His hands were working at the ties on his leggings when she snapped, "All right, this has gone far enough!"

"You are wrong. It has not."

Edwina struggled to control the trembling that beset her as Night Raven's leggings fell to his feet and he stood naked before her. Forcing her chin a notch higher, she declared with as much poise as she could manage, "Whatever your intentions are—"

Edwina's statement came to a premature halt when Night Raven turned unexpectedly, abandoning her to her presumptions as he walked into the water, then dived out of sight.

Humiliated, Edwina seethed. He was so clever! He knew the full power of his virile appeal. She doubted he had ever known the need to pursue a woman. To the contrary, a single day in the camp had made it clear that one reason the women in the camp hated her was jealousy of the attention he showed her.

Edwina watched with growing agitation as Night Raven moved at a leisurely pace through the water, almost as if she was not present on the bank. She wondered what he hoped to achieve by this outing. Did he think that the intimacy of the encroaching darkness would draw her to him? Did he believe she would be helpless against the sheer power of his masculinity, as so many women had obviously been before her? Did he truly think that she would forget she was a captive who had arrived in the camp the previous day, bound and thrown over his horse like so much baggage? Did he really think that she would—

Edwina's raging thoughts stopped cold. She stared a moment longer at Night Raven swimming near the center of the pool, then glanced around her. During her brief excursion with

Running Deer early that morning, she had noted that the men of the camp had turned the horses out to graze on a nearby rise the previous night. From the leisurely manner in which they walked out to retrieve them as the dawn brightened, it appeared to be a nightly custom, one that could work to her advantage.

Edwina's heart began a rapid pounding. The rise where the horses grazed was not far away. If she could start in that direction before Night Raven realized her intent, she would gain the time she needed before he could reach the bank. Naked as he was, he would have to clothe himself before pursuing her, thereby allowing her more precious minutes.

A glance at Night Raven revealed that he wasn't looking her way. Breathless with anticipation, Edwina looked around her as she devised a simple plan. With a quick scramble up the path and a sharp right turn near the top so she would be hidden from view of the camp, the horses should be within sight. If she could get to them before Night Raven reached her—

Edwina's heartbeat thundered in her ears. Her attempt at escape had failed once before. She could not fail again.

Could she do it?

She took a breath.

Yes!

Edwina bolted up the path. Cursing as she stumbled on a loose stone, she did not dare look back as she neared the top and branched abruptly to the right. Fighting her way through the tall grasses, Edwina was breathing heavily when she emerged into the clearing beside the camp and looked up at the nearby rise where the horses grazed. Incredulous when she heard no sound of pursuit, she withheld a snort of jubilation at the mental image of Night Raven racing back to the bank.

With a last glance at the camp behind her, Edwina started running. Nearing the crest of the rise, she slowed her pace, fearing to frighten the horses grazing only yards from her reach.

Her heart pounding, her breathing ragged, Edwina forced herself to walk as she drew close to the grazing animals. She spoke softly to the horses judging by the twitch of their ears and their nervous shuffling the likeliest animal to approach. A pinto mare glanced her way, appearing to accept her advance, and she extended a trembling hand toward it. The mare snorted under her touch, but she didn't move, and Edwina's heart leaped with anticipation.

Grasping the animal's mane with a flush of pure triumph, she was about to pull herself up onto its back when a deep voice behind her said, "No, Edwina, you will not ride without me tonight."

Turning with a gasp, Edwina met gold eyes filled with fury.

Lifted astride the mare in a flash, Edwina was incapable of reply when Night Raven mounted behind her and dug his heels into the animal's sides, jolting them into motion.

The night breeze whipped wet spirals of hair back from Night Raven's shoulders as he forced the mare relentlessly forward. Ignoring the perils of the darkened terrain, he clutched Edwina tight against his bare chest. The knot of rage within him tightened in recollection of the moment when he had looked toward the bank and sensed her intention to flee. The thought that she might escape him had caused a momentary feeling of panic, and his fury had soared.

Digging his heels into his mount's sides, Night Raven set a frantic pace that cast all caution to the buffeting wind. Immune to the fear that stiffened Edwina's slender body, he felt only the need to evict that memory with the pure power of speed.

Reason returned abruptly when the mare stumbled and Night Raven was thrust forward so sharply that he was almost unseated. He heard Edwina's frightened gasp and her grunt of pain when his arm crushed painfully tight around her ribs. He felt her weakness when the mare regained its footing and she leaned back against him in a moment of unguarded relief.

His mindless rage broken, Night Raven

closed his arms around Edwina and held her possessively close. Still breathing hard, he urged the mare toward a wooded copse nearby and then drew the animal to a halt. He swept Edwina from the mare's back, not bothering to place her on her feet as he carried her to the base of a tree and laid her on the ground beneath it.

Leaning over her, staring down at her with a hunger he could no longer deny, Night Raven rasped, "You cannot escape me, Edwina."

A great silver moon cast Night Raven's form in stark relief as he crouched over her. Disoriented by the rapid progress of events, her ribs aching from his unrelenting grip and her head throbbing, Edwina looked up at Night Raven's intimidating outline. The darkness was his ally. It brought into intimidating focus the overwhelming size and power of the man: his massive shoulders overshadowed her, his muscular arms pinned her against the ground as effectively as iron bars; his mammoth chest heaved with emotion he could not conceal.

Night Raven raised his hand and Edwina steeled herself against an expected blow. She gasped when his hand met her cheek to cup it almost tenderly. His unexpected gentleness stunned her. She stared, transfixed, at the dark silhouette above her as Night Raven's deep voice throbbed softly into the undulating darkness.

"This encounter was meant to be, Edwina. It is a challenge we must meet." His hand slid into the hair at her temples as he whispered more softly, "But do not fear. It is a loving challenge to be faced moment by moment . . . the moment that is now before us."

Mesmerized, Edwina was unable to respond as Night Raven's fingers slipped deeper into her hair, as they tangled in the heavy mass to hold her still while he lowered his head toward hers. His mouth brushed her lips. It was warm, reassuring. She closed her eyes as his kiss deepened; her lips gradually separated under his insistent gentleness. She felt the press of his strong body as Night Raven lowered himself against her. She heard his soft groan as she allowed his tongue to explore her mouth. She felt the rapid beat of his heart when he ripped his lips from hers to taste her fluttering lids, the rise of her cheek, the curve of her jaw. A breathless anticipation pounded within her as his mouth circled hers, then found her lips to indulge deeply once more.

Tasting, teasing, hungering, Night Raven's loving homage moved to the column of her neck, to the curve of her shoulders. She made no protest when her bodice slipped away as if of its own accord and Night Raven found the warm flesh of her breasts. She gasped aloud when his mouth met a waiting crest, when he kissed and suckled the sweet flesh until her hunger matched his own.

The cool night air touched her bared flesh, and Edwina gasped at the sudden rush of heat that filled her when Night Raven's tautly muscled form met hers fully at last. He stroked her body with his hands, seeking the rise of her breast, the curve of her hip, the soft skin of her stomach before sinking lower, to the warm delta between her thighs, and she welcomed his touch. He found the nub of her desire and explored it briefly with his fingertips, and a new trembling began inside her. He slipped down to taste her womanly heat with his mouth and she caught her breath. She remained motionless as he cupped her buttocks with his broad palms to allow himself full access, then drew deeply from her with deep, hungry kisses.

Shuddering at the wealth of emotions Night Raven's intimate ministrations evoked, Edwina felt control slipping away and a sudden panic beset her. Suddenly struggling, she attempted to push Night Raven from her, but he clasped her hands in his, restraining her protests as he whispered, "You first appeared to me in the shadows, Edwina. It is fitting that I claim you fully as my own while the shadows prevail."

When her trembling hands still resisted,

Night Raven's voice dropped a throbbing note lower. "This time is ours, Edwina. Do not oppose me. We but meet our destiny this night."

Somehow impotent against his earnest plea, Edwina remained motionless as Night Raven lowered his mouth to taste her once more. She breathed deeply at the sensual play of his lips, groaning softly as she writhed in the expanding delirium of sensation he evoked. Yielding to his passion at last, she separated her thighs, allowing him the freedom he desired, and her wonder soared.

Shuddering as control began to escape her, Edwina called Night Raven's name in sudden alarm. The panic in her voice raised Night Raven's head toward her with a whispered entreaty.

"Yield, Edwina. Give to me, and I will give to you in return."

His mouth flush against her once more, Night Raven suckled deeply, drawing from her with selfless ardor that left Edwina helpless against the ecstatic spasms gaining control. She caught her breath as emotion burst into flame in sudden, pulsing climax under Night Raven's lips, and he drew her body's nectar within him.

Numbed by the mind-drugging emotions holding her in thrall, Edwina struggled to regain control as Night Raven slid himself atop her. She muttered a soft word as Night Raven entered her moistness full and hard, in a single thrust.

Moonlight flickered through the rustling leaves overhead, briefly illuminating Night Raven's countenance. Edwina's heart skipped a beat at the desire that tightened his chiseled features as he held himself motionless within her. She was unable to look away as he began moving slowly, stroking with each thrust, his features contorting with passion as he swelled inside her.

The first cataclysm of ecstasy that shook Night Raven reverberated within her. Consuming her with its intensity, it pulsed through her with ragged heat, lifting her anew to join him in heart-stopping climax that left her motionless and replete, breathless in the warm bower of his arms.

Night Raven lay motionless and spent atop Edwina when reality returned. The night was dark. This man . . . this faceless shadow . . . this *enemy*, had taken her body as no man ever had before. He had claimed her in the darkness—in the most primitive of ways—and she had welcomed him!

Trembling, Edwina attempted to slip from beneath Night Raven's massive bulk. Suddenly struggling, she pushed and shoved at his weight, to no avail. She halted abruptly when Night Raven lifted himself to peer down at her once more. Straining to make out his features, she succeeded in seeing only a flash of gold eyes as he whispered simply, "Edwina . . . this night has just begun."

Margaret shivered in the dim light before dawn. Clutching her shawl more tightly around her shoulders, she stood still in the silent fort yard as Craig checked the supplies on his pack horse. Satisfied at last, he turned toward her.

Craig's smile was forced. Margaret managed a smile, too, as he slipped his arm around her and drew her against his side.

"You won't worry too much, will you, darling?" he whispered.

"No, I won't."

Drawing her closer, Craig kissed her, his mouth lingering. His earnest expression touched her heart when he drew back at last and said, "I'll return as soon as I can, and I'll bring Edwina with me. I won't disappoint you."

"You could never disappoint me, Craig."

A smile tugged at Craig's lips. "Never?"

"Never."

Mounting abruptly, Craig signaled the guard. Margaret shivered again as the gates opened. Craig looked down at her with a frown.

"Go back inside. You're chilled."

"I'm fine."

His brown eyes locked with hers. "I'll come back. I promise."

Her reply lost in a mist of tears, Margaret watched the fort gates swing closed behind him.

The pinto mare moved forward at a steady pace beneath them as the sky began to brighten with morning. Holding Edwina in the circle of his arms, Night Raven supported her weight easily as she sagged against him in sleep. The hours previous had been filled with passion. He had taken Edwina in the darkness of night, when there were only shadows between them. He had taken her again as the night began to merge with light, and he had taken her the last time when the night sky yielded at last to slender fingers of dawn—yet his hunger for her was not sated.

After her first, feeble protests, Edwina had accepted him in silence, allowing her body to speak more eloquently than words—but he had felt a gradual change in her as daylight brightened, a stiffening that softened only when sleep overwhelmed her.

The image of the raven battered his mind unexpectedly, and Night Raven's expression gradually hardened. No, he could not afford to indulge gentler emotions. Edwina's body was soft, but her will was strong. She would not surrender easily.

Edwina stirred, as if sensing his thoughts. She glanced up at him with a frown. Refusing to allow it, Night Raven caught her cheek with his palm and held it fast as he lowered his mouth to hers—but the act meant to demonstrate his dominance achieved only partial victory as the sweet taste of her again filled him with yearning.

Allowing Edwina to draw back when she resisted the deepening of his kiss, Night Raven kept their mount to their steady pace. Edwina shifted, adjusting herself as she rode. Her breasts brushed his arm, and Night Raven curved his palm around the warm flesh. Edwina attempted to remove his hand when he caressed her gently. Her protest stoked the heat within him, and his caress became more intimate. Her resistance was nil when he found the hardened crests at last and massaged them through the fabric of her dress.

Night Raven felt Edwina's heartbeat thundering against his hand as she turned toward him in near panic and whispered, "No . . . please. We're nearin' the camp. Someone will see us."

Capturing her mouth with his, Night Raven held her hot and tight against him. Exhilaration soared at his increasing power over her senses, at her impassioned gasp as he slid his hand underneath the hem of her dress to find the bare skin of her midriff. She stiffened, attempting to steel herself against his caresses when he found the warm delta he had explored so lovingly in the darkness—when he drew her back against him to allow himself better access—but he knew the battle was nearing its end when her body shuddered in response. She quivered when he touched the moist, womanly nub between her thighs, her shivering growing more pronounced as his caresses deepened. Lying back against him at last, she surrendered fully to his searching touch.

His own body hardening, Night Raven held her tight against him as his penetration deepened. Edwina's breathing grew sharp and quick. Her passion was near its peak when he halted abruptly and whispered against her ear, "Tell me you want me, Edwina."

No response.

"Your body hungers. You want to feel me inside you."

Edwina shook her head stiffly.

"Tell me."

"No."

Night Raven stroked her again and Edwina gasped.

"Tell me."

"Whatever game you're playing, you think you've won, but you haven't."

"Haven't I, Edwina?"

With a soft grunt of anger, Edwina made a futile attempt to remove his hand. His own heartbeat escalating, he widened his caress until she was again pliant under his touch.

Edwina was moist and ready. Night Raven

felt the first quaking that shook her. Dismounting abruptly, Night Raven swung Edwina down
from the horse and carried her to the shadow
of a nearby tree. She was beyond resistance
when he pressed her back against the trunk
and raised her skirt.

A thrill shuddered down Night Raven's spine
at Edwina's gasp when he slipped himself
inside her, as his body swelled and he possessed her completely, holding her fast. The
glorious blue of Edwina's eyes met and held
his. Her eyelids grew heavy as he moved within
her. He watched as they drooped closed, shut-
ting the glorious color from his sight as her
body met and absorbed the impetus of his
powerful thrusts.

Holding himself rigidly in check as culmina-
tion neared, Night Raven rasped, "Look at me,
Edwina."

Edwina's eyes slowly opened.

"See the glory between us. Watch as it soars,
and remember . . ." His own breathing short,
he rasped, ". . . that in the darkness or the light,
you are mine."

Bringing them to full, shuddering fruition
with a final thrust, Night Raven clutched
Edwina close until they were both sated and
still.

Edwina was limp against him when he withdrew from her body at last. Lifting her into his
arms without a word, he carried her to the

horse. Again mounted behind her, he felt her breath brush his neck as her head lolled back against him.

Supporting her with ease, Night Raven urged the mare forward.

Chapter Eight

"You're sure you're all right, ma'am?"

Corporal Lee leaned toward Margaret Rice, his expression concerned. It was early morning, just past dawn, and Mrs. Rice was standing at the gate as the guard changed and the first morning patrol made its exit. It was not the first time she had appeared there, a somehow desolate sight with her extended abdomen protruding from the shawl wrapped around her shoulders and her expression forlorn. Her conversation never exceeded a simple "Good morning," and she never asked any questions, but he knew why she came. She was hoping that when that gate opened, Captain Rice would be there, waiting to come in. But he wasn't, as he hadn't been there for the full two weeks since he had left, and Mrs. Rice was disappointed again.

"Ma'am?"

Margaret Rice turned toward him as if she had just heard his voice. He saw the shadows under her eyes that hadn't been there when the captain left, and he noted her pallor. He smiled, encouraging her to smile in return as he said, "I wouldn't worry about the captain, ma'am. He's a real good officer, and he knows what he's doin'. If anybody can find Miss Keene, he can."

"Thank you, Corporal." Mrs. Rice's smile was halfhearted, but he was encouraged anyway as she turned away, then turned back toward him to say, "You've been very kind durin' my husband's absence—as have Corporals Anderson and Murray. And I want you to know I appreciate your confidence in my husband. I'll make sure to mention it to him when he returns."

"Ma'am . . ." Corporal Lee fidgeted uncomfortably, then said, "You've been walkin' in the yard at night . . ." At her surprised glance, he said, "I couldn't help noticing it. My sister, Emily, had trouble sleepin' when the time was nearin' for her first baby, with her back hurtin' her the way it did and all. Well, I just figured maybe that's what's been keepin' you up to all hours, and gettin' you up so early in the mornin'."

Margaret Rice's pale skin warmed as she

said, "I didn't realize you were keepin' close track of my comin's and goin's, Corporal."

Corporal Lee shrugged. "Captain Rice asked me and a couple of the others to watch out for you, and it's my pleasure to do so, ma'am. I just wanted to say that Captain Rice was worried a bit about you walkin' in the fort yard alone at night."

"Oh, that was only after the Sioux attack."

"I've got the feelin' he still might not be comfortable knowin' you're alone in the dark, especially in your condition. I just wanted to say that if you feel the need to walk, any one of us, either Murray, Anderson, or I, would be happy to walk with you, so's we can be sure you're safe."

"That's very kind of you, Corporal. I'll remember . . . and I'll try not to cause you any more worry."

"It's my job to worry, ma'am."

Margaret Rice's smile was more heartfelt when she turned away, and Corporal Lee sighed inwardly. Captain Rice was a good man and a good officer. It was his private opinion that the captain was probably the best officer in the fort—without exception—and he knew for a fact that Captain Rice was married to the nicest woman in the fort. Maybe she wasn't as pretty as Miss Keene, but he always did like the look of freckles on a lady, and her smile was just about the prettiest he had ever seen.

Watching as Margaret Rice waddled out of sight, Corporal Lee shook his head. Captain Rice was a good officer, but he was worried about him.

Yes, he was very worried.

Edwina awakened slowly. The small circle of sky above her head was just beginning to brighten with the new day as Night Raven stirred where he lay beside her. She closed her eyes, pretending sleep as Night Raven slid his hand down her body, his rough palm brushing the naked flesh pressed so warmly to his. She willed her eyes to remain closed, hoping the pretense would deceive him. She dared not allow herself to respond. Memory of the previous night, and the two weeks of previous nights spent in intimate exchange after her first heated encounter with this enigmatic Sioux, revealed only too clearly that she had no resistance to his touch, or to the throbbing passion in his voice when their bodies were so close.

Edwina's heart began a slow pounding. This part of herself was new to her—this desire that Night Raven awakened. It was as if he somehow touched a chord within her that only he could reach. She did not understand it. She could not account for it. She felt the need to struggle against it. In the presence of others, this man was her enemy; yet when they were alone, there was no distance between them that could not be overcome by the sound of his voice, the unexpected gentleness of his touch, and the taste of his mouth on hers.

Night Raven's touch grew more intimate, and Edwina's heart began a heady pounding. She was powerless to resist as he turned her toward him, onto her side so they lay face to face. His sweet breath bathed her lips as he whispered, "Open your eyes, Edwina. I feel the pounding of your heart, and I know the need builds within you as it does in me."

Her pretense useless, Edwina opened her lids. She felt Night Raven harden against her. She felt his probing, and she restrained a gasp as he slipped himself inside her.

The almost indiscernible twitch of his cheek the only sign of his escalating ardor, Night Raven whispered, "See how your body accommodates mine, Edwina, yet you resist." Taking her arms, Night Raven slipped them around his neck and pulled her closer. He licked at her lips, then tasted her mouth. He pressed his lips to her chin and nipped her sharply, raising a protest that he swallowed with the heat of his kiss. She felt him swell inside her as his kisses deepened, and he asked again, "Tell me you want me, Edwina."

The same question. She remained silent. Speaking the truth would be a final capitulation she could not bear.

Night Raven was moving slowly inside her, and Edwina felt a familiar euphoria rising.

"Tell me."

"Does it matter?" Breathless, Edwina grated, "You take me at your will."

"It is *your* will I seek."

"Would it matter if I did resist you?"

"Only to you, because the pleasure would be *taken*, not shared."

Edwina's face flushed hot and Night Raven's gaze turned to molten gold.

"You do not deny your pleasure. You cannot."

Edwina remained silent.

"But you will not declare it."

"Because it isn't my choice!"

Night Raven's sensuous stroking ceased. "Then tell me to stop, Edwina."

She was trembling.

The molten gold hardened. "Tell me to leave you now, and I will."

Edwina did not respond.

"Tell me you do not yearn for the fire between us to continue. Tell me and I will cease, Edwina."

Trembling, wanting desperately to be able to speak those words, Edwina did not respond.

"Your hunger is in your eyes. It will soon be on your lips, Edwina, and when that day comes—"

Night Raven's words halted abruptly as his passion soared past control. Carrying her with him, he drove himself home to shuddering relief within her.

They were still joined when Night Raven again covered her mouth with his. She was powerless under the assault of his kiss when he drew back from her, then separated himself from her and stood up abruptly. She knew what was coming then—the coldness in his eyes and in his voice, the distance between them the moment the passion ceased—the anger without a name that glowed in his eyes as he slipped on his buckskins and left the tipi without a word.

She heard light footsteps—women of the camp going for living water. She heard the heavier tread that followed—the men of the camp as they walked out to retrieve their mounts.

The morning ritual of the camp was reassuring to Seeing Woman. Each dawn she celebrated the new day and the life that had almost been taken from her.

Seeing Woman's brief smile faded when she remembered the darkness that had enclosed her as she lay in Lone Dog's tipi. In it she had floundered, her spirit drowning in the cries of sorrow. The cries had grown ever louder as her body weakened. She had been able to hear none of the voices calling her back—save one.

Seeing Woman breathed deeply. She walked to the entrance of the tipi and lifted the flap.

271

The rising sun shone on her face and she allowed its glow to warm her. Blue Fawn, daughter of Blue Shell, would soon arrive to guide her to the stream where she would begin the day's chores. Blue Fawn was a happy child who was pleased with the responsibility placed in her small hands. In the girl's pleasant company, she would attempt to put her unhappy thoughts behind her.

A familiar step. Seeing Woman's smile flashed and she reached out her hand. She felt the callused palm that touched hers, and a true warmth flushed her face as Jumping Bull's deep voice sounded.

"The sun touches your cheek with color. You heal well, Seeing Woman."

"I am well." Seeing Woman took a step toward him. She felt the spontaneous tightening of Jumping Bull's touch as he warned, "Take care."

Seeing Woman's smile dimmed. "My step is steady. The darkness is my friend. You need not fear."

"The darkness once betrayed you."

Seeing Woman did not reply. She drew back her hand. She felt the silence. It hung heavily between them before Jumping Bull said, "Do not be angry. I suffer the memory of days while I feared you would be lost. The thought haunts me. I would not have it happen again."

"Do not fear for me." Seeing Woman's smile

returned without its true glory. "I would not be a burden to you."

"Your words slice at my heart, Seeing Woman. You know where my true burden lies. All else pales beside it."

Seeing Woman felt the heat of tears as she whispered, "My true burden lies in the truth that I do not wish to cause you torment."

Jumping Bull's touch on her shoulder was heavy and warm. Its warmth spread through her as the sound of a step beside them interrupted their exchange.

Seeing Woman felt Blue Fawn touch her arm. She turned toward the child, and Jumping Bull's hand fell away. She mourned his silent retreat and the secret she withheld from him as she picked up the clothing to be washed in the stream and followed Blue Fawn's lead.

The morning sun was rising. The pale light filtered through his office window as Major Locke sat stiffly at his desk, staring down at the official communication that had reached him the previous day. The wire had been forwarded by express messenger in the same manner in which he had sent his own communication to Washington announcing Night Raven's capture only three weeks earlier. He had received the congratulatory wire granting him his request to assume personal responsibility for Night

Raven until he was delivered for trial. It came only days after Night Raven escaped.

The congratulations had since ceased.

". . . and the delivery of Night Raven to trial remains your personal responsibility. Failure to restore him to custody will be considered your personal failure. Further depredations attributed to him and their effect on the stability of the frontier will also be taken into consideration. All negative conclusions reached will be noted in your file."

Washington idiots who had no concept of what the "frontier" truly was!

Inflamed with rage, Locke slammed his fist onto the desk, then stood up abruptly. Stomping toward the window, he scrutinized the fort yard. Two weeks, and each successive patrol remained as ineffective as the last in its attempt to find the Sioux camp. He had railed at his men. He had taken Lieutenant Ford to task for his unexpected inadequacy. He had noted the fellow's displeasure, but he cared little. His only satisfaction during that time had been the fact that Captain Rice had not returned.

Locke's bearded chin twitched. It was his sincere hope that the next patrol would discover Rice lying on the open prairie with a Sioux bullet in his heart. At least then the fellow would serve the useful purpose of distracting attention from his own failure.

Locke's chest heaved with growing agitation. But he knew where his true failure lay—in allowing himself to be influenced by Edwina Keene. He also knew that when and *if* she was found, he would see to it that she paid for the blight she had brought on his career.

Striding toward the rise where his mount was grazing, Night Raven refused to look back at the camp behind him.

The danger deepens.

Forcing aside the warning voice that sounded in his mind, Night Raven reviewed the days since he had brought Edwina to his camp. His people's mourning was gradually fading. Scouting parties from the camp had returned to report that bluecoat patrols ranged out from the fort with new vigor each day, only to return each night in defeat—and he scorned the ineptitude that left the bluecoats at such a loss that they wandered aimlessly in search of him.

Fools that they were, the bluecoats were unaware that Jumping Bull's scouts observed their pitiful efforts, that they waited to report an opportunity for vengeance against the fort.

In the same two weeks, Seeing Woman had regained enough strength to return to her tipi. Night Raven's spirits briefly warmed at the thought. But the relief he and Jumping Bull felt was tempered by concern for the subtle changes in her demeanor—the prolonged silences and the long absences of her smile.

His own physical wounds had healed, leaving only an angry mark where blood had once flowed so freely. Yet he took little satisfaction in his body's recuperative powers, when his body failed him in other ways.

The danger deepens.

The disturbing voice sounded again in his mind, and Night Raven's frustration mounted at the truth it expressed. That morning had begun with yearning despite the passion he and Edwina had shared the previous night. Edwina turned willingly into his arms, but the game he played was beginning to go awry. Edwina was his captive, but the need to conquer her spirit grew weaker with each night she slept in his arms, and with the realization that with each new day his desire for her was becoming a torment that exceeded any he could hope to inflict.

He had come so close that morning. The words he had urged Edwina to say—the final concession to a passion both sought to deny—had almost slipped from his *own* lips as their bodies pulsed to mutual satiation.

His surrender, when he sought hers . . .

The grazing horses turned toward Night Raven as he approached, and he called his mount softly as he neared. The animal remained motionless as he mounted. Submitting to the weakness of a backward glance at the camp as he turned away, he saw Edwina emerge from his tipi with White Bear beside her.

White Bear had become Edwina's keeper and her friend, but the boy's loyalty to him knew no challenge.

Night Raven frowned as he turned his mount. Edwina could not escape White Bear's watchful eye, but even if she should, invisible bars of hatred and envy surrounded her in the daylight hours, and his own arms were as effective as prison bars at night—bars that held her passionately confined.

It was increasingly clear, however, that there could be no victory over this woman who threatened his destiny while his own inner conflict raged.

Night Raven urged his mount toward the distant horizon. His body was healed. Only the wounds of his spirit remained. He knew what he must do.

"Lone Dog told me to bring you to his tipi, Miss Keene. He *told* me to!"

Bobbie walked beside her. He had arrived minutes earlier at the tipi she shared with Night Raven, as had become his custom. Bobbie had become her guide around the camp, her protector in Night Raven's name, her teacher in explaining the ways of the Sioux; and, despite her initial reluctance, her ally. She had had little contact with Running Deer since Night Raven's dismissal of her, and she was relieved—but the woman's vitriolic glances followed her wherever she went, and the hatred she openly displayed was never far from mind.

Edwina glanced down at Bobbie's earnest expression and frowned. "I'm not comfortable with this, Bobbie."

"Mornin' Bird's daughter is sick. Lone Dog's been tryin' to help her, but none of his medicine's doin' any good. Little Sun's only four years old, Miss Keene. She needs your help."

"Mornin' Bird . . ." The name struck a familiar chord in Edwina's mind. "Isn't she Eagle Heart's widow, the one who—"

"That's her, but she ain't bad like she seemed. She didn't mean it when she came after you with stones in her hand that first day. She was grievin' for Eagle Heart and she wasn't thinkin' clear."

"She was thinkin' clearly enough." Edwina's step slowed. "Lone Dog wants me to look at the girl. I won't be able to do anythin' for her because I don't have my bag or any of my medicines. I can only guess what'll happen if the girl gets worse after I leave."

"She's gettin' worse anyway. Besides, if Mornin' Bird comes after you, Night Raven will stop her."

"Night Raven's not here, and there's no guarantee that—"

"Little Sun's only four years old, Miss Keene."

They had arrived at Lone Dog's tipi. The familiar fragrance of scented smoke met her nostrils and Edwina unconsciously sighed. For all her protests, she knew she had no choice.

Two steps into Lone Dog's tipi, and Edwina's skin chilled. The child was lying on the sleeping bench. Her barking cough and labored breathing left no doubt as to the cause of her distress. With only a fleeting glance at Lone Dog, Edwina kneeled beside her. Round-faced, her hair plastered to her small head with perspiration, her skin bright with fever, and her petite features contorted in her struggle to breathe, the girl fought for each breath.

Croup.

"Little Sun fails."

Edwina glanced up at Lone Dog. She hesitated, then addressed him soberly. "I've seen many children among my people suffer the same disease. There's only one thing I can do for her here. I'll need some water to boil over the fire, and a blanket to make a tent over her so I can moisten the air."

Lone Dog's eyes blinked. He nodded. "I will ready the sweat lodge."

The child's breathing grew more strained and Edwina urged, "Quickly, Lone Dog. Her heart is poundin' too hard."

Edwina was bathing Little Sun with cool

cloths when she heard an angry exchange outside the tipi that preceded Morning Bird's frantic entrance. Her eyes wild, the squaw started
toward her, only to be halted by Lone Dog's
sharp command.

Standing beside the sleeping bench, Edwina
watched the exchange between the frail
shaman and the distraught squaw. Unable to
understand a single word, she did not notice
that Bobbie came to stand supportively beside
her until his hand touched her arm.

"Don't worry, Miss Keene, Lone Dog's
standin' up for you. He won't let Mornin' Bird
do nothin'."

"The girl can't last much longer. We have to
get her to that sweat lodge quickly."

"That's what Lone Dog's tellin' her."

Morning Bird turned toward her abruptly.
Edwina felt the heat of her stare. She saw the
woman's sharp step toward her that was halted
by Lone Dog's grunted command. The woman's
gaze pinned her as Lone Dog continued talking.

The child made a croaking sound that turned
Edwina back toward her abruptly. Dropping to
her knees beside the sleeping bench, Edwina
looked up, her voice harsh as she addressed the
squaw flatly.

"Your daughter will die if you don't let me
treat her soon."

Lone Dog's brief translation snapped the
woman toward her with a burning gaze that

held Edwina motionless. She did not realize she was holding her breath until the woman stepped back unexpectedly to clear the entrance, and she took a deep breath.

The heat of the child's limp body frightened Edwina when she scooped her up and followed Lone Dog across the camp. Ignoring dark stares sent her way, she entered the sweat lodge and placed the child on the mat beside the center pit. She scrutinized the dome-shaped structure briefly. Made from willow poles much as a tipi was constructed, it was covered with buffalo robes in such a manner that it appeared airtight, yet the steam within was limited and inadequate for her purpose. Her silent dismay was abruptly dismissed when Lone Dog dipped a horn into a pouch of water nearby and flicked it onto the heated stones in the pit. Great clouds of steam filled the lodge and Edwina released a relieved breath.

Edwina turned at the sound of Bobbie's voice beside her.

"Will Little Sun be all right now?"

The child's labored breathing continued, and Edwina shook her head. Dipping a cloth into the pouch nearby, Edwina bathed the child's fevered face as she replied simply, "I don't know."

Blue Fawn held Seeing Woman's hand tightly as they walked the path back to the camp. The girl's small fingers were intertwined with hers, and Seeing Woman's heart was touched by the sincere concern for her welfare that the child evinced.

Seeing Woman's smile was genuine, but it dimmed as the path turned and they heard sounds of great agitation at the edge of the camp. Blue Fawn's step slowed as the angry voices grew louder, and her fingers tightened.

Seeing Woman asked, "What do you see, Blue Fawn?"

"The women of the camp gather, speaking harshly. Laughing Water and Spear Woman berate Morning Bird. They say she has given up Little Sun to the enemy."

"To the enemy?"

"To Night Raven's woman." Blue Fawn continued slowly, "The women surround Morning Bird with angry taunts, and Morning Bird steps back as their words grow fierce. Running Deer nears Morning Bird and speaks softly. I cannot hear what she says, but the women are listening." Blue Fawn gasped. "Running Deer places a club in Morning Bird's hands! She picks up stones, and the other women follow. They go to the sweat lodge, to punish Night Raven's woman and to rescue Little Sun!"

Seeing Woman trembled. "Take me forward into their midst. I would speak to them."

"They are angry, Seeing Woman." The child's

voice was hoarse with fear. "They will attack you if you speak against them!"

"Take me forward!"

The silence that fell when Seeing Woman walked into view was more revealing than words. Anger swelled around her as Seeing Woman ordered, "Cast away your clubs and your stones! You err in believing Night Raven's woman is Little Sun's enemy."

"You are old and you are blind!" White Antelope grated harshly. "And you have been too long without a man in your tipi to still feel the pain of its emptiness."

"The pain of my tipi's emptiness is ever fresh in my heart, but the white woman had no part in the battle that took Spotted Wolf from me. Nor does she bear blame for your tipis' emptiness."

"She was at the fort! She is one of them!"

"She belongs to Night Raven."

"She is the enemy, yet she walks freely among us! She learns our ways so she may turn them against us! Now she steals our children!"

Seeing Woman's sightless eyes narrowed at the sound of the last voice. She turned, addressing Running Deer directly.

"You are not a widow and you have no children, Running Deer, yet your voice sounds loudest in protest."

"I speak out against the white woman so we may guard all the children of our camp."

"You speak out for reasons that are your own."

"I speak for the safety of the camp!"

"You speak for the betterment of one person only."

The angry crowd stilled.

"You . . ." Running Deer's voice drew nearer. "You are the one who speaks with one person in mind, Seeing Woman. You speak for Night Raven, who thinks only of the pleasure the woman brings him on his sleeping bench. You defend him . . . but he is not worth your defense!"

Gasps and muttered protests sounded, echoing Seeing Woman's own as Running Deer continued, "You see only what Night Raven wishes you to see, and you hear only his fawning words."

Anger replacing her distress, Seeing Woman responded, "I am blind, but I see many things more clearly than those with sight. I am old, but I know many things others do not know—things that some fear might one day be revealed. Yet, amid all I know and see with my sightless eyes, nothing is more clear or more true than what I tell you now. The white woman is not the enemy of the Sioux. I saw her coming while I lay in the world of endless sleep, unable to awaken. The bright color of her hair was the only light in my darkness as she stood just beyond my reach. My ears were closed to all the voices that called me back and I despaired, until she advanced toward me. My darkness lightened with each step she took. I saw the bright color of her eyes—the same color as the sky above—and I saw her smile . . . and when she spoke to me at last, I awakened."

Running Deer's contempt was in her voice as she spat, "An old woman's dream!"

"I saw her! I awaited her approach, and when she came, she brought healing."

"She brings the wrath of the bluecoats down upon us!"

"The Sioux do not fear the bluecoats' wrath. There is only one thing they need fear—Night Raven's ire if his woman is harmed."

The silence grew deafening. Running Deer spoke in solitary dissent.

"The white woman holds Morning Bird's child hostage!"

"The white woman comes to heal!"

Sounds of grudging assent and shuffling steps followed. The footsteps gradually faded from Seeing Woman's hearing. Sensing the moment of Running Deer's departure, Seeing Woman released a tense breath.

Blue Fawn's voice held a note of awe when she spoke at last. "The women have dropped their stones and dispersed."

Still trembling, Seeing Woman did not voice her fear that she had not seen the last of their hostility.

* * *

Another false trail.

His brow beaded with sweat as he sat his weary mount, his fair skin burned from the sun, and his usually fastidious grooming suffering from his extended trek in the wilderness, Craig raised his hat from his head and wiped his forehead dry with his sleeve. He paused to survey the rolling plains thick with undulating grass that surrounded him, then looked up at the endless sky that stretched blue and bright as far as his eye could see. Not a cloud or a sign of civilization in sight.

Sardonic amusement twisted Craig's dry lips. He had spent two weeks wandering in this hostile wilderness, and one mile still looked the same as the last to him.

His fleeting amusement replaced by a sigh of frustration, Craig unconsciously shook his head. He had charted his direction carefully on the maps available to him before leaving the fort and he had followed his course meticulously. The maps were woefully inaccurate, as he'd expected, and he had made careful notation or every error he encountered. What he had not expected was the number of Sioux trails he found and followed until they faded into obscurity; and what he had failed to take into account was the supreme vastness of the country the Sioux called their home.

No, he wasn't smiling. He was sick to the

heart and worried almost out of his mind. Edwina had been Night Raven's captive for two weeks. He knew Edwina. She wouldn't make it easy for herself in that savage camp— beautiful Edwina, whose spirit would not be compromised.

Craig's throat choked tight. In the silence of the previous night, he had forced himself to face another, equally distressing possibility— that Edwina might not be with Night Raven any longer. He had heard about the practices of those savages. Their propensity was to use their captives and then sell them to the highest bidder. If that was the case, Edwina might be lost among one barbaric tribe or another for the rest of her life.

Unable to bear that thought a moment longer, Craig forced Margaret's image to mind. He had been gone two weeks. Margaret would be frantic by now, but she'd be doing her utmost to conceal it. He deeply regretted the need to put her through such turmoil in her condition, and a familiar conflict returned. Margaret loved him, and he loved her, yet Edwina had wedged herself so deep inside him that she had also become a part of him.

And Margaret was safe, while Edwina was not.

No, he could not abandon Edwina.

Craig scanned the horizon. His gaze settled on a wooded copse in the distance; then he glanced up at the merciless sun. He needed to find some shade for a while. His horse was spent, and so was he. He had checked his supplies that morning. They wouldn't last much longer.

Making a quick decision, Craig kicked his mount into motion and headed for the cool respite of the trees. He needed to regroup. He needed to define his next course of action. He needed to check his direction.

He needed to find Edwina.

The sacred hillside underneath his horse's hooves was green and familiar. Dismounting, Night Raven secured his mount and walked slowly to the summit. His thoughts lost their driving intensity at the feel of the familiar terrain under his feet, and peace gradually permeated his mind. He remembered his preparations for the vision quest he had made in this holy place when he was little more than a boy. Four times he had smoked the sacred pipe in the sweat lodge. Four times Lone Dog had sprinkled water on the hot rocks. Four times Lone Dog had sung songs of purification while he prayed—but he had been alone in his heart when he ascended the sacred hill for the *hanbelachia*.

Fasting for four days and four nights, he had awaited the sign that would reveal the course of his destiny. It was then that the raven appeared to him for the first time, flying over the battlefield littered with the bodies of his enemies.

His purpose then clear, he had pursued his life path avidly. He had met the bluecoats with bravery and courage, knowing the satisfaction of vengeance as it was meant to be. It was not until long afterwards that the vision came to him in the night, taunting him in its new form. Under its assault, his confusion had been profound.

Proceeding to the crest of the rise, Night Raven paused to strip off his buckskins so the brisk breeze could buffet his skin, so the bright sun overhead could bathe him, so the sweet scent of the earth could be absorbed into his heart. His powerful body so exposed, his dark hair fluttering in the shifting currents of air, he focused on the cloudless sky above, his arms raised in supplication.

An eternity passed as Night Raven continued his prayerful song. His muscles stiffened and his voice grew hoarse.

Swirling steam filled the sweat lodge as Lone Dog sprayed the heated stones anew, and Edwina caught her breath. Her worry that the steam might be inadequate had been dismissed. She would have laughed at the thought of how wrong she had been—if she wasn't too hot and weary for the effort.

The aged shaman had been relentless in his efforts through the long afternoon as he transported the heated stones from the outside fire with a dedication that knew no bounds. Her respect for him had grown with each passing hour.

Little Sun was again convulsed by a paroxysm of coughing, and Edwina frowned. The barking sound had softened and Little Sun's small features were no longer contorted with the effort to breathe, but the child still drifted in a fevered sleep. She had bathed the girl's skin with cool water as the temperature of the lodge rose, but she was uncertain of the prognosis.

Little Sun's breath rattled in her throat unexpectedly, and Edwina felt a jolt of panic. Lowering her head to the girl's chest, she listened intently, relieved at the steady beat of her heart.

Perspiration dropped from her brow and Edwina wiped it away, realizing for the first time that her hair lay in wet strands against her scalp. She noted with surprise that her clothes adhered wetly to her skin as well. The heat was almost overwhelming, but she dared not halt her ministrations. Lone Dog was right. The child had been close to death—and she could not be certain how close to the edge the child still teetered.

Edwina scrutinized Little Sun more closely. She was such a pretty girl with her clear skin and sweet features.

The child's almond-shaped eyes flickered open briefly, and Edwina wished she could see her delicate lips curve into a smile, could hear the sounds of her strained breathing transformed into laughter.

In direct contradiction of her thoughts, Little Sun's small body twitched, and she convulsed unexpectedly in another coughing spasm that snapped her eyes open wide as she gasped for breath. The spasm ceased as suddenly as it had occurred, and the child went still.

Momentarily unable to move, Edwina stared at Little Sun's motionless face. The beating of her own heart seemed to still as she lowered her ear to the child's chest. A gasp of pure elation escaped her lips at the sound of Little Sun's heart beating evenly and strongly.

Tears briefly blinding her, Edwina clasped the child's hand tight and closed her eyes. Little Sun had passed the crisis. She would get well.

Lone Dog's gaze met hers when she again opened her eyes. Uncertain of the thoughts behind his sober expression, she raised her chin and spoke to him softly.

"We can take Little Sun back to her tipi now, but I need a dry blanket to wrap around her so she won't take a chill." She paused, then said, "Little Sun will need special care. Can I depend on Mornin' Bird to obey my instructions?"

Lone Dog's gaze did not falter. "Morning Bird will listen, and she will obey."

Edwina turned back to the child as Lone Dog slipped out of the lodge and closed the flap behind him.

Standing concealed among some trees, Running Deer watched as the flap of the sweat lodge was raised and the white woman emerged with Little Sun in her arms. The child was wrapped in a blanket, and the woman carried her with feigned tenderness. She watched as the women of the village observed in silence while Morning Bird approached them, then cried out her joy when her child smiled.

Running Deer inwardly raged. They were fools, all of them! Was the deceit in the white woman's eyes obvious to her alone? Could they not see that she sought to lull them into a sense of safety while she walked among them, so she could betray them more easily? Did they not realize that the woman had even managed to cast a spell on the cruel and heartless Night Raven, who had spurned all other women before her?

Gnawing jealousy expanded within Running Deer. The time of reckoning had been at hand earlier. She had seen her opportunity and she had taken it when the women had gathered in protest against the white woman. She had cast aside her fear that Jumping Bull might discover the part she played, believing the risk worthwhile if the women of the camp would finally deal Night Raven's captive the justice she deserved—but her plan had been foiled.

Seeing Woman had walked boldly into their midst and turned the women against her with her blind stare and cryptic words. But Seeing Woman didn't fool her. In her weakness, the old hag sought to cling to those who were strongest in the camp—Jumping Bull and Night Raven. She hoped to keep those men to herself, and she had done well. Night Raven's heart had been cold to all but her, and Jumping Bull put no one before her—not even his wives.

Oh, yes, the old woman was clever. With the arrival of the white woman, she had noted Night Raven's intoxication with the woman's pale flesh. She had then seen Jumping Bull support him, and she had developed a plan to remain in their favor.

A movement in the foliage caught Running Deer's eye. She caught her breath with a snarl of pure antipathy at the realization that Seeing Woman stood partially concealed there, as if watching the scene at the sweat lodge unfold before her sightless eyes. Seeing Woman's stare was so intense that Running Deer could almost believe the witch did see Edwina Keene carrying Little Sun across the camp.

The white woman slipped from view into Morning Bird's tipi, and Seeing Woman turned toward the familiar path nearby that led to the area where clothing washed earlier at the stream was spread out to dry in the sun. The old woman's cautious, seeking steps revolted her, and Running Deer grunted.

The sightless hag . . .

The sun had begun its gradual descent over the sacred hill when Night Raven saw the vision. Ignoring the weariness of his body, he had maintained his prayerful stance through the long afternoon hours.

The vision appeared gradually. Halting his song of supplication, he waited silently as it became so vividly intense that there could be no mistaking it.

Night Raven stood motionless as the vision faded. Lowering his arms at last, he picked up his buckskins and dressed. Mounting, he did not look back as he left the sacred hill behind him.

Emerging from Morning Bird's tipi, Edwina stood, suddenly shaken in the aftermath of the anxious hours recently past. She had carried Little Sun out of the sweat lodge only minutes earlier. She had halted abruptly when she saw the women of the camp gathered and waiting, their expressions unreadable.

Drawing strength from Lone Dog's presence, she had followed him, only to halt again when Morning Bird stepped into her view. She had clutched Little Sun closer then, determined not to surrender her, determined to protect the child at any cost, even from the good intentions of her mother, which might cause harm in her delicate condition. Trembling, she had resumed her steps boldly as Morning Bird ran toward her and called her child's name. The child stirred at the sound of her mother's voice. Morning Bird had reached their side as Little Sun opened her eyes and smiled into her mother's teary face.

Edwina swallowed against welling emotion. She had had no need for an interpreter when Morning Bird spoke to her then. Joy was in her eyes and in the sound of her voice. When Edwina had left Little Sun in Morning Bird's tipi, the happy mother had humbly requested that she return.

"Are you all right, Miss Keene?"

Bobbie was again beside her.

Edwina managed a smile. "I'm all right, I . . . I'm just tired."

Bobbie grinned. "I told you Morning Bird wasn't really bad. She's real happy that you helped Little Sun. She was thankin' you over and over, and all the other women were feelin' real ashamed of the way they acted."

Edwina took a weary breath. "I'm glad."

"You're all sweated, Miss Keene." Bobbie frowned. "Night Raven will be comin' back soon and he won't like seein' you that way. I'll take you down to the pool if you want. I'll wait for you to wash up. I won't peek, I promise."

Discovering she wasn't too weary to be amused by the boy's candid manner, Edwina replied, "Thanks, Bobbie."

Discovering that she wasn't too weary to tease, either, Edwina nudged him when they reached the pool. "Remember, you promised not to peek."

Surprising her, Bobbie blushed. With his back resolutely turned, he was walking back up the path to establish a discreet distance between them when she recalled his words.

Night Raven will be comin' back soon, and he won't like seein' you that way.

She hadn't protested that statement. She hadn't even thought to protest it.

Frowning, Edwina dropped the blanket she had taken from Night Raven's tipi, stripped off her clothes, and walked into the pool.

Smiling, Seeing Woman carefully negotiated the familiar trail to gather the clothes she had left to dry. She had heard Morning Bird's joyful cries when Night Raven's woman brought Little Sun out of the sweat lodge only minutes earlier. She had then listened intently as voices that had formerly been raised in anger against Edwina Keene, sang her praises.

They called her "healer."

A flush of pleasure spread through Seeing Woman. She had deliberately maintained her distance from Edwina Keene in the time since she had recuperated. When Night Raven spoke the woman's name, she had heard in the sound of his voice a note that was too delicate to address. She had chosen silence in other matters as well, but with her silence had come a guilt that had often stolen her smile.

Seeing Woman reached the brush where clothing she had washed earlier in the stream was spread. She touched the familiar garments, identifying them immediately. She gathered them carefully, halting abruptly at a sound behind her.

She turned as Running Deer addressed her in a voice of grating anger.

"You said the white woman came to heal, and now the women of the camp call her 'healer.' You are clever, but your cleverness does not fool me."

"Yes, I am clever." Seeing Woman faced Running Deer soberly. "I was clever when I forced the women of our tribe to cast aside their hatred so they could view Edwina Keene as the woman she is, instead of the woman they believed her to be."

"The woman they believed her to be *is* the woman she is! The white woman does not heal. She deceives, awaiting the opportunity to deliver us to the bluecoats."

"Night Raven's woman heals. She tended Night Raven's wounds—"

"So Night Raven could be delivered to a more humiliating death!"

"She helped Little Sun."

"To gain acceptance."

"She drew me from the darkness."

"She did no more than speak your name."

"She has healing in her heart."

"She deceives."

". . . as *you* deceive, Running Deer?"

Seeing Woman felt Running Deer go still.

"I do not deceive. I speak to save our people."

"Is that why you struck me in your anger that morning and knocked me to the ground—so roughly that I hit my head and was gravely injured? Is that why you reported falsely that I had stumbled, rather than reveal your malicious act?"

"I did not strike you! Your mind plays tricks!"

"My mind is clear."

"If your mind is clear, why did you not accuse me? Why did you not report the falsehood you claim?"

"I was greatly tempted. My stomach rebelled at your feigned concern for my welfare when I awoke. Were it not for my respect for Black Dog, whose noble memory you betray with your evil deeds . . . were it not for the pain I chose to spare Jumping Bull . . . were it not for my fear of Night Raven's retribution, I would have spoken."

A sneer was evident in Running Deer's voice. "You withheld the truth to save me . . ."

"No, I didn't."

"You said—"

"I withheld the truth to save Jumping Bull and Night Raven the discomfort of knowing the depth of your deceit."

Running Deer laughed.

"But I begin to see the error of my ways."

Seeing Woman heard the sharp step Running Deer took as she rasped, "You seek to threaten me with this secret you withhold."

"I seek to warn you."

Running Deer laughed again. "A blind, old hag whose mind is touched with visions seeks to warn me."

"An old, blind woman who has the trust of the two you most revere now speaks her final warning."

Seeing Woman heard Running Deer close the remaining distance between them. She felt the heat of the younger woman's breath on her cheek, but she held her ground as Running Deer spat, "Listen closely, old woman, for now I warn you as well! Do not attempt to speak against me to my husband. I am young and I am beautiful. My husband desires me, and he forgives me anything for the use of my body!"

Seeing Woman was amused.

"Do not attempt to turn Night Raven's wrath against me, for you will turn him against Jumping Bull as well, and in a contest between them, Jumping Bull would emerge victorious."

Seeing Woman's amusement faded. Her response was cold.

"Act wisely, Running Deer."

Not awaiting a response, Seeing Woman turned back in the direction from which she had come, unmindful of the darkness that shaded her way as she left Running Deer behind her.

Standing silent and unseen where he had witnessed Running Deer and Seeing Woman's angry exchange, Bobbie clutched his small fists against his sides. He saw Running Deer watch Seeing Woman with true malevolence as the older woman returned to her tipi. He held his breath as Running Deer followed the same path with a furious step. Running Deer turned in the opposite direction and also slipped from sight, and he breathed freely once more.

Bobbie blinked, incredulous at what he had overheard. He hadn't meant to listen. He had walked up from the pond to a place where he could wait for Miss Keene to finish bathing. He hadn't wanted to be seen waiting for her because he knew the other boys in the camp would tease him. He had seen Seeing Woman arrive to collect her clothing, and he had been about to make himself known when Running Deer advanced on the blind squaw so hatefully. Unable to move without intruding on the angry encounter, he had remained motionless . . . and astounded.

Running Deer's vicious words flashed again across his mind, along with Seeing Woman's sober replies. The true account of what had happened the day when Seeing Woman was so badly injured scared him. Seeing Woman was blind and helpless. Running Deer had hurt her without showing any sign of regret—and she was still angry. She might hurt Seeing Woman again.

Bobbie's anxiety heightened. He didn't know what to do. He could tell Night Raven, but Seeing Woman didn't want Night Raven to know. He could tell Jumping Bull. He didn't believe what Running Deer said about Jumping Bull forgiving anything bad she did, just because he wanted to take her to his sleeping bench. Jumping Bull didn't even *like* Running Deer— but he was only a boy and he couldn't be sure.

Bobbie's eyes clouded and his fair brow knit in a frown. He couldn't tell Miss Keene. He'd only get her in trouble. And the truth was, Seeing Woman might get mad at him if he told anybody at all.

Bobbie rubbed his forehead, in a true quandary. He was a Sioux. He should know what to do!

He didn't.

Bobbie thought a moment longer, then raised his chin. He was White Bear, and he would behave as a Sioux brave should. He would not act if he could not act wisely.

He would keep silent . . . and wait.

Dammit! His horse was limping.

Craig drew his mount to a halt. Pausing to scrutinize the surrounding terrain with extra caution, he dismounted. After his brief pause to regroup earlier in the day, he had followed another of the many Sioux trails he had discovered. This one, however, had begun looking more promising than the others, and if the tingling in his spine was any indication, there was a possibility that this was the right one. His mount could not have come up lame at a worse time.

Satisfied that there was no threat in the immediate vicinity, Craig checked his mount's leg, then cursed again. The obvious injury had probably come about when the animal stepped into a prairie dog hole earlier.

Craig glanced at his pack horse. He had no choice but to ride that sluggish animal until his own mount was fit to ride again. In the meantime, he couldn't afford to remain out in clear view while he unloaded and reloaded his gear.

Spotting a wooded patch that would provide adequate protection, Craig remounted, gritting his teeth as he forced his limping horse forward. He had almost reached the clump of trees when his mount snorted unexpectedly, then reared with fright.

Suddenly aware that the animal's injured leg would not hold him, Craig attempted to jump from the saddle—but it was too late. The animal came down on its side, pinning Craig underneath him.

Light-headed from a burst of pain, Craig extricated his leg from the tangled stirrup the moment before his horse regained its feet—but Craig knew instinctively from the position of his twisted limb that he wouldn't be able to do the same.

Craig closed his eyes against the dizzying pain. Damn it all, his leg was broken!

Gritting his teeth, he attempted to drag himself into a position of greater safety when his horse snorted and reared again. He turned, glimpsing the reason for the animal's panic just before the rattler struck him.

"What's the matter, Bobbie?"

Bathed and securely wrapped in the dry blanket she had taken from Night Raven's tipi on her way to the pond, Edwina carried her wet clothing as she walked back to the camp with Bobbie at her side. The clothes had been rank with the perspiration of her vigil in the sweat lodge, and she had washed them quickly, knowing they would be dry enough to wear when morning came if she spread them on the bush beside Night Raven's tipi. She had then called Bobbie to accompany her back up the path. Feeling much refreshed, she had been about to tease him again when she noted his pensive expression. He was unnaturally subdued, and she was concerned.

Edwina asked again, "What the matter? Why are you so quiet?"

"I ain't quiet." Bobbie's eyes avoided hers. "I just ain't got nothin' to say."

Edwina coaxed his smile. "Havin' nothin' to say isn't like you, Bobbie."

"Yes, it is. I ain't always so talkative, and Night Raven says a brave don't need to say nothin' if he ain't got nothin' to say."

Edwina didn't doubt that those were Night Raven's words.

"And he said a brave shouldn't act if he can't act wisely."

Edwina nodded, suddenly as sober as he.

"Are you tryin' to tell me somethin', Bobbie?"

Bobbie turned toward her, suddenly resolute. "My name's White Bear, Miss Keene. I ain't Bobbie no more. I'm a Sioux, and my name's White Bear."

"I'm sorry." Edwina spoke sincerely. "I forgot."

Bobbie—White Bear—nodded. "I'm sorry, too. I didn't mean to sound so mad."

"That's all right. You have a right to be called by the name you choose."

"It ain't the name I choose, Miss Keene." White Bear's expression grew earnest. "It's who I *am*."

"I apologize."

Walking in silence a few steps more, White Bear looked up again at Edwina. "You're a nice lady, Miss Keene. I wish—"

"Yes, White Bear . . . what do you wish?"

"Oh . . . nothin'."

They had reached the head of the trail when White Bear said, "Look, there's Night Raven! He's back!"

His relief apparent when Night Raven started toward them, White Bear flashed a smile. "I'll be goin', Miss Keene. Night Raven can watch out for you now." He glanced at Lone Dog, who stood closeby. "It looks like Lone Dog told him what you did for Little Sun. Night Raven will be glad."

But Edwina wasn't listening. Mesmerized as Night Raven strode toward her, she saw that his skin was darkened by the sun to a mellow hue that gave an eerie quality to the gold eyes that held her in their fixed gaze. Her heart leaped a beat.

Night Raven's hand closed on her damp shoulder when he reached her side, and she stammered, "I . . . Bobbie took me to bathe. I was hot and sweaty."

Night Raven curved his arm around her and led her toward his tipi. She saw the bowls of food from Trailing Mist's cooking pot that were waiting, as they had been each night. She reached toward them, but Night Raven shook his head.

Unable to read his expression, she remained silent as Night Raven turned her to face him. Her lips parted in a gasp when he slid his fingers into her damp hair and clenched his hand. Her eyes drifted closed as he loosened the blanket she clutched around her and bared her naked flesh.

Edwina could think no further than the pounding of her heart when Night Raven whispered three simple words.

"You are mine."

Chapter Nine

Rain clouded his vision as Night Raven again viewed the battlefield littered with the dead and dying. The raven alighted on the wounded soldier, and his anticipation mounted.

No!

But his cry of protest went ignored as the raven spread out its wings to shield the soldier from the falling rain.

Awakening abruptly, Night Raven looked down at the sleeping bench beside him. He knew what he would see—Edwina, her pale beauty exquisite in the silver light of dawn.

Night Raven's frustration soared. The vision he had seen on the sacred hilltop the previous day was clear. In it, his battle shield emerged triumphant. Seeing it, he had been possessed of a new strength of will to fulfill his destiny. He had returned to the camp, knowing he would prevail. He had then been met by Lone Dog, who related Edwina's triumph in the camp. Conflicting emotions had heated within him, and he had taken Edwina's body with his—but his intention had been reversed once more.

Warm in his arms, Edwina had responded to his lovemaking with true fervor—but without speaking the words he wished to hear. So consumed had he been with the intensity of their intimate moments, he had allowed himself to believe what he wished to believe, that Edwina's ardor was real, that she was not the true challenge to his destiny.

But the raven had returned to haunt him.

Edwina stirred. The glorious blue of her eyes mingled with the gold of his gaze. The colors of the sacred hilltop came to mind, and Night Raven's resolution was abrupt and decisive.

Night Raven urged, "Rise, Edwina. We leave."

Edwina's sleep-drugged gaze was uncertain. "Leave? Where are we goin'?"

Refusing to respond, Night Raven stood up and drew Edwina to her feet beside him. Her naked body glowed in the dim light, and Night Raven touched his hand to a firm breast. At her intake of breath, he whispered, "The time and the place await us."

Mounted, Edwina riding astride in front of him and a pack horse trailing behind, Night Raven left the camp.

Lieutenant Ford stared at Major Locke. The sounds of the morning patrol mounting behind him in the fort yard faded from his hearing as he scrutinized Locke's shadowed expression in the gray light before dawn.

The grim tone of Locke's voice could not be mistaken as he repeated, "I said I'm sick and tired of ineptitude! Both you and Lieutenant Johnson have proved yourselves worthless. Your failure to find Night Raven and his captives has become *my* failure, and I'll stand for it no longer!"

"Sir, Lieutenant Johnson and I have been takin' out alternate patrols, but we've been conferrin' on the territory we've covered. It won't be long now before we find those heathens and trap them like the rats they are, and then—"

"I'm tired of hearing you say 'and then,' Lieutenant! What I'm concerned with is now, and it's obvious that if I want to find Night Raven *now*, I'll have to do it myself!"

"Sir—"

"I'm done talking! Step out of the way! I'll be taking the patrol out this morning."

"Sir—"

"Don't worry"—Locke almost smiled—"I won't remove you from the place of honor at my side. I won't humiliate you in front of the patrol—not yet!" Locke's smile faded. "But I'm warning you: look sharp! Someone's going to suffer for this debacle with Night Raven, and if you don't prove your worth better than you've been doing, it just might be you!"

"Yes, sir."

"Lieutenant Ford . . ."

Halting the burly officer as he turned toward his horse, Locke added, "I'll expect an in-depth briefing as we ride. I'll expect you to explain the full extent of the penetration you've conducted into enemy territory. I'll expect you to make sure that we do not retrace a single foot of ground you've already explored, except for the trail that leads us to and from this fort—is that understood?"

"Yes, sir."

When Lieutenant Ford did not move, Locke questioned sharply, "Is there something you don't understand, Lieutenant?"

"Sir, I was just wonderin' who'll be left in charge of the fort while you're accompanying the patrol."

"While I'm *leading* the patrol, Lieutenant!"

"Yes, sir."

Locke's smile was tight. "There hasn't been an Indian sighted around this fort since Night

Raven escaped. I doubt the Sioux are lying in wait for me to leave so they can attack. In any case, Lieutenant Johnson will remain in command during my absence."

Ford's lips tightened.

"Does that irk you, Lieutenant? Well, if it does, show some gumption! Show me the same kind of soldiering that got you to that Sioux hunting camp you found a while back. See to it that the Sioux won't be the only ones getting themselves more scalps! Then we might be able to put these weeks of ineptitude behind us. It's up to you, Lieutenant."

"Yes, sir."

The rustle of leather and clatter of horses' hooves was joined by the buzz of low conversation as Major Locke's horse was brought forward. Mounting with a flourish and without a backward look, Major Locke signaled the patrol into motion.

"What does it mean, Corporal?"

Her expression tight and her face pale, Margaret was at Corporal Lee's side the moment the fort gates closed behind the morning patrol.

"Ma'am, are you all right?" Scrutinizing her startling lack of color, Corporal Lee took Margaret's arm instinctively. "Are you feelin' faint or somethin'?"

Margaret pressed, "Why is Major Locke

leadin' the patrol? Does it mean Lieutenant Ford thinks he's found somethin'? Does it mean Major Locke's just gettin' desperate?" Margaret paused. "Or does it mean they think somethin' has happened to Craig?"

"I don't know, ma'am."

"Well, what do you think? Tell me somethin', Corporal!"

"Ma'am . . ."

Struggling to control her trembling, Margaret rasped, "I'm sorry. Please forgive me. I don't know what's come over me. It's just that when I came out this mornin' and saw Major Locke ready to take out the patrol, I thought—" Margaret halted abruptly. She swallowed with obvious difficulty and whispered, "I don't know what I thought. Please . . . tell me what *you* think."

"Ma'am . . . I talked to Lieutenant Johnson last night. Neither he nor Lieutenant Ford's been able to find anything—just old tracks leadin' in the same old circles. They ain't seen a sign of Injuns."

"Then why is Major Locke takin' out the patrol?"

" 'Cause he thinks he's a real Injun fighter and he thinks he can do what Lieutenant Ford and Lieutenant Johnson can't, and because . . . because he's a horse's ass, ma'am."

Margaret's eyes flicked open wide.

"If you'll excuse the expression."

Margaret nodded.

"He ain't goin' to find nothin' that them patrols didn't find—not unless some Injun huntin' party comes stumblin' right down into his path. I figure there ain't much chance of that."

"Then why . . . who—"

"Ma'am, them Injuns had a big defeat when they attacked this fort. They lost too many warriors for them to forget it too fast. They're probably just gettin' over their mournin', and they ain't dumb enough to try somethin' when they ain't at full strength."

"What about Night Raven?"

"I ain't goin' to lie to you, ma'am. From the look of that fella when I was standin' guard over him in Miss Keene's quarters, I'd say he ain't the kind to forget what happened too easy. He'll be comin' back for more, sooner or later."

"Sooner or later . . ."

"But I'm thinkin' it'll be later, ma'am."

"About Craig . . ."

"Like I said, Captain Rice is a good officer."

"I know."

"Don't worry about him, ma'am. He'll be back. It's just that he ain't the kind to give up easy."

"I know." Margaret's eyes lit with another thought. "Do you think that maybe Major Locke's patrol might run across Craig? If he did, he'd tell Craig to come back, wouldn't he?"

"Ma'am, I'm thinkin' Captain Rice is probably deeper into Injun territory than Major Locke will ever let himself get, unless he's draggin' that cannon and half the fort behind him."

"So you're sayin'—"

"I'm sayin' Major Locke ain't half the man Captain Rice is . . . not even near."

Margaret's eyes filled. "Thank you for that, Corporal."

"Don't worry about the captain. He knows what he's doin'."

"All right."

Margaret forced a smile. Corporal Lee was right. Craig was a good officer, and he was doing what he had to do. He was probably fine . . . just fine.

He heard voices.

No, he didn't.

His fever was rising, and the pain . . . Craig gasped. It was almost more than he could bear.

Craig raised his head in the semidarkness. It was getting light. He had managed to pull himself under the protection of some foliage where he had lain all night, just waiting for morning. Now morning was here . . . or was it?

Craig fought to clear his head. He glanced at his mount, which grazed nearby. The big chestnut was well trained. He wouldn't go far unless something spooked him again. His pack horse was gone.

Voices again . . . voices.

Craig glanced around him. His body jerked as pain spread through his veins like liquid fire. He thought he heard Margaret calling him. He knew what that meant. Hearing voices . . . the pain and swelling in his arm and leg . . . a thirst that he couldn't seem to satisfy, even after almost draining the canteen that had fallen from his mount during the commotion.

He was in trouble.

Craig looked at his arm again. The rattler had done a good job. The punctures were just above his wrist. He had managed to tie it off and draw out some of the poison, but he knew he hadn't done enough. His hand was swollen grotesquely and his leg was broken.

Laughter bubbled in Craig's throat. He remembered. He had been hoping that by morning he'd be strong enough to pull himself up on his horse and start back to the fort, but the opposite had happened. He was weaker, and he was getting more confused.

Damn that fever!

He was in trouble.

Craig twisted the cap off the canteen. It hurt his hand.

He raised the canteen to his lips and drank. It was almost empty, and he was still thirsty.

He wondered, was Edwina thirsty? Was she waiting for morning? Was she waiting for him to come rescue her? He had failed her. He couldn't rescue her now. He couldn't even rescue himself.

Was that Margaret calling him?

No . . . he was out of his head.

A wave of pain convulsed through him, and Craig caught his breath. He couldn't give in. He had to try to get up . . . get on the horse. If he didn't, he didn't have a chance.

But he was tired.

Was that Margaret calling him?

No . . . no, it wasn't.

Was it morning? Where was his horse? He was supposed to start back.

No, he'd wait until he felt stronger.

He was in trouble.

Yes, he was.

White Bear awakened slowly. He glanced around the tipi with a frown. Many Faces had already left to get his horse, and Singing Bird wasn't on her sleeping bench. He glanced up at the small patch of sky above the smoke hole. It was late. He had slept poorly and his stomach wasn't feeling too good. That was probably the reason he hadn't gotten up in time to accompany Many Faces to get his horse.

White Bear stood up. He looked at Singing Bird when she entered the tipi. He answered the question in her eyes in spontaneous Sioux.

"I'm all right. I guess I was more tired than I thought, that's all." He shook his head when

Singing Bird offered him a steaming bowl. "No, thanks, I ain't hungry."

Outside the tipi minutes later, White Bear walked toward Seeing Woman's tipi. He was angry with himself for sleeping so late. He saw the women of the camp already returning with living water, but Seeing Woman wasn't at the entrance of her tipi waiting for Blue Fawn, as was her custom.

White Bear walked faster. His stomach twisted tight and fear crawled up his neck. Seeing Woman was always ready and waiting when Blue Fawn came. He remembered Running Deer's voice when she spoke to Seeing Woman. She was so mad . . . almost like she was crazy. If anythin' happened to Seeing Woman, and if she—

The flap of Seeing Woman's tipi moved. Seeing Woman appeared in the opening, and White Bear took a relieved breath. Embarrassed when he realized that his eyes were damp, White Bear turned toward the trail behind him and slipped out of sight.

The midday sun beat warmly down upon them. Night Raven's strong body was warm against her back as their mount moved at a steady pace, but Edwina felt little of the comfort the day afforded.

Night Raven's touch had been gentle, but his eyes had been hard when he lifted her up onto his mount earlier that morning. The pack horse carried supplies for several days, but she was uncertain of his intent. Night Raven had spoken hardly a word since the inception of their journey, and with each mile that passed, Edwina's anxiety mounted.

She shifted and Night Raven's grip tightened, reminding her of the truth that she forgot each night that she lay in his arms: She was Night Raven's captive. He was her enemy. Her fate was as uncertain as it had always been, despite the husky tremors that shook Night Raven's voice when he spoke her name in the darkness, and despite the part of her that responded instinctively to the sound.

Disgusted by her own weakness, determined that she would no longer succumb to it, Edwina forced a coolness to her tone when she asked abruptly, "Where are we goin', Night Raven?"

He made no reply.

"Night Raven . . ."

"Be silent, Edwina," Night Raven responded mildly. "Look around you. Absorb the beauty."

Night Raven's hand moved in a stroking motion against her midriff. He cupped her breasts with his hand. The familiar lethargy that his touch induced began rising, and Edwina fought it with all her strength.

"I want to know where you're takin' me."

"Why, Edwina?" Night Raven's breath was

warm against her ear. "Do you wish to plan your escape?"

"I want to know where we're goin' . . . why you took supplies for a camp."

"Perhaps we go to hunt."

"I don't believe you."

"Perhaps . . . I am bringing you back to the fort."

Edwina's heart leaped.

"Perhaps I am not."

Anger flared.

"Or perhaps I take you to a special place where the conflict between us will be settled at last."

"The conflict between us?"

Cupping her chin with his hand, Night Raven turned Edwina to face him as he whispered, "You cannot deny the conflict within you. I feel it in the beat of your heart. I hear it in your voice."

"Yes, I feel conflict." Her heart racing, Edwina rasped, "I'm not used to bein' a prisoner, and I don't like it."

"And the conflict is?"

Edwina's face flamed. She was somehow unable to move when Night Raven lowered his mouth to hers and drank deeply from her lips. Drawing back from her at last, he whispered, "The conflict is one that I share, Edwina."

Edwina whispered, "Let me go, Night Raven.

Let me take the pack horse and ride back to the fort. I won't betray the position of your camp. I wouldn't do that. I couldn't be responsible for the deaths of any of the people in your camp— you know I couldn't!"

Night Raven's posture grew rigid. "You seek to return to the bluecoats who mock the Sioux as savages, but they are the fools they claim the Sioux to be. They speak loudly with their cannon, but without them, they flounder."

"They aren't fools."

"They ride in circles in their pursuit."

"They don't! They have maps—"

"Their maps are worthless and their sense of direction is poor. Jumping Bull's scouts have watched their useless forays each day, and they have seen the posture of defeat with which the bluecoats return each night."

"Jumpin' Bull's scouts have been watchin' the fort?"

Night Raven did not reply.

"He's plannin' to attack the fort again?"

Silence.

"You're just waitin', aren't you? You're waitin' for the mournin' to end and for the anger to build so you can attack."

"The Sioux are not fools, Edwina. We have faced the cannon and we know its worth."

"Then you won't attack the fort."

Silence.

Edwina struggled for control. "You're waitin'

for somethin'. What is it? Are you waitin' for another tribe to join you? The result will be the same, you know. The cannon will—"

"We will not face the cannon again."

"Whatever you're plannin', you can't succeed, don't you see that?" Edwina continued earnestly. "Tell Jumpin' Bull . . . tell your people that the cannon at Fort John Carter is only one of many that will be comin' to the frontier. Too many will die if you try to fight against them! This country is so big. Tell Jumpin' Bull to take your people north. The army won't pursue you there. You'll be safe!"

"Do you want me to be safe, Edwina?"

Edwina went abruptly still.

"I am an enemy of your people. I have killed many."

Edwina closed her eyes.

"It is in my heart to kill many more."

Edwina's eyes snapped open.

"I seek the day when the white man's forts will be burned and the bluecoats driven from the land of the Sioux."

"No!"

"Yes, Edwina." Night Raven paused, his expression intense. "That is the true conflict between us."

Suddenly trembling, Edwina whispered, "Let me go back to the fort, Night Raven."

"No."

Night Raven's reply was still reverberating

within her when he changed direction abruptly.

"Where are we goin'?"

White Bear adjusted the feather in his headband as he walked through the foliage a distance from camp. His smile was absent. It was only midday. The hours of morning had passed slowly. He had gone to Night Raven's tipi earlier, as was his custom, with the expectation of extending his protection to Miss Keene until Night Raven returned, but she wasn't there. He was surprised when Trailing Mist told him that Night Raven had taken supplies with him when he left with Miss Keene. He supposed they'd be gone for a while—hunting, maybe. He probably wouldn't have to be watching out for Miss Keene much longer, anyway, because things were changing in the camp, and there probably wouldn't be a need to protect her while Night Raven was gone.

White Bear's expression grew pensive. He was only a boy, but he didn't believe what some of the women of the camp said about Night Raven and Miss Keene. He had the feeling that maybe Running Deer was the one who got them to thinking Night Raven was only using Miss Keene for his servant and all. He had seen the way Night Raven looked at Miss Keene. He liked her. Night Raven didn't want people to know it, but he did. And he had the feeling

Miss Keene liked Night Raven, too, even if she was his captive.

But . . . it wasn't Miss Keene he was worrying about.

White Bear unconsciously shrugged. He had spent the greater part of the morning lingering at the edge of the camp, where he could watch people's comings and goings. He had told himself that he wasn't really watching Seeing Woman to make sure she was safe, but he knew he was.

Stopping short, White Bear saw Lone Dog moving slowly through the low stretch of foliage, his concentration intent. He was picking leaves for medicine and for the healing smoke. This was Lone Dog's special place. He had known Lone Dog would be there.

Lone Dog turned toward him as he approached, his eyes intent. White Bear halted, suddenly uncertain.

"Come forward, White Bear. I have been waiting."

"You didn't know I was comin' to see you!" White Bear was disbelieving. "How could you know?"

"A boy who wears a smile through the day is troubled when he frowns. A boy who enjoys the conversation of others is unlike himself when he is silent."

"I don't talk that much."

Lone Dog almost smiled. "And a boy who

avoids the presence of youthful friends and lingers near an old man, undecided whether to speak, bears a heavy burden on his mind."

"I guess you're right."

Lone Dog did not reply.

White Bear started slowly. "I need to know some things, Lone Dog. I wasn't always a Sioux, so there're some things I need to ask." White Bear took a breath, frowning again. "I was wonderin'... what would a good Sioux brave do if he knew a secret that he wasn't supposed to know?"

"Silence keeps all secrets safe."

"But if the secret was important... if somebody might get hurt if it wasn't told?"

"If the secret is not his to tell—"

"But if somebody already hurt a real nice person, a person who couldn't watch out for herself... if somebody might hurt that nice person again if the secret wasn't told..."

Lone Dog slowly straightened. "A good Sioux brave protects the weak and helpless of his camp."

"But if the Sioux brave wasn't sure, and... and if the Sioux brave was only a boy..."

"A good Sioux brave listens to the urging of his heart and chooses."

"He'd make a choice... he'd decide whether to tell or not if he was a good Sioux brave?"

Lone Dog nodded.

White Bear considered his choices.

* * *

She had never seen a more beautiful place.

Night Raven halted his mount, then slipped to the ground and swung her down beside him, and Edwina was momentarily unable to speak. The brilliant green of the hillside stole her breath, as did the wild proliferation of flowers in every color and hue at its base. Strangely, the rays of the sun seemed to beat with particular brilliance at the summit, as if its concentration there was more intense.

Turning toward Night Raven, Edwina questioned, "What is this place?"

"It is a hillside."

"Night Raven . . ."

"It is a place where many seek answers that elude them. It is a place where visions are seen by those who prepare themselves well. It is a place that many hold sacred . . . yet it is a hillside of earth and grass like any other."

"Why did you bring me here, Night Raven?"

"It is a place where the conflicts of many are resolved."

"Our conflicts?"

"We will camp here."

Edwina pressed, "Why did you bring me here?"

Night Raven walked to the pack horse and began unloading.

"Night Raven . . ."

Night Raven turned on her with unexpected

anger. "You press for answers when there are none, Edwina!"

"I press for answers that go unspoken."

"No, you do not." Advancing suddenly toward her, Night Raven gripped her arms almost painfully tight as he rasped, "You wish to evade a truth that shudders through you each time we are near."

"No, I—"

"You seek to deny, Edwina . . . even now, when your heart pounds at my touch."

"I'm angry!"

"The anger you feel is at yourself, for the hunger that rises within you."

"No!"

Slipping his hand to her cheek as he held her fast, Night Raven caressed her gently and whispered, "You shudder at the thought of the intimacy between us—as I do. You decry the need that builds within you—as I do. You seek an answer to the strife within—as I also seek."

Night Raven drew her closer. His lips only inches from hers, he rasped, "We will seek the answers together in this place of truth, Edwina. We will separate ourselves from all else as we breathe the air and feel the earth of this sacred ground underneath us—and we will accept the truth that emerges."

"Truth?" Edwina was trembling. "What truth could emerge in a place of solitude, when the same conflicts will return as soon as the world intrudes? You're foolin' yourself, Night Raven, and you're hopin' to fool me as well."

"It is not my aim to fool you."

"But you—"

Night Raven closed the distance between their lips, silencing Edwina's words of protest, and she struggled under his kiss as a flush of protest raged within her. She would not submit to the spontaneous heat between them. She would not allow reason to be overwhelmed by need.

Edwina gasped aloud as Night Raven's mouth slipped to her neck, as his hands worked at the buttons on her dress and his lips met the warm flesh of her breasts at last. She was still protesting as he suckled her gently, as he swept her up into his arms and walked the few steps to a leafy bower. She gasped words of protest when his naked length met hers at last and he thrust himself inside her with an ecstatic gasp that echoed in her heart.

Uncertain of the moment when her arms slipped around Night Raven's neck, Edwina felt him swell within her. So true was her passion that all denial was dismissed when, with a few penetrating strokes, he brought her to full fruition, his eyes golden embers in the silence as her body pulsed to rapturous climax.

His own passion building, Night Raven whispered against her lips, "Such is the conflict between us, Edwina."

Night Raven throbbed his completion within her as Edwina grasped him ecstatically close. She was still clutching him tightly when he separated himself from her at last and whispered, "Rise, Edwina. We have yet many hours before us during which we will seek the answers that we—"

A sound in the brush halted Night Raven's words. All trace of passion erased from his expression, he remained motionless, crouched above her as the rustling in the brush continued. He was on his feet in a moment. Edwina saw the flash of his blade as he moved silently toward the sound and disappeared from sight.

Hastily donning her dress, Edwina was on her feet when Night Raven emerged from the foliage. Her breath caught in her throat at the sight of the pack horse he led into view—an animal outfitted in military gear.

"Wh . . . where did it come from?"

Dressing quickly without replying, Night Raven turned to his mount.

"Where are you goin'?"

Anger flushed hot and swift within her when Night Raven mounted his horse and turned back into the brush. She rasped, "I asked you—"

Night Raven disappeared in the foliage and Edwina made a swift decision. Grasping the reins of the pack horse Night Raven had secured only moments earlier, Edwina mounted and urged him into the brush also. She saw the angry look Night Raven flashed in her direction when she reached him. His glance warned caution. She heeded it as he followed a trail through the thick underbrush. They emerged into the open at last.

Sensing Night Raven's next move, Edwina was on her feet at the same moment that Night Raven touched the ground, knife drawn. She was behind him as he raced toward a blue-coated form lying facedown, almost obscured beneath low-lying bushes. She halted the swift, downward stoke of his blade with her shocked cry.

Her heart pounding at first sight of the soldier's bright shock of hair, Edwina moved between Night Raven and the motionless form, rasping, "Put down your knife!" When Night Raven's knife remained poised, she rasped, "If you kill this man, you'll have to kill me, too!"

Without a thought for the glinting blade that remained poised above him, Edwina turned the soldier toward her.

Her breath escaped in a sob.

"Craig!"

"Is it true?"

Jumping Bull's voice vibrated with anger, and Seeing Woman stepped back at the intensity of the sound. He had entered her tipi moments earlier and she had turned toward him with a smile that faded the moment she heard his rasping breaths. She could not see his face, but she knew. He was enraged. And his fury was directed at her!

Filled with remorse at his agitation, Seeing Woman whispered, "I have offended you, Jumping Bull, but I do not know how."

"Is it true?" Jumping Bull repeated his question as he advanced toward her. She felt the radiating heat of his anger as he stood so close that their bodies almost touched. "Is it true that you allowed me to believe a falsehood told by one who shares my tipi—a falsehood that endangered your life?"

Seeing Woman's voice trembled with emotion. "I wished to spare you pain."

His hands clamped heavily onto her shoulders. Jumping Bull grated, "Falsehood causes me pain! One who lives within my household and acts in evil ways causes me pain! Words of remorse spoken without truth cause me pain! But of all these things, none matches my pain at the thought of endless days without the comfort of your smile. You knew all this, yet you allowed the threat against you to continue!"

Her sightless eyes filled with tears at the quiver in Jumping Bull's deep voice. "I wished to spare you," Seeing Woman whispered.

Jumping Bull rasped, "How could you not see that in hoping to spare me a moment's pain, you risked causing me a grief I could not endure?"

Jumping Bull's rough palm smoothed tears from Seeing Woman's cheek that she did not realize she had shed. His voice suddenly devoid of anger, he whispered, "Take care not to err in this way again, Seeing Woman. You test my restraint when my most cherished dream is threatened."

Jumping Bull's hands dropped unexpectedly from her shoulders, and Seeing Woman felt the abrupt change in his demeanor as he turned away.

Seeing Woman halted him with a soft plea. "Youth often acts in ways that are unwise—in ways that maturity may alter."

Jumping Bull left without reply.

Silent, unmoving, Night Raven observed Edwina's frantic ministrations to the injured bluecoat. Her shocked cry as his blade descended had halted its downward thrust, but the words she spoke had numbed him.

If you kill this man, you'll have to kill me, too.

Night Raven's jaw tightened. He remembered this bluecoat. This man had come to Edwina's room at the fort. He had looked at him with contempt and called him "savage," and he had spoken to Edwina with an affection that surpassed simple friendship.

Jealousy filled him. Night Raven took a step toward the wounded man as Edwina turned toward him.

"It's Craig Rice, my friend, Night Raven. He's unconscious." Edwina swallowed convulsively. "He's been bitten by a snake, but he managed to tie off the point of puncture. And his leg's broken." She took a short breath that was close to a sob. "He needs our help or he'll die."

Hardening himself to Edwina's plea, Night Raven replied, "Your friend needs *your* help— not the help of one he calls 'savage.' "

"I don't have time to argue, Night Raven. I . . . I need to build a fire so I can heat some water. I need to set the break in his leg, and I need something that'll keep his leg immobile, so he won't injure it further."

Standing up abruptly when Night Raven made no reply, Edwina walked the few steps to the army pack horse. He heard the relieved sound that escaped her throat when she discovered a leather water pouch that was still full. When she turned back to him, her eyes were hard and cold.

"I know what you're thinkin'. This man's your enemy. You made it clear what you feel in your heart for your enemy, so I'm not goin' to ask you for help. I'm only goin' to ask you for one thing. Stay away from him. I'll do the rest."

Night Raven watched dispassionately as Edwina quickly gathered wood for a campfire, as she struck it to a blaze and removed a metal pot from the pack horse's back and filled it with water. He saw her tender ministrations as she returned to the bluecoat's side and bathed his face, speaking to him softly as she did. He saw the moment when the bluecoat's eyes opened and he spoke her name, and he saw Edwina's hand tremble as she stroked the bluecoat's cheek.

Turning away, Night Raven chose to watch no more.

A smile on her lips, Running Deer returned from the pool and crossed the camp with a confident step as afternoon waned. Enraged by Seeing Woman's threat, she had spent the night in thought, and the day in planning. Satisfied that she had devised a way to diminish Seeing Woman's image so her words would be dismissed as the rantings of the aged hag that she was, she had shed her anger in the cool water and emerged refreshed.

Running Deer smiled. She had taken great care so she could present herself at her best when she next saw Jumping Bull. She had brushed the tangles from her hair with great patience until the strands lay smooth and glowing against her shoulders. She had rubbed the smooth skin of her body until it shone, and she had pressed scented blossoms to intimate places of heat that would emit their fragrance when Jumping Bull held her close. Certain of her physical worth, she had then scrutinized her image in the clear water to reassure herself that her expression reflected only the innocence Jumping Bull sought. When she approached him as he lay on his sleeping bench that night, she would serve his body in a way his other wives would not—in a way he could not refuse.

Running Deer's smile lost all trace of innocence as her fingers squeezed tight around the seeds she had secretly gathered. She knew their potency. It would not be difficult to drop them into the bowl to be delivered to Seeing Woman from Trailing Mist's campfire that night. When Seeing Woman first felt their effects, Running Deer would be lying in Jumping Bull's arms. She would rise with the same shocked horror as the others when Seeing Woman stumbled through the camp with her mind afire, shaming herself before all and destroying whatever credence her words had once carried.

She would be sympathetic to Seeing Woman's affliction. She would cater to her needs, bringing her food from Trailing Mist's campfire—and with careful use of the seeds, she would see to it that Seeing Woman's power over Jumping Bull ended forever.

Running Deer drew her slender frame up proudly. Her time of triumph was near.

Her steps momentarily slowing when she

saw Jumping Bull standing beside her tipi, Running Deer felt a rush of heat. Jumping Bull awaited her. Time had stretched long since they had lain together. He had tired of the sight of aged skin and grunting responses to his body's needs. He sought youth this night, and she would not disappoint him.

Approaching her tipi eagerly, her smile bright, Running Deer stopped abruptly when Jumping Bull turned toward her. The camp fell silent behind her as she took a step in retreat, cowering at the rage in her husband's heavy features as he raised his arm to strike her.

Jumping Bull stayed his powerful arm, and Running Deer fell to her knees in fear. She had not the strength to speak a word when Jumping Bull addressed her in a tone that bespoke unyielding fury despite its softness.

"You chose to scorn my warnings, Running Deer. You are the daughter of a proud warrior and a good friend, but you defile his name. Now only shame remains."

True terror contorting her features, Running Deer cried, "I am innocent of wrongdoing! I choose only to exalt your name in all I do!"

Jumping Bull took a theatening step. "Only Black Dog's blood protects you."

"I have been a good wife!"

"You degrade what you claim to exalt! In your decision to deceive me, in your effort to mold my affections to your selfish designs, in your hope of fostering in me an infidelity to those who have served me loyally, in your hostile act against one whom I esteem, you have committed true evil against me."

"Lies told by one who wishes me harm!"

"Truths, revealed by the most unlikely of sources!"

"I have been true to the bond between us!"

"There *is* no bond between us!" Pausing so Running Deer might absorb his statement fully, Jumping Bull continued, "I do not wait to 'beat the drum' before all to make my declaration. I say it here and now! You are no longer my wife. It is only my respect for Black Dog that saves you from punishment for the infidelity you have practiced."

"I have not been unfaithful!"

"You have been unfaithful to me in every way, except with your body, and you will pay the price."

Running Deer shuddered. The punishment for infidelity—to have her nose severed—a disfigurement that would shame her forever!

Running Deer covered her face with her hands in true horror, realizing a moment too late that the seeds she had clenched so tightly spilled to the ground.

The silence surrounding Running Deer grew acute as Jumping Bull snatched the spilled seeds up from the ground. Staring at them for long moments, he then dropped them back into the dust and crushed them with his heel.

When Jumping Bull spoke again, it was in a voice deep with finality.

"You have decreed your own fate with this last evil act you intended. This camp will no longer shelter one who shames it so deeply. You will take Black Dog's mount and pack horse and the articles of your household, and you will leave this camp before darkness falls. You will heed my words, for if you remain at the rise of the new day, the punishment for infidelity will be carried out."

"No!" Staggering to her feet, Running Deer approached Jumping Bull with tears streaming. "You are wrong! I did nothing!"

Incredulous as Jumping Bull turned his back and walked away, as all others who had stood in observance did the same, Running Deer stood swaying uncertainly.

She called out into the silence.

"Jumping Bull errs!"

Her words reverberated. When there was no reply, she called out again.

"I did nothing!"

The silence continued.

Running Deer stood motionless and alone.

The import of the moment inescapable, Running Deer closed the distance to her tipi in a few shaky steps.

* * *

Twilight was fading to darkness as the mounted contingent made its weary trek back through the gates of Fort John Carter. Riding in the lead, Major Locke drew his horse up without a word and dismounted.

Striding through his office doorway moments later, he dismissed Lieutenant Johnson's report with a wave of his hand and slammed the door closed behind him. He paused a moment, then sat down at his desk and picked up his pen. He wrote furiously, livid at the humiliation of the day's failure.

Slapping the pen down when the letter was completed, he shouted to the guard at the door, "Get a messenger in here . . . now!"

Locke's expression hardened to stone. He'd had all he could take from the bureaucrats in Washington. This letter would set them straight. And when it did, he'd settle the Sioux problem on the western frontier—once and for all!

Running Deer surveyed the encroaching darkness surrounding her as she urged her mount forward along the trail. She recalled her panic at Jumping Bull's decree that she leave the camp before sundown, never to return. She had gone to her tipi and gathered all she could quickly transport from her household. She had secured it on the horses provided while waiting each moment for Jumping Bull to come and rescind his judgment. But he had not come, and she had left the camp as the sun began its descent toward the horizon.

Jumping Bull's raging countenance flashed momentarily through her mind and Running Deer shivered. No, she would not be intimidated by a future that now loomed dark and empty. Her displacement was only temporary. She had only to make her way to the Sioux tribes in the north, where Black Dog's name was known, and she would be treated with the respect she deserved. She would explain that a witch had cast a spell on her husband and caused him to act unwisely, and they would understand. Her beauty would avail her of her choice of braves, and she would choose the greatest and strongest, and she would see that he meted out to Jumping Bull the justice he deserved. It was only a matter of time.

The memory of her solitary departure from the camp abruptly returned, and true malevolence clawed at Running Deer's heart. She thought back, seeking the first seed of her present debasement, and a solitary figure loomed brightly. Night Raven. In casting her aside so coldly, Night Raven had set the pattern for all that had followed—and it was Night Raven who would suffer her ultimate vengeance!

Controlling her fear as the wavering shadows of night closed in around her, Running Deer drew her mount to a halt and dismounted. She would make her camp. She would keep to her northerly direction until her journey was done. She would survive to wreak her vengeance.

Yes, it was only a matter of time.

Hardly aware of Night Raven's activities, Edwina bathed Craig's face with cool water. He was mumbling incoherently in his delirium, his eyes opening for brief periods, then closing again in a feverish sleep. She had set the break in his leg and bound it firmly, bracing it with wooden rods she had fashioned and strips of cloth from Craig's pack.

Edwina glanced at Craig's hand. She had cleansed the wound as carefully as she could, but his hand was still purple and grossly swollen. He was in great pain, but it wasn't the bite that caused her the most concern. Craig had survived whatever poison had filtered into his system, but the circulation in his hand was not returning. She feared that she had arrived too late . . . that the extremity was impaired beyond repair. She knew what she would be forced to do if the circulation could not be restored.

Edwina's heart began a heavy pounding. She needed to get Craig back to the fort, where she had medicine that would relieve his pain and fever, where she would be better equipped to help restore the circulation in his hand. And, if she could not, where she had the tools to perform the operation that would break her heart.

Edwina caught her breath on a sob. Craig had come out into this desolate wilderness alone, in the hope of finding her and bringing her back. She knew that without a doubt. He had risked his life for her, because he felt responsible for her safety, and his life now hung in the balance while Margaret awaited his return.

Briefly overwhelmed, Edwina closed her eyes. She needed to take Craig back to the fort. She needed to start out at dawn so she could make the fastest progress possible. She needed—

"Edwina . . ."

Craig's eyes were open. He rasped, "Don't . . . don't cry, Edwina. I don't want to see you cry."

"I'm not crying, Craig. I'm fine. Just close your eyes and rest. We'll talk tomorrow."

Craig's eyelids fluttered closed, and Edwina's throat tightened to the point of pain. She stood up and walked toward the fire—realizing abruptly that Night Raven had established their camp during the long afternoon while she had devoted herself to Craig's care. She accepted the dried beef Night Raven put into her hand and sat abruptly on the blanket he had spread, too exhausted to eat.

"The bluecoat sleeps. You must sleep as well."

"I can't let myself sleep." Edwina raised a hand to her throbbing temple. Hardly aware of her actions, she leaned against Night Raven when he sat beside her. Suddenly desperate, she looked up at him and pleaded, "Craig came here to find me . . . to bring me back. He's sick, Night Raven. I have to take him back to the fort or he might die."

No response.

"Night Raven . . . please."

"You must sleep now, Edwina."

"Night Raven . . ."

Silence.

Edwina leaned back against Night Raven's chest. She closed her eyes in an attempt to shut out a reality that was suddenly too overwhelming to endure. She whispered, "He might die. I couldn't bear it if he did."

The night had darkened. Edwina sat leaning limply back against him, her breathing deep and steady. Exhaustion had assumed control. She was sleeping.

Laying her down on the blanket, Night Raven stretched out beside her and took her into his arms. She whimpered softly in her sleep, and Night Raven tightened his arms around her. He had watched in silence as Edwina worked diligently through the long afternoon, seldom leaving the bluecoat's side. He had seen the love in her eyes when she

342

looked down on the bluecoat's pale face, and he had heard that same love returned when the bluecoat spoke to her—but his jealousy was no longer stirred. He recognized a love between them that was deep and true but without any passion to threaten that which Edwina and he shared.

Night Raven looked again at the bluecoat. He was sleeping soundly, without the spasms that had formerly tormented him. Edwina would sleep as well . . . for a little while . . . and he would hold her.

Night Raven looked up at an overcast sky empty of stars. He frowned and drew the blanket up around them.

Night Raven awakened at the first drops of falling rain. Glancing at Edwina beside him, he saw that she slept soundly. Dislodging himself from her warmth, he retrieved a soft hide from the supplies nearby and spread it carefully across the low-lying branch above their blankets to provide protection from the rain.

Night Raven glanced at the bluecoat. The man did not move, and he walked closer. The buttons on the man's jacket glinted in the meager light of the dying campfire, and Night Raven grew still. His hand moved to the knife at his waist as bitter memories flashed across his mind. He remembered a day of bloodshed and fire years earlier, when the bluecoats raided their hunting camp. The buttons on their coats had glinted in the sun as they rode amongst the tipis, burning and slaughtering. When silence again reigned, only he survived— and his vow of vengeance against all who wore the blue coats he despised was born.

His knuckles whitening, Night Raven clenched his knife tighter. But he remembered something else as well. He remembered the gentleness of Edwina's touch when she bathed the bluecoat's cheek. He recalled the sound of her voice when she spoke softly to him, although the bluecoat could not really hear her.

I don't want you to cry, Edwina.

The bluecoat's words struck a chord within Night Raven as raindrops struck the dry ground around him with greater frequency. The bluecoat reacted as they struck his face, mumbling . . . frowning. They fell harder and the bluecoat jumped, the suddenness of the movement causing his pale face to crease with pain.

Another raindrop. Another.

Turning back toward the piled supplies, Night Raven withdrew the oiled cloth the soldiers used to protect themselves from the rain. Crouching, he spread it over the wounded man to shield him from the rain.

The bluecoat's restless movements stilled.

Night Raven was still crouched beside the

sleeping man when the import of the moment struck him a staggering blow.

The rain was falling in earnest when Night Raven stood up in stark incredulity. He, who had so despised the dream that haunted him, had become the hated raven of his vision! The eye of the raven had become his own!

Chapter Ten

Sounds of movement interrupted Edwina's restless sleep. She opened her eyes to the rising sun, then jolted to full wakefulness when the events of the previous night returned with full clarity. She sat up, her head brushing the hide covering stretched out above her. She stared at the ground around her. It had rained during the night. Night Raven had spread the hide to shield them, and she had not awakened.

Glancing at Craig, Edwina saw that he was mumbling and moving restlessly. Panicked, she scrambled to his side to find his fever again soaring—although his body was dry. She touched the oilskin covering him, then glanced at Night Raven, who continued working, attaching freshly cut wooden poles to the pack horse's back with leather thongs. He did not look in her direction, but she knew it was his hand that had spread the protective covering over Craig as well, and her throat choked tight. Momentarily unable to speak past the tightness, Edwina pressed the cup to Craig's lips and whispered, "Drink, Craig. You'll feel better if you do."

Craig's lips parted. He swallowed convulsively, his breathing ragged. His eyes opened briefly, but he was lost in a world of fevered dreams. His condition was worsening.

Edwina stood up. She turned toward Night Raven as he approached.

"Craig's worse, Night Raven. If I don't take him back to the fort soon, he'll die."

Night Raven's eyes met hers coldly. Chilled by the unexpected animosity in their depths, she was momentarily speechless when Night Raven responded, "I have prepared a travois so you may take the bluecoat back to the fort."

His reply startled her, and Edwina stammered, "You . . . you're sayin' you're goin' to let us both go?"

Night Raven did not reply. She watched with a sense of unreality as Night Raven drew the travois up beside Craig's twitching figure, as he lifted Craig as easily as if he were a child and placed him on the blanketed conveyance, then secured him in place.

Edwina glanced around her, suddenly aware that the camp had also been packed while she slept. Facing Night Raven when he was again standing, she said, "Thank you . . . for covering Craig during the night. If not for you, he—"

Interrupting her, his gaze frigid, Night Raven grated, "We leave now."

Her discomfort increasing with each plodding step her horse took, Running Deer seethed. Her first night on the trail had been filled with difficulties. Accustomed to the protection of the camp, she had been abandoned to her own defenses in the wilderness for the first time. Ordinary sounds became those of demons that screeched and yowled in the night, sounds that were muted only when the rain began. Lying beneath a rough hide covering, she had lain awake in the hours that followed, steeped in bitterness and cursing the Sioux camp from which she had come.

Her hatred knew no bounds when morning dawned. She had resumed her trek, her hair disheveled, her skin unclean, and her clothing smelling of the dampness that permeated her bones. But with the light of a new day, memory of the fear that had held her rigid through the night made her flush with shame.

Running Deer kicked her mount to a faster gait. She was the daughter of Black Dog, who was a stranger to fear. She had always stood as proud and fearless as he—until the previous night.

Hatred spiraled within Running Deer, expanding hotly. Night Raven had caused this breach with the spirit of her warrior father. Because of him, she had been left with no choice but to accept Jumping Bull's suit—a union destined to fail. Because of Night Raven, Jumping Bull had discarded her, and her name was forever marked with shame.

Running Deer glanced upward as the sun rose brightly, rapidly erasing all trace of the stormy night past, but the storm in Running Deer's heart lingered. In the absence of a son, Black Dog had taught her much of a warrior's ways. She could follow a trail easily, and the use of weapons was not unknown to her. She had no cause for unreasonable fear. She would follow the trail on which she was set, sacrificing all to haste so she might reach the safety of her new home in the north. She would establish herself comfortably there—to pursue the vengeance that would be hers.

"Corporal . . ."

His hands freezing on the bucket he held, Corporal Lee turned at the sound of the unsteady voice behind him. Straining to see clearly in the limited light of the stable, he stared at the small, bulky figure standing in the morning shadows behind him.

"Ma'am?" He placed the bucket on the ground and advanced toward Margaret Rice, uncertain. She hadn't been at the gate in the early hours when the morning patrol started out. It hadn't missed his notice that Lieutenant Johnson had also looked toward the corner of the fort yard where she usually stood. He had thought he saw a flash of concern in the lieutenant's expression, but he dismissed the officer's concern—and his own—with the thought that the captain's wife had probably had a bad night and was sleeping late.

Advancing toward her, Corporal Lee squinted in an attempt to see Margaret Rice's shadowed features more clearly. "This ain't no place for you, ma'am. It ain't clean in here, and with you in your condition and all . . ." He paused. "Is somethin' wrong, ma'am?"

"You said to come to you if I needed anything, Corporal." Margaret Rice paused. Appearing peculiarly breathless, she continued, "I wasn't feeling well this morning, so I decided to sleep late, but my uneasiness worsened." Margaret paused again. "Corporal . . . help me, please."

Corporal Lee reached out in time to catch Margaret Rice as she slid limply to the ground.

Edwina sat her horse stiffly as their small entourage continued onward along the wilderness trail. She looked at Night Raven, who rode silently beside her. Unable to dismiss the sense of unreality with which the day had begun, she stared at his emotionless expression, recalling the passion she had formerly seen reflected there.

In this place, we will settle the conflict between us . . . a conflict that torments me as well.

Was that what had happened when he had taken her into his arms the previous night and drawn her back against his chest . . . when she had relaxed against him in total trust . . . when she had drifted into an exhausted sleep and awakened to find that he had protected her . . . and Craig . . . from the night storm?

Edwina glanced back at Craig; from time to time he groaned softly with the bump and sway of the travois. She shook her head, her thinking muddled. She should be glad that Night Raven was releasing them, shouldn't she? She should be thankful that he was allowing her to take Craig back to the fort where she would have a real chance to save his life. He was doing what she, in her exhaustion, had *begged* him to do.

Edwina took a shuddering breath. But . . . she hadn't begged Night Raven to *dismiss* her. She hadn't expected that the heat that had blazed between them would turn to ice, and she had not dreamed that she would be left so cold inside that she feared her heart would shatter.

Without conscious intent, Edwina prompted, "Night Raven . . ."

Night Raven turned toward her with the eyes of a stranger, freezing her tongue. Glancing up at the sun as it made its rapid ascent in the sky, Edwina strove for a normal tone when she asked, "How much longer will it be before we reach Fort John Carter? We've been ridin' for hours. Craig's not doin' well."

Strong features, which had formerly reflected loving emotion remained unresponsive. Lips, which had formerly covered hers with tender hunger, remained stiffly set. His powerful body, which had once taken hers with a passion that knew no bounds, remained unyieldingly posed as Night Raven replied, "We will soon reach the trail the bluecoat morning patrol takes each day. It is well marked. You will meet them before the sun reaches its high point."

"You're sayin' the mornin' patrol from the fort is ridin' toward us right now?"

Silence.

Suddenly overwhelmed by a great sadness, Edwina struggled against tears as she rasped, "The conflict between us has been settled, hasn't it, Night Raven?" When there was no reply, she added, "And now that the conflict is gone, there's nothin' left."

Night Raven's features hardened to stone.

Edwina averted her gaze. She did not speak

when they reached the trail at last. Nor did she look his way when Night Raven turned his mount and, without a word or a backward look, rode away.

Bertha Charles stared at Corporal Lee. Her hands on her hips, her oversized bosom jutted imperiously forward, she boomed, "I don't care if Mrs. Rice asked you to stay. You have no business here. Get out of this room!"

His fair skin heating, Corporal Lee glanced at the bed nearby, where Margaret Rice lay. He noted her gallant effort to deny the pain that had caused her to collapse in his arms. He had carried her to her quarters and called for help—only to have the bellicose Bertha move in to assume command with her usual arrogance. He had never felt more out of his element than he did at that moment, but the realization that Mrs. Rice had turned to him when she was in need infused him with determination. "Sorry, ma'am. Mrs. Rice don't want me to leave." He turned belatedly toward the bed for confirmation. "Ain't that right, ma'am?"

"Yes."

Mrs. Rice's breathless response heightened Corporal Lee's concern as he turned back to his buxom adversary and said, "This ain't the time for arguin', anyways. Ain't there nothin' you can do for Mrs. Rice? She's in pain!"

Bertha glared. "Havin' babies is all about pain!"

"But"—Corporal Lee lowered his voice—"it ain't her time yet."

"Babies don't come on schedule."

Suddenly angry, Corporal Lee grated, "Ain't there nobody in this fort who knows nothin' more about havin' babies than you do, ma'am?"

Bertha's glare deepened. "I'm the best this fort's got to offer now—and I say you leave, Corporal!"

Corporal Lee was about to respond when a voice from the bed behind them rasped, "I say he stays, Bertha." After a short, breathless silence Margaret added, "If you don't mind, Corporal."

Glaring into Bertha's livid expression, Corporal Lee replied, "I ain't movin' from this spot, ma'am."

Running Deer glanced up at the sky, at the sun that neared its summit. Her discomfort mounted. So agitated had she become, so determined was she to reach the Sioux camp in the north as quickly as possible, she had made a grievous error. She had recalled from her childhood a trail through this area that Black Dog had once taken to reach their camp—a trail that had been rough and arduous but had brought them home in haste. She had chosen to deviate from the trail commonly used to follow it, and the mistake had been grave indeed. She had not remembered that the terrain was so rocky and unsafe underfoot. She had not recalled the stress it placed on the horses. She had not realized that she would find herself shaky and uncertain as she stood on a high, rocky outcrop, unsure how to get down.

Seeing no recourse, Running Deer dismounted and peered at the rocky terrain where it crossed a trail below. She was studying the path intently when she first saw *her*.

Running Deer remained motionless, unwilling to look away from the apparition riding steadily nearer until identification was certain. Yes, it was she!

True venom pulsed through Running Deer's veins, and her heart pounded. It was Night Raven's woman! She rode, dragging a travois behind her on which a bluecoat lay.

Trembling, Running Deer could hardly believe her eyes. A clear view of the surrounding terrain revealed that Night Raven was nowhere near, yet the travois was obviously built by his hand. There could be only one explanation. Night Raven had freed the woman so she could bring an injured bluecoat to the fort. He had surrendered to the woman's wiles as he had never surrendered to hers, and the woman's victory was now complete.

She would not allow it.

Scrambling toward the pack horse behind

her, Running Deer searched the hastily wrapped articles of her household. Her heart leaping when her trembling fingers touched cool metal at last, Running Deer withdrew the rifle that had been Black Dog's most prized possession. She had refused to surrender it, knowing that it would gain her favor with the young warriors in the northern camp—but it would serve another purpose this day.

Shaking with frenzied agitation, Running Deer located the leather pouch she sought. She went abruptly still when she shook the contents into her hand. Three bullets. Only three!

Recalling the days when Black Dog had taught her the rifle's use, Running Deer raised her chin defiantly. Three bullets would be enough. The first would stop the white woman's heart. The second would put an end to the bluecoat's life as well. And the third . . .

Running Deer smiled. The third would be for the true joy the moment would bring her!

A sudden calm replacing her former agitation, Running Deer loaded the rifle and strode back to observe the scene below. Edwina Keene continued her steady pace, the travois bumping at each rut in the trail behind her.

Steady and determined, Running Deer crouched at the edge of the overhang, exulting in the unobstructed view. Setting the bright gold of the woman's hair in her sights, Running Deer gradually lowered her aim. She would demonstrate to all that the white woman had not beaten her, and she would deal Night Raven an unexpected and irreversible blow to the heart when her bullet went crashing home.

Running Deer steadied her aim. So intent was she that she did not hear the first warning cracks. Her finger was tightening slowly on the trigger when the outcrop under her feet shifted, knocking her to her knees. Her eyes widening as the rifle slipped from her grasp, Running Deer fought to regain her feet. She was still scrambling for a steady foothold on the crumbling rock when it collapsed beneath her with a great roar of sound, and she went plummeting downward.

Her breathing ragged, her thinking unclear, Running Deer felt no pain as she lay partially covered by the fallen boulders. She was unable to move, but her hearing was strangely acute. She heard the chatter of birds nearby, the rustle of a fleeting breeze through the foliage surrounding her . . . and, accompanying her final breaths, the echo of steady hoofbeats and the scraping sound of a travois as Edwina traveled on.

Edwina's horse skittered sideways as the groan of falling rock vibrated underfoot. Holding the reins firmly, she squinted against the brilliant rays of sun hindering her view of the dust cloud rising in the aftermath of the slide. The gritty cloud spewed its contents into the air. She brushed away the sandy particles delivered by the shifting breeze, allowing them only fleeting notice as her attention was caught by figures riding into view on the trail ahead.

Her heart pounding, Edwina urged her mount to a faster pace.

Lieutenant Johnson negotiated the familiar trail in silence. The mood at the fort was grim, and Major Locke's humor was worse. He had little confidence that this day's patrol would be any more successful than all the others in locating any sign of Night Raven or his camp, but he maintained a dim hope that they might meet up with Captain Rice.

Lieutenant Johnson's mind lingered on that thought. He had made a definite effort not to become involved in the conflict that had erupted between Major Locke and Captain Rice upon the captain's arrival at the fort. He had maintained his distance from Mrs. Rice during the captain's absence, but his sympathies for her were sincere, and he had already made up his mind that if she faced any difficulties while the captain was gone, he would stand at her side. He had not seen her in the fort yard that morning. That worried him. He respected Margaret Rice's courage and her loyalty to her friend, and he hoped Captain Rice would soon realize, as he did, that Edwina

Keene would not be returned until Night Raven chose to surrender her. Since that possibility was remote, and since he—

Lieutenant Johnson's meandering thoughts halted abruptly. His hands stilled on his reins. His eyes narrowing, he stared into the distance, then snapped at the soldier riding beside him, "Do you see what I see ahead, Corporal?"

"Sir, it looks to me like that's a woman ridin' toward us. It looks like it might be—"

"It is!"

Lieutenant Johnson signaled the patrol into a gallop.

The last light of day was fading when Night Raven rode into the Sioux camp. Making no attempt to respond to the inquiring glances sent his way, he unpacked his horses and released them to graze. He strode back into the camp, halting briefly when White Bear approached.

White Bear's expression was sober. "Nobody was expectin' you back so soon, Night Raven, but Jumpin' Bull will be glad to see you. A lot's happened since you left."

When Night Raven did not respond, White Bear glanced around them. "I ain't seen Miss Keene."

Night Raven's silence continued.

"She ain't with you?"

No reply.

"Oh . . ."

Averting his gaze, his head drooping, White Bear turned away without comment as Night Raven raised the flap of his tipi and went inside.

"Are you in pain, Margaret?"

Struggling to conceal her growing concern for her dear friend, Edwina took Margaret's hand and squeezed it tightly. Daylight had faded, but not her incredulity at the rapid progress of events since first light that morning.

She had fallen asleep in Night Raven's tender embrace, and she had awakened to the gaze of a cold stranger who had turned his back on her without a good-bye. She had traveled a wilderness trail alone, hoping to reach the fort before Craig's injuries claimed his life. She had then met up with the fort patrol, just as Night Raven had said she would, and had arrived back at the fort to discover that Margaret's condition was dire.

In a whirlwind of activity since then, she had given Craig the medicine he needed and surrendered him to the fort women with strict instructions as to his care. Properly ashamed of their previous conduct, and despite Bertha Charles's protests, the women had accepted her authority without complaint, allowing her the freedom to return to Margaret's side. She had dismissed a relieved Corporal Lee from the scene with the promise to call him if needed. Meanwhile, the danger of Margaret's condition prevailed.

"Margaret . . . everythin's goin' to be fine. The baby's a few weeks early, but we've got everythin' ready. It'll be all right."

Her face pale, Margaret rasped, "T . . . tell me about Craig."

"Night Raven and I found him seriously injured, Margaret." Edwina did not attempt to lie. Margaret had always been able to see through her, and she would know immediately. She continued, "I was afraid for him for a while, but now that he's back at the fort where he can get the proper medicine and care, he'll be all right."

Margaret scrutinized her breathlessly. "A . . . are you all right?"

Edwina's throat tightened. "I'm fine."

"Night Raven—"

"He was . . . kind to me. He didn't let anyone abuse me. When we found Craig badly injured, he cared for him while I slept. When he realized Craig's life was threatened, he took us as far as the trail back to the fort and let us go."

"W . . . why?"

"Why did he help Craig?"

Margaret nodded.

"I don't know."

Margaret gasped in the throes of another contraction, and Edwina squeezed her friend's hand tighter.

"I'm afraid, Edwina . . . for the baby."

"Don't worry."

"I don't want to lose Craig's child."

"You won't. I promise."

Her freckled face pale, Margaret rasped, "Don't make a pro . . . promise you can't keep."

"I didn't."

Margaret gasped again, unable to respond.

The silence within his tipi seemed deafening; Night Raven turned toward his sleeping bench. His body was stiff and his spirits were low. The camp had still been in shock over the revelation of Running Deer's deadly intentions toward seeing woman. Jumping Bull's rage at the depth of Running Deer's duplicity had been visible when he'd related the events of the previous evening.

His own rage flaring at the realization that Running Deer had intended Seeing Woman further harm, Night Raven had visited Seeing Woman's tipi briefly, and emerged both relieved and astounded at her calm reaction to all that had come to pass.

Gnawing deeply within was Night Raven's knowledge that Running Deer's fury had extended to him as well—and that in his dismissal of the danger, he had put Edwina at risk.

Edwina.

The ache within Night Raven twisted tight. Though her absence was well noted, no questions had been asked of him, and he had not expected otherwise. But he knew the time of explanation would soon come, and he searched his heart for the words.

His life path had been clear from birth, and he had met his destiny boldly. He had faced the challenge of the vision that haunted him, never fearing defeat. He knew now, however, that his mistake had been in failing to consider the power of the emotions that would come to life when he held Edwina in his arms. He had not taken into account the reality that Edwina might respond to him as well, that she would be as helpless as he to combat their emotions when she lay in his arms. Nor had he allowed himself to consider that his passion for Edwina, and his respect for her honesty and courage, would merge into an overpowering emotion that would bring about his final downfall.

Stripping away his buckskins, Night Raven lay down on his sleeping bench and closed his eyes. It was over and done. He had failed the test. Edwina was back among her own, and the emptiness within him was the penalty for his defeat.

Margaret's soft, grunting sounds as the contractions increased . . . the heat of the room as

Margaret's labor became intense ... the tension building as the babe's small head crowned ... anxious, anxious moments until Margaret gave a fierce, final push and the babe was in Edwina's arms.

"It's a girl!"

But the babe made no sound and Edwina's heart leaped with anxiety. Working frantically, she massaged and thumped the infant's breast, but its color didn't improve. The babe wouldn't cry.

"Edwina ... is she all right?"

The babe shivered. She was so small ... almost too small and delicate to survive.

"Edwina?"

Edwina heard the babe's first, mewling whimper. The sound rattled to a halt within the infant's fragile form, and Edwina worked harder. The babe whimpered again. The sound grew louder, gradually building until it became a full, angry wail.

Her tears joining Margaret's, Edwina knew that the supreme beauty of the moment when she placed Margaret's small, perfect girl-child into her arms would be enshrined forever in her heart.

Lying abed in the darkness of her room, Edwina allowed those thoughts to linger. The long day was behind her. Mother and child were doing well. Craig was responding to the medicine and care he'd received. His temperature had dropped, and the worst of his pain had been alleviated. She was still concerned about his hand, but she had promised herself that she would wait for the new day to face that worry.

Another problem yet to be faced was Major Locke, whose arrogant summons to his office she had totally ignored while tending to matters of greater concern. She knew that would not sit well with him, and she knew he would attempt to make her pay. She also knew she cared not a damn what he did, and she cancelled him from her mind.

Edwina glanced at the window. The darkness of night was already tempered by dawn. She could not sleep, despite her exhaustion; her memories would allow her no respite. She heard Night Raven's voice throb with passion as he whispered:

Stronger than prison bars, my arms will hold you captive.

Prison bars that had held her lovingly.

You cannot escape me.

In her heart, she had not really tried.

You are mine, Edwina.

But . . . she was his no longer.

The conflict was over, and with it had gone the love.

Yes . . . the love.

Edwina fought the tears that tightened her throat. Night Raven had cast her aside, but she would not—she could not—forget the side of him that Night Raven had revealed to her alone. The intimacy of body and spirit they had shared was a cherished gift. She would treasure it always.

And she would mourn its loss.

Her heart a heavy weight in her breast, Edwina closed her eyes. Yes, she would mourn its loss.

Chapter Eleven

Prepared, cleansed in body and spirit, Night Raven ascended the sacred hillside. His gaze on the crest where the sun shone with startling luminescence from a cloudless sky, he allowed his thoughts to wander.

Empty days and endless nights had limped by since he had allowed Edwina to ride from his life. During that time he had searched for a new direction, but he had found none. Edwina was gone. The image of the raven had deserted him. His heart was barren. There was only one thing left for him to do.

Arriving at the summit, Night Raven paused, then discarded his buckskins. The breeze buffeted his body and his mind, stripping away the

367

shadows as he gazed upward at the brilliant sun. He remained motionless as the rays bathed him, cleansing him. He breathed deeply, absorbing the sweet scent of the earth into his heart. Standing so exposed, he offered himself with true humility.

"I don't believe a word of it!"

Livid, Major Locke stared at Edwina Keene's adamant expression. He had been infuriated when Lieutenant Johnson's patrol returned the previous week with the arrogant witch in tow. He had stepped out into the fort yard as Captain Rice's fevered form was being carried into the infirmary, with Edwina Keene snapping orders boldly as she walked behind. She had totally ignored his summons to his office, leaving him to hear secondhand what had ensued:

Edwina Keene had made the first positive step in improved relations with the Sioux while she was Night Raven's captive.

Edwina Keene's matchless skill had saved the life of her dear friend, Margaret Rice, and of the premature daughter that was born to her.

Edwina Keene had effected a cure of Captain Rice's multiple injuries that was almost miraculous. Her skill as a medical doctor was unmatched.

Edwina Keene was a hero!

It was all damned, fool nonsense that turned his stomach. He had spoken to the newly beatified Miss Keene briefly after that first night, but he had lost patience quickly and the interview had been brief. Now, having gained support within the fort, the arrogant witch had entered his office again with her bold claims and even bolder demands.

Major Locke repeated with deepening antagonism, "I don't believe a single word of any of the nonsense you spout!"

"I didn't come here to discuss myself, Major. What you believe or don't believe doesn't concern me. What I want to know is—"

Interrupting hotly, Major Locke sneered, "Then it won't bother you to learn that I see through you and your personal agenda in this affair."

"My personal agenda . . ."

Locke continued hotly, "You don't fool me with all this noble talk, you know. I've seen the blood that these Sioux savages have shed—the blood of honest soldiers who sought nothing more than to protect others against their savage depredations. I will not forget what I have seen."

"I can't forget what I've seen, either, Major. I've seen the Sioux people suffering at the loss of their loved ones, just as we suffer. I've seen hatred that comes from seein' the blood of their warriors shed, men who want nothing more than to protect their homes against depredations being practiced against them."

"So, you are an Indian lover, after all."

Edwina Keene restrained her spontaneous retort, saying instead, "I want to know if the rumors are true. I want to know if you've written to Washington for reinforcements so you can march against the Sioux in force."

"I'm proud to say they are!"

"You want Night Raven's blood, and the blood of all the Sioux."

"I want Night Raven, all right, and I'll get him! I'll see to it that he goes to trial so the whole frontier can witness his hanging." Locke advanced an angry step closer. "And I know something else, as well. *You* are the mysterious confederate who aided Night Raven in his escape from this fort. You've been working with Night Raven all along. His pretended kidnapping of you was a farce calculated to destroy me because you disagree with my tactics."

"You must be insane!"

"Insane, am I? Night Raven couldn't have escaped without help!"

"White Bear—Bobbie Ray—helped him, and he was proud to do it. He did it to repay Night Raven for saving his life."

"To put the blame on a child . . . it's despicable!"

"White Bear isn't a child, not in the normal sense. He—"

"You're wasting your breath, Miss Keene! Since you pressed for this interview so boldly,

I'll clarify my position once and for all. Night Raven is a savage killer. There is no thought in his mind that takes precedence over his need to kill as many of the 'bluecoats' as he can. He will not stop until he's *forced* to stop, and we can force him to stop in only one way. His escape is a blemish on my record that I will erase at any cost. I've sent my report to Washington with the *true* explanation of everything that's happened here. I expect a response at any time, and when I receive the reinforcements I've requested, I'll advance against the Sioux with cannon and enough men and firepower to end the Sioux resistance forever."

"If you do that, you'll destroy any chance of peace."

"Peace with the Sioux is a daydream of ignorant bureaucrats and Indian lovers who would sacrifice their own people for heathen devils who'll turn on them in the end."

"I won't let you do what you're planning, Major."

"Try to stop me, Miss Keene."

Trembling with anger, Edwina was about to speak again when Major Locke shouted to the guard at his door. "You may escort Miss Keene to her quarters now, Corporal." And in a lower voice he said to Edwina, "The reply to my requests is on its way. It's only a matter of time."

* * *

371

"I have to go, Craig. I have to!"

"Edwina . . ."

A flush colored Craig's pale face, and Edwina felt a pang of remorse. Craig was healing well. His temperature had been normal for three days, his leg was causing him less pain, and his hand had almost returned to normal size. She was still uncertain if he would regain full mobility, but that concern paled in light of his almost miraculous recovery. He was still weak, but she needed to let him know what her intentions were before she left.

"It won't do any good, Edwina. Whatever appeal you intend to make to Major Locke's superiors will be wasted. He's an experienced military professional and you're only a frontier doctor—and a woman doctor, at that."

"Not you, too, Craig."

"Edwina . . ." Craig gripped her hand and held it tight. The warmth of his concern brought moistness to her eyes as he whispered, "You know how I feel about your abilities. You're special in every way. I knew that the first time I saw you. You saved my life—"

"I only did what any doctor would do."

"You saved my life, and I don't believe any other doctor would have had the courage to stand up to Night Raven for me."

"Night Raven is—" Edwina paused, then began again. "It's important to me that you understand. Night Raven's not a savage, Craig. He wants what's best for his people—and the Sioux are just people like any other. They're fighting for their lives, just as we are, yet we're fighting against each other. The Army has to be made to understand that!" Edwina paused again. "I can't tell you why Night Raven released me when your life was endangered because I don't know why. What I do know is that I can't let Major Locke get away with the wholesale slaughter he's intendin'—not without givin' him the fight of his life!"

Craig searched Edwina's gaze intently. She saw the flicker of something she couldn't identify as he whispered, "All right. You'll do what you believe you have to do, whatever I say." Craig gripped her hand tighter. "But I want you to be careful, Edwina. And I want you to remember: If you need me—for anything—I'll never be sick enough that I can't come to you if you call." He paused, then insisted, "Tell me you won't forget that."

"I won't forget it . . . not ever, Craig."

A whimpering cry from behind them turned Edwina toward Margaret and the babe that moved briefly in the cradle beside her. Edwina whispered, "You understand, don't you, Margaret?"

"Yes, I understand."

"I'll leave tomorrow with the mornin' patrol."

"All right."

Suddenly unable to say more, Edwina left the room.

In the silence that followed, Margaret went to Craig's bedside. He gripped her hand and met her sober gaze with his.

"I know why Night Raven let Edwina take me back to the fort."

"I do, too."

"I wish—"

"I know."

Craig's gaze deepened. "I love you, Margaret."

With those hoarsely whispered words, Craig gathered Margaret into his arms.

Frowning, Jumping Bull stared at the two horses grazing on the hillside nearby. The animals had been found and driven back to camp earlier that day. Their arrival had stirred soft conversations and a wagging of heads that had not yet ceased. Their arrival had raised a conflict within his heart as well, and his sorrow increased.

Turning at the sound of footsteps behind him, Jumping Bull saw Seeing Woman approaching with Trailing Mist beside her. His gaze caught by Seeing Woman's sober expression, he hardly noticed when Trailing Mist faded back and moved away. He had avoided Seeing Woman for the week since he had driven Running Deer from the camp, and his heart had ached at the deprivation. He broke the silence between them with a simple declaration.

"Running Deer's horses were found wandering loose. Many Faces and Gray Elk brought them back."

Jumping Bull studied Seeing Woman as she nodded silently. The joy of her smile was absent as he continued, "I have sent Iron Shell and White Horn to trace the trail Running Deer was to take, but I fear the effort will be wasted."

"What would you have them do if they find her? Would you have her brought back here?"

"No!" Jumping Bull's response was spontaneous. "Running Deer decreed her own fate with her evil intentions."

"Then there is no need for the guilt that plagues you." Seeing Woman approached with a step that was steady and true, despite the darkness in which she walked. Resting her hand against Jumping Bull's chest as was her custom when her words were heartfelt, she said more softly, "You must cast the guilt from your heart."

Jumping Bull paused with wonder at the clarity of vision this woman possessed despite her sightless eyes. He responded, "The guilt that tears at my heart has been well earned."

"No."

His words emanating from a deep well of remorse within, Jumping Bull rasped, "Guilt has kept me from your company these many days, Seeing Woman—a guilt I can ignore no longer—for on that day when Running Deer's betrayal was fully revealed, I saw clearly the result of my love for you."

"Jumping Bull . . ."

"No, I must speak! Because of my love for you, because of my need to keep you close to my heart, you have suffered. In my selfishness, I have compromised the vow you so faithfully keep. Because of me, the curse befell you, and the sight was taken from your eyes."

"No!"

"And because of my selfishness, your life was almost taken by one who was jealous of my love for you."

"No."

"You deny, but I know the depth of my guilt, and my heart weeps for the pain I have caused you."

"Jumping Bull, listen to me, and understand." Seeing Woman whispered more softly, "My love for Spotted Wolf was deep and true. I flowered under its glow, and the memory of it is a sun that will forever shine in my heart. I chose to 'bite the knife' in my grief, to remain ever faithful to the love Spotted Wolf and I shared. I do not regret the vow I took."

Jumping Bull nodded, the words touching his heart with pain.

"But another love lives within my heart as

well. It shared a place with my love for Spotted Wolf even while my husband walked beside me. Spotted Wolf knew of this love. He did not protest it, or ask that I expell it. He did not, because he knew I *could* not. I have been true to the two loves that live in my heart, each in its way. I will remain true to them always."

Seeing Woman paused. Her smile returned, as bright as the sun that warmed his skin as she said, "I have lost my sight, but the blessings are many. Do you not realize that to my unseeing eyes, the world will never grow dark? The sun will always shine, the flowers will always bloom, the earth will always burst with bounty, and the snows will always remain as unsullied as the day they fall. The beauty of all that is unseen will remain ever pure . . . and those I love will never grow old."

Her voice momentarily quavering, Seeing Woman whispered, "You are not as fortunate as I. You will be forced to trace the passage of the years on my visage. You will see me wither and age, and you will bear that burden as it grows ever heavier—while in my sight, you will always be as you are now, a great and powerful warrior who is forever young. I will always see love when you look down at me and speak my name. I will always feel that same love in your touch and hear it in your voice, and my world is rich beyond all imaginings for this gift that has been given to me."

"Seeing Woman . . ."

"Do not withdraw from me for imagined injuries you have caused, Jumping Bull. Instead, remember that the love you offer me is a love of the spirit, which I accept fully." Her voice dropping an earnest note softer, Seeing Woman whispered, "Know that it is returned in kind. Allow your heart to be at peace in the knowledge that the love we share will remain always pure, that it serves no one harm, and that it benefits all who would bask in its light."

The ache within him almost more than he could bear, Jumping Bull caressed Seeing Woman's lined cheek, remembering the smooth blush of youth that had formerly glowed there. He stroked the graying stands at her temple, recalling ebony strands of silken glory. He dwelled long and deep on the eyes that had once glowed with life and now could see no more. Yet he felt their wonder.

Jumping Bull's heart raced. All Seeing Woman had said was true—but he knew something else as well—that the beauty within this woman overshadowed all that time might alter, and to him, Seeing Woman would be forever young.

With no further need for words between them, Jumping Bull drew Seeing Woman close against him. He held her gently, sharing her peace, while sharing another truth that had gone unspoken.

In each other's eyes, they would be forever young—and in their hearts, they would be forever one.

Night had come and dreams invaded.

Edwina felt Night Raven's mouth against hers, and she sighed. She felt his familiar touch and her heart sang. She heard his voice whisper her name.

"Edwina . . . awaken."

Edwina resisted. She did not want to awaken, to be shaken from this dream in which she was in Night Raven's arms once more.

Edwina opened her eyes to the darkness. Her dream had been so real. She could almost see Night Raven's familiar outline crouched over her, his broad shoulders blocking out the slim shafts of moonlight filtering through the window of her room.

"Edwina . . ."

Edwina gasped.

"Do not be afraid."

"What are you doin' here? How did you get in?"

"I know this room well. Do you remember?"

She remembered. Her heart ached with the memories she had reviewed over and again in her mind during the endless week past. But the memories had hardened her when she considered the contrast between the deep passion of intimate moments in Night Raven's arms and his cold dismissal of her that last day.

"Do not harden your heart against me, Edwina. I have come to speak to you, to say things that went unspoken when we parted."

"You shouldn't be here, Night Raven." Edwina glanced again at the window, panic rising. "It'll be mornin' soon. The patrol will be lookin' for me. They'll send somebody to my door if I'm not out in the yard and ready to travel with them at first light."

"Travel?"

"I'm leavin' Fort John Carter. I'm goin' back east for a while." Edwina urged, "You have to leave. Major Locke's determined to find you again. He's determined to avenge the humiliation your escape caused him."

"I will not be recaptured."

Fear jolted through Edwina. "What're you sayin'? Why did you come? Don't you realize how dangerous it is for you here?"

"I came to bring our time full circle."

Anger flaring, Edwina rasped, "Our time *has* come full circle, Night Raven! I'm back where I belong now." Her ire fading as abruptly as it had occurred, Edwina whispered, "I was angry when you sent me away so coldly, but I'm not angry anymore. I reviewed all you said over and over in my mind. I laughed at myself for lettin' the moments we shared touch my heart. I told myself I was a fool—and then I began seein' how foolish my anger was. You were right to send me back to the fort. It's where I belong."

"I was not."

"Yes, I—"

Pressing his fingers against her lips, Night Raven halted Edwina's further protest as he whispered, "When all was dark without you, when I could no longer see the true reason for all that had transpired, I went again to the sacred hill. There, I received the answer I was seeking."

Night Raven's fingers slipped into her hair, holding her fast as he continued, "There are many things you do not know, Edwina. I have always known that mine is not a common destiny. Lone Dog's vision of a raven at the moment of my birth foretold triumphs and challenges that would exceed those of all others in my tribe, and I accepted that fate as my own. The vision of the raven appeared to me, guiding my way, and I followed it devoutly— but it mocked me as I matured. It looked at me with eyes that were my own, while scorning the vengeance I had sworn against the bluecoats who shed the blood of my people. Yet it was not until the vision expanded that my torment became complete."

His voice deepening, he described his recurring dream. "*You* were my torment, Edwina. Long before I saw your face, your image taunted me. It gave me no respite through long, anxious nights, and my heart was turned against you."

At Edwina's incredulity, Night Raven drew her closer. "My heart leaped in realization of the moment at hand when I opened my eyes to see you standing over me in that prison cell. I saw all you did with suspicion when you nursed my wounds and restored my strength. I viewed the intimate exchange that was to come between us as the true challenge of my destiny."

His voice dropping, Night Raven rasped, "I fought you more fiercely than I had fought any foe, striving even in the moments of our intimate joining to expel the need for you that expanded within my heart. But, to my dismay, only the reverse proved true, and my need for you grew greater. I struggled to escape the truth that grew clearer with each day that you stood beside me, and with each night that you lay in my arms. Yet my self-loathing was not complete until the moment when I looked down at the injured bluecoat you had tended and felt no hatred at all, then covered him to protect him from the falling rain."

Night Raven's intensity pierced the semi-darkness as he continued, "My rage was overwhelming when I realized that I had become the raven of my vision that I had so despised! Acknowledging defeat, I sent you away—only to suffer even greater torment."

Night Raven leaned closer. His aura surrounded her, touched the cold, aching knot within her. "The raven of my vision will batter me no more, Edwina, for the truth has been revealed to me at last."

His words trembling with the fervor of the moment, Night Raven rasped, "You were, indeed, the challenge of my destiny, Edwina, but the contest was not as I first viewed it. The true challenge did not lie in conquering, but in the joining of your spirit with mine—so truly that we might discard the differences in our paths, and walk together—so I could lead my people on that same path as well. I came to see that the true test was not of my worthiness to lead my people in battle but of my worthiness to lead my people in *peace*."

Night Raven continued earnestly, "You asked if I had settled the conflict between us and found nothing left—but the reverse was true. In settling the conflict between us, I discovered not the end but the *beginning*."

Passion flaring in his gold eyes as Night Raven urged, "Come with me, Edwina. Leave with me now so we may take this beginning that is offered to us. Let us accept our true destiny—a destiny that can be fulfilled only in each other's arms."

Night Raven's words touched Edwina's heart and set it racing. They were tender words that she had dreamed of hearing, words filled with a love and yearning that she shared, but fear overshadowed her joy as she responded, "I . . . I can't! Major Locke intends—"

"I know what he intends. He seeks to destroy the Sioux, but in so seeking, he will only destroy himself."

"But—"

"Come with me now, Edwina."

The tone of his voice . . . the hunger . . .

Edwina's lingering protest was silenced by the warmth of Night Raven's arms, by the passion of his kiss, by the response that quaked through her in return—and by the realization that she was where she was meant to be.

Slipping through the shadows of the fort yard with Night Raven minutes later, Edwina halted as they reached the rear wall they had scaled once before. A ladder . . . a rope, and Edwina dropped into the darkness to be caught by Night Raven's waiting arms.

Mounted beside him, Edwina turned to meet a gold-eyed gaze that filled her heart to bursting.

It promised truth.

It promised love.

It promised all Night Raven had to give.

It promised . . . forever.

Epilogue

Poor timing, that's what it was! Just poor timing.

Major John Randolph Locke stood behind his desk unconscious of the brilliant shafts of morning sunlight slanting through his window. A month had passed since Edwina Keene had disappeared into the night with the infamous Night Raven—leaving only a brief note behind.

His posture rigidly erect and his bearded face composed in a scowl, Locke muttered an obscene curse as he glanced around his office, reviewing in his mind the aggravations that had grown steadily greater in the time since.

The most recent directive from Washington was to sue for peace with the Sioux. Locke laughed aloud. The Sioux didn't know what the word meant. Every man who had ever set foot in Sioux territory knew they were bloodthirsty savages who could never be civilized. Washington was ignorant of that fact—a truth that needed to be impressed upon them with utmost rigor.

Locke snorted. The truth was that the bureaucrats in Washington had erred from the beginning. They had monitored his activities with a continually critical eye and had disregarded his reports and subsequent requests to the point that he had been rendered ineffective. He'd make sure he told them that, too.

Rounding the desk with his customary swaggering step, Locke paused to adjust his uniform. His spotless blue jacket fit him smartly and the brass buttons were polished to a high sheen. His trousers were sharply creased, his boots polished, and his hat freshly brushed. Completing the adjustment to his appearance, his hair was neatly cut and his beard meticulously trimmed. He was the epitome of the military professional—the exact picture that Washington desired.

Locke's expression faltered. Bad timing, that's all it was. He had been agitated beyond caution when he'd returned with the morning patrol that had gone out in search of Night Raven that day. He had imagined he could *hear* the Sioux laughter rebounding when each trail they had followed disappeared as if into thin air. Frustrated, aware that his image was suffering badly, he had come back to the fort in a rage. He had written that letter to Washington, demanding that his command be doubled in size, that more cannon be provided, and that he be given a free hand to handle the Sioux menace in the manner he saw fit, so the savage tribe could be wiped from the face of the American West forever! He had supported that demand with a letter of resignation, to become effective if his conditions were not met. He had been certain his threat of resignation would make the bumbling bureaucrats sit up and take notice. And it did.

Locke gathered the last of his papers and stuffed them into his case. He didn't regret writing that letter. He regretted the timing, that was all. It was the most inopportune twist of fate that had brought Edwina Keene back to the fort so unexpectedly afterwards, dragging a badly injured Captain Rice behind her with a tale that Night Raven had saved Captain Rice from exposure to the elements and then freed her so she could take him back to the fort where he could get the care he needed. Preposterous! It still amazed him that her letter to his superiors in Washington had carried so much weight—that they had chosen to believe her letter over his report—especially since he had clearly stated that he believed Edwina Keene had been in league with Night Raven all along. He intended to reiterate that point and drive it home to his satisfaction at his first opportunity.

Major Locke raised his well-trimmed chin. He had been recalled to Washington. He wasn't worried about that. His resignation would never be accepted. He was a proven Indian fighter. He was too valuable to lose.

In the meantime, as a result of Edwina Keene's report, a moratorium had been called on all unprovoked forays against the Sioux tribe from Fort John Carter. The directive had also stated that a peace parlay was to be offered at the discretion of the interim fort commander—Captain Craig Rice—who had recovered from his injuries with unexpected speed.

Well, good luck to him! It would never work.

Striding to the door, Major Locke drew it open and proceeded out into the fort yard. His horse was waiting, as was the small contingent that would accompany him directly to the closest rail station, where he would claim the accommodations back to Washington that awaited him.

Mounted, his belongings packed in smart cases bearing his initials in gold, Major Locke barely glanced at the few curious soldiers who had risen early to observe his departure. Among them was Corporal Lee, the fool who had been so openly pleased when Margaret

Rice announced her new daughter's name. Edwina *Lee* Rice. The sentiment made him ill.

It did not miss his notice that the detachment assigned to accompany him had among its number Corporal William Smart, whose hatred for the Sioux matched his own, but who had been put on report for his unacceptable conduct toward both the prisoner and Edwina Keene while guarding Night Raven. Corporal Buddy Thompson, whose antipathy for Night Raven was well known, was also included, as was Sergeant Westley Charles, the poor bastard who was married to the buxom and bellicose Bertha. In command of the detachment was Lieutenant Ford, who had been officially reprimanded by Washington for the slaughter of the unprotected Sioux camp earlier in the year. It was a sorry contingent meant to embarrass him—and the truth was, it did.

With his last look at Fort John Carter, Major Locke sneered. He had not realized how primitive the fort truly was. He would see that it was raised to a higher standard when he returned.

As for the last line in his letter of recall, stating that he would be met with a full inquiry as to his practices on the frontier, he dismissed it. He'd be back. He knew he would.

Saluting sharply, Major Locke spurred his mount into motion. He did not spare a backward glance as the fort gates closed behind him.

* * *

Mounted beside Night Raven, watching unseen from a lookout point, Edwina observed the scene being enacted in the fort yard. Satisfaction surged as the fort gates closed and the mounted contingent escorting Major Locke proceeded down the trail. She knew what Major Locke's recall meant. He wouldn't be back.

In his new position as interim fort commander, Craig had already forwarded a preliminary invitation to Jumping Bull and the other Sioux war chiefs to come to the fort so they might discuss a peaceful settlement of their differences. Night Raven had spoken to the council in favor of accepting the invitation.

She had been in touch with Craig and Margaret in the month since she had left the fort, and she knew all was well. She had needed to tell them that all was well with her, too. She would go back to visit when the time was right—when the peace parlay was ready to proceed. She had faith that it would be soon.

She had come to terms with the women in the Sioux camp—even the last holdouts who had resented her most. She had a great affection for Seeing Woman, and the greatest respect for Jumping Bull. She saw in that strong leader the image of the man Night Raven would one day be, and her heart was filled with pride at the thought that when that day came, she would be standing beside him.

As for Bobbie—White Bear—he would be a great Sioux chief one day. She was certain of it. But in the meantime, he was a darling boy whom she had come to love dearly.

Love . . .

There were many she had grown to love, but only one person who stirred her heart with enduring passion.

The mounted contingent gradually faded from view, and Edwina turned toward Night Raven to see him looking at her in sober silence. Reaching toward her unexpectedly, he swept her from her horse to seat her across his mount in front of him. Cradling her gently in his powerful embrace, he whispered, "The past now fades into the distance and the future lies before us. It is an uncertain future, but make no mistake"—his gaze singed her—"however it proceeds, *you are mine*."

"Night Raven—"

His gaze abruptly softening to a familiar glow, Night Raven whispered, "And however it proceeds, Edwina, we will make our own peace . . . together."

Edwina parted her lips to the hunger of Night Raven's kiss. Love swelled within her at the knowledge that the eye of the raven had indeed become his own . . . and that it looked at her with love.

WINGS OF A DOVE
ELAINE BARBIERI

On the harrowing train ride from the slums and tenements of New York City to the wide open farmland of Michigan, Allie Pierce and Delaney Marsh form a bond that no one can break. Traveling to find a new life of opportunity and adventure in the heartland, the two orphans uncover their hearts' only desire. From childhood to adulthood, their friendship grows into something neither have planned or expected. For without Allie, Delaney is nothing more than a street tough, striving to prove his mettle. And without Delaney, Allie is little more than a sad wisp of a girl, frightened and alone. But together, the two will be able to carve opportunity from misfortune, understanding from discord, and ultimately find a passion that will last a lifetime.

___52323-X $5.99 US/$6.99 CAN

AMBER FIRE

ELAINE BARBIERI

Melanie Morganfield has grown from a precocious child to a beautiful woman in Asa Parker's lavish home. Melanie is grateful to Asa for all he has done for her, and in her devotion, she longs to make happy the final years of the man who has cared for her in every way that he could. But when she meets Stephen Hull, his dark and youthful sensuality heats her blood in a way which she can neither ignore or deny. She knows instinctively that she must not ever see Stephen again, or she will be fanning the flames which are destined to lead to amber fire.

___52290-X $5.50 US/$6.50 CAN

Dorchester Publishing Co., Inc.
P.O. Box 6640
Wayne, PA 19087-8640

Please add $1.75 for shipping and handling for the first book and $.50 for each book thereafter. NY, NYC, and PA residents, please add appropriate sales tax. No cash, stamps, or C.O.D.s. All orders shipped within 6 weeks via postal service book rate. Canadian orders require $2.00 extra postage and must be paid in U.S. dollars through a U.S. banking facility.

Name_____
Address_____
City_____State_____Zip_____
I have enclosed $_____ in payment for the checked book(s).
Payment <u>must</u> accompany all orders. ❑ Please send a free catalog.

WISHES ON THE WIND

ELAINE BARBIERI

Born of Irish immigrant parents, Meghan O'Connor's background dictates her hatred of the affluent Lang family. When a mining accident devastates her family, she realizes her friendship with David Lang places them both in peril. But as friendship blossoms into love Meghan will have to listen to her own conscience and follow her heart. . . .

Pampered heir David Lang lives in a world of opulence and luxury. But in Meghan O'Connor he finds the one person to whom he can entrust his heart and soul. Torn between loyalty to his family and love for the wrong woman, David knows his dreams of sharing the passion of a lifetime with Meghan are more than wishes on the wind.

RECKLESS LOVE

MADELINE BAKER

"Madeline Baker's Indian romances should not be missed!"
    —*Romantic Times*

Joshua Berdeen is the cavalry soldier who has traveled the country in search of lovely Hannah Kincaid. Josh offers her a life of ease in New York City and all the finer things.

Two Hawks Flying is the Cheyenne warrior who has branded Hannah's body with his searing desire. Outlawed by the civilized world, he can offer her only the burning ecstasy of his love. But she wants no soft words of courtship when his hard lips take her to the edge of rapture...and beyond.

_3869-2 $5.99 US/$7.99 CAN

White Flame

Susan Edwards

Searching for her missing father, the determined Emma O'Brien sets out for Fort Pierre on the Missouri River, but when the steamboat upon which she is traveling runs aground, she is forced to travel on foot. Braving the wilderness, the feisty beauty is soon seized by Indians. Surrounded by enemies, Emma learns that only Striking Thunder can grant her release. The handsome Sioux chieftain offers her freedom but enslaves her with a kiss. He takes her to his village, and there, underneath the prairie's starry skies, Emma learns the truth. The danger Striking Thunder represents is greater than the pre-war bonfires of the entire Sioux nation—and the passion he offers burns a whole lot hotter.

___4613-X $4.99 US/$5.99 CAN

PRICKLY PEAR

RONDA THOMPSON

Daddy's little girl is no angel. Heck, she hasn't earned the nickname Prickly Pear by being a wallflower. Everyone on the Circle C knows that Camile Cordell can rope her way out of Hell itself—and most of the town thinks the willful beauty will end up there sooner or later. Now, Cam knows that her father is looking for a new foreman for their ranch—and the blond firebrand is pretty sure she knows where to find one. Wade Langtry has just arrived in Texas, but he seems darn sure of himself in trying to take a job that is hers. Cam has to admit, though, that he has what it takes to break stallions. In her braver moments, she even imagines what it might feel like to have the roughrider break her to the saddle—or she him. And she fears that in the days to follow, it won't much matter if she looses her father's ranch—she's already lost her heart.

___4624-5 $4.99 US/$5.99 CAN

Dorchester Publishing Co., Inc.
P.O. Box 6640
Wayne, PA 19087-8640

Please add $1.75 for shipping and handling for the first book and $.50 for each book thereafter. NY, NYC, and PA residents, please add appropriate sales tax. No cash, stamps, or C.O.D.s. All orders shipped within 6 weeks via postal service book rate. Canadian orders require $2.00 extra postage and must be paid in U.S. dollars through a U.S. banking facility.

Name_____
Address_____
City_____State_____Zip_____
I have enclosed $_____ in payment for the checked book(s).
Payment <u>must</u> accompany all orders. ❏ Please send a free catalog.
CHECK OUT OUR WEBSITE! www.dorchesterpub.com

SONYA BIRMINGHAM

Song of the Lark

When the beautiful wisp of a mountain girl walks through his front door, Stephen Wentworth knows there is some kind of mistake. The flame-haired beauty in trousers is not the nanny he envisions for his mute son Tad. But one glance from Jubilee Jones's emerald eyes, and the widower's icy heart melts and his blood warms. Can her mountain magic soften Stephen's hardened heart, or will their love be lost in the breeze, like the song of the lark?

___4393-9 $5.50 US/$6.50 CAN

SWEET FURY

CATHERINE HART

She is exasperating, infuriating, unbelievably tantalizing; a little hellcat with flashing eyes and red-gold tangles, and if anyone is to make a lady of the girl, it will have to be Marshal Travis Kincaid. She may fight him tooth and nail, but Travis swears he will coax her into his strong arms and unleash all her wild, sweet fury.

___4428-5 $5.99 US/$6.99 CAN

Dorchester Publishing Co., Inc.
P.O. Box 6640
Wayne, PA 19087-8640

Please add $1.75 for shipping and handling for the first book and $.50 for each book thereafter. NY, NYC, and PA residents, please add appropriate sales tax. No cash, stamps, or C.O.D.s. All orders shipped within 6 weeks via postal service book rate. Canadian orders require $2.00 extra postage and must be paid in U.S. dollars through a U.S. banking facility.

Name_____
Address_____
City_____State_____Zip_____
I have enclosed $_____ in payment for the checked book(s).
Payment <u>must</u> accompany all orders. ❑ Please send a free catalog.
CHECK OUT OUR WEBSITE! www.dorchesterpub.com

FRANKLY, MY DEAR...

SANDRA HILL

Selene has three great passions: men, food, and *Gone With The Wind*. But the glamorous model always finds herself starving—for both nourishment and affection. Weary of the petty world of high fashion, she heads to New Orleans. Then a voodoo spell sends her back to the days of opulent balls and vixenish belles like Scarlett O'Hara. Charmed by the Old South, Selene can't get her fill of gumbo, crayfish, beignets—or an alarmingly handsome planter. Dark and brooding, James Baptiste does not share Rhett Butler's cavalier spirit, and his bayou plantation is no Tara. But fiddle-dee-dee, Selene doesn't need her mammy to tell her the virile Creole is the only lover she gives a damn about. And with God as her witness, she vows never to go hungry or without the man she desires again.

___4617-2 $5.50 US/$6.50 CAN

Dorchester Publishing Co., Inc.
P.O. Box 6640
Wayne, PA 19087-8640

Please add $1.75 for shipping and handling for the first book and $.50 for each book thereafter. NY, NYC, and PA residents, please add appropriate sales tax. No cash, stamps, or C.O.D.s. All orders shipped within 6 weeks via postal service book rate. Canadian orders require $2.00 extra postage and must be paid in U.S. dollars through a U.S. banking facility.

Name_____
Address_____
City_____ State_____ Zip_____
I have enclosed $_____ in payment for the checked book(s).
Payment <u>must</u> accompany all orders. ❑ Please send a free catalog.
CHECK OUT OUR WEBSITE! www.dorchesterpub.com